LECTURA
DANTIS
AMERICANA

LECTURA DANTIS AMERICANA

Inferno

II

RACHEL JACOFF
and
WILLIAM A. STEPHANY

With a new translation of the canto by
Patrick Creagh and Robert Hollander

UNIVERSITY OF PENNSYLVANIA PRESS

PHILADELPHIA

Translation of *Inferno,* Canto II,
© 1989 by Patrick Creagh and Robert Hollander

The Italian text of the *Commedia* reproduced here is that established by
Giorgio Petrocchi and originally published by A. Mondadori, Milano, 1966.
It is reprinted by the kind permission of La Società Dantesca Italiana.

Library of Congress Cataloging-in-Publication Data

Jacoff, Rachel.
    Inferno II / Rachel Jacoff and William A. Stephany; with a new
translation of the canto by Patrick Creagh and Robert Hollander.
        p.   cm. — (Lectura Dantis Americana)
    Bibliography: p.
    Includes index.
    ISBN 0-8122-8177-2
    1. Dante Alighieri, 1265–1321. Inferno.   I. Stephany, William A.
II. Title.   III. Title: Inferno two.   IV. Title: Inferno 2.
V. Series.
PQ4445 2d.J34   1989
851'.1—dc19   89-5558
                                                                  CIP

LECTURA
DANTIS
AMERICANA

a series of readings in Dante's *Commedia*
under the auspices of the
Dante Society of America

For our parents

Who would not say that glosses increase doubts and ignorance, since there is no book to be found, whether human or divine, with which the world busies itself, whose difficulties are cleared up by interpretation? The hundredth commentator hands it on to his successor thornier and rougher than the first one had found it. When do we agree and say, "There has been enough about this book; henceforth there is nothing more to say about it"?

Montaigne, "Of Experience"

It is only personal weakness that makes us content with what others or we ourselves have found out in this hunt for knowledge. . . . There is no end to our researches; our end is in the other world.

Montaigne, "Of Experience"

∗   ∗   ∗

". . . un sol volere è d'ambedue."

Inferno II, 139

CONTENTS

Inferno II and translation by Patrick Creagh and Robert Hollander   *xi*

Preface   *xxi*

1   The Canto of the Word   *I*

2   *Tre Donne Benedette*   20

    Problems in Interpretation   *20*

    The Question of Allegory   *43*

3   Pilgrim and Poet: Definition by Dialectic   *57*

    The Pilgrim as Aeneas and Paul   *57*

    The Poet's New Mission   *72*

Afterword   *91*

Abbreviations   *93*

Notes   *95*

Bibliography   127

Index   141

INFERNO

II

and

TRANSLATION

Lo giorno se n'andava, e l'aere bruno
   togliea li animai che sono in terra
   da le fatiche loro; e io sol uno   *3*
m'apparecchiava a sostener la guerra
   sì del cammino e sì de la pietate,
   che ritrarrà la mente che non erra.   *6*
O Muse, o alto ingegno, or m'aiutate;
   o mente che scrivesti ciò ch'io vidi,
   qui si parrà la tua nobilitate.   *9*
Io cominciai: "Poeta che mi guidi,
   guarda la mia virtù s'ell' è possente,
   prima ch'a l'alto passo tu mi fidi.   *12*
Tu dici che di Silvïo il parente,
   corruttibile ancora, ad immortale
   secolo andò, e fu sensibilmente.   *15*
Però, se l'avversario d'ogne male
   cortese i fu, pensando l'alto effetto
   ch'uscir dovea di lui, e 'l chi e 'l quale   *18*
non pare indegno ad omo d'intelletto;
   ch'e' fu de l'alma Roma e di suo impero
   ne l'empireo ciel per padre eletto: *21*
la quale e 'l quale, a voler dir lo vero,
   fu stabilita per lo loco santo
   u' siede il successor del maggior Piero. *24*
Per quest' andata onde li dai tu vanto,
   intese cose che furon cagione
   di sua vittoria e del papale ammanto.   *27*
Andovvi poi lo Vas d'elezïone,
   per recarne conforto a quella fede
   ch'è principio a la via di salvazione.   *30*
Ma io, perché venirvi? o chi 'l concede?
   Io non Enëa, io non Paulo sono;
   me degno a ciò né io né altri 'l crede.   *33*
Per che, se del venire io m'abbandono,
   temo che la venuta non sia folle.
   Se' savio; intendi me' ch'i' non ragiono." *36*
E qual è quei che disvuol ciò che volle
   e per novi pensier cangia proposta,
   sì che dal cominciar tutto si tolle,   *39*
tal mi fec' ïo 'n quella oscura costa,
   perché, pensando, cosumai la 'mpresa
   che fu nel cominciar cotanto tosta.   *42*

Daylight was fading, and the darkening air
Released all living things that are on earth
From their labors; and I, lone among men,   *3*
Was readying myself to face the struggle
Both of the way itself and of the pity,
Which memory, unerring, will retrace.   *6*
O Muses, O lofty genius, now sustain me.
O memory, that recorded what I saw,
Here shall your true worth be made apparent.   *9*
I began: "Poet, O you who lead me,
Assess my powers, whether they be sufficient,
Before you commit me to the lofty crossing.   *12*
You yourself say that Silvius's father,
Still subject to decay, went to the deathless
Realm, and was there in his own body.   *15*
But that the adversary of every evil
So favored him, considering what high sequel
Would spring from him, and who and what he was,   *18*
Seems not unjust, to a man of understanding;
For he was chosen in empyrean heaven
To be father of holy Rome and of her empire: *21*
The one and the other, if we tell the truth,
Were established in the sacred place
Where the successor of greatest Peter sits.   *24*
From this journey, with which you credit him,
He learnt of things ordained to be the cause
Of his own victory, and of the papal mantle.   *2,*
There, later, the Chosen Vessel went,
Thence to return with comfort for that faith
Which begins the journey toward salvation.   *30*
But I, why should I go there? Who permits it?
I am no Aeneas, I am no St. Paul.
Not I, not any one, thinks me worthy of it.   *33*
Therefore, if I resign myself to coming,
I fear it may be madness. You are wise,
You understand things better than I can say them."   *36*
And, like one who unwishes what he wished for
And changes his intent on second thoughts
So that he quite gives over what he'd started,   *39*
Such I myself became on that dark slope,
For, by thinking, I sapped the undertaking
Which had been so prompt in its inception.   *42*

"S'i' ho ben la parola tua intesa,"
    rispuose del magnanimo quell' ombra,
    "l'anima tua è da viltade offesa;   45
la qual molte fïate l'omo ingombra
    sì che d'onrata impresa lo rivolve,
    come falso veder bestia quand' ombra.   48
Da questa tema a ciò che tu ti solve,
    dirotti perch' io venni e quel ch'io 'ntesi
    nel primo punto che di te mi dolve.   51
Io era tra color che son sospesi,
    e donna mi chiamò beata e bella,
    tal che di comandare io la richiesi.   54
Lucevan li occhi suoi più che la stella;
    e cominciommi a dir soave e piana,
    con angelica voce, in sua favella: 57
'O anima cortese mantoana,
    di cui la fama ancor nel mondo dura,
    e durerà quanto 'l mondo lontana,   60
l'amico mio, e non de la ventura,
    ne la diserta piaggia è impedito
    sì nel cammin, che vòlt' è per paura;   63
e temo che non sia già si smarrito,
    ch'io mi sia tardi al soccorso levata,
    per quel ch'i' ho di lui nel cielo udito.   66
Or movi, e con la tua parola ornata
    e con ciò c'ha mestieri al suo campare,
    l'aiuta sì ch'i' ne sia consolata.   69
I' son Beatrice che ti faccio andare;
    vegno del loco ove tornar disio;
    amor mi mosse, che mi fa parlare.   72
Quando sarò dinanzi al segnor mio,
    di te mi loderò sovente a lui.'
    Tacette allora, e poi comincia' io: 75
'O donna di virtù sola per cui
    l'umana spezie eccede ogne contento
    di quel ciel c'ha minor li cerchi sui,   78
tanto m'aggrada il tuo comandamento,
    che l'ubidir, se già fosse, m'è tardi;
    più non t'è uo' ch'aprirmi il tuo talento. 81
Ma dimmi la cagion che non ti guardi
    de lo scender qua giuso in questo centro
    de l'ampio loco ove tornar tu ardi.'   84

"If I have understood your words aright,"
Replied the shade of that great-hearted one,
"Your spirit is impaired by cowardice,   *45*
A thing which often so impedes a man
That it turns him from some noble enterprise
As a beast sees false and shies away from shadow.   *48*
That you may be delivered from this fear
I will tell you why I came, and what I heard
At the first instant I felt pity for you.   *51*
I was one of those who are suspended,
When a lady called me, one so beautiful,
So blessèd, that I begged her to command me.   *54*
Her eyes shone forth more brightly than the star,
And sweetly, softly, she began to speak
With the voice of an angel, in her native tongue: *57*
'O courteous Mantuan spirit,
Whose glory still continues in the world
And will continue while the world endures,   *60*
A friend of mine, who is no friend to Fortune,
Upon the desolate slope is so impeded
On his way, that he has turned back in terror.   *63*
Judging from what I have heard of him in heaven,
I fear he is already so far astray
That I may have risen too late to be of help.   *66*
Go now, and with your polished speech
And whatever else is needed for his safety
Come to his aid, that I may be consoled.   *69*
I, who send you forth, am Beatrice.
I come from a place where I would fain return.
Love it was that moved me, that makes me speak.   *72*
When I am once again before my Lord
Often will I speak to Him in praise of you.'
Then she fell silent; and then I began: *75*
'O lady by whose virtue and nought else
The human race surpasses all that lies
Within the smallest compass of the heavens,   *78*
Your commandment is so pleasing to me
That, were it done already, it would seem late.
You have only to express your wishes to me.   *81*
But tell me the reason why you are not wary
Of descending here, into this center,
From the spacious place you are burning to return to.'   *84*

'Da che tu vuo' saver cotanto a dentro,
  dirotti brievemente,' mi rispuose,
  'perch' i' non temo di venir qua entro.   *87*
Temer si dee di sole quelle cose
  c'hanno potenza di fare altrui male;
  de l'altre no, ché non son paurose.   *90*
I' son fatta da Dio, sua mercé, tale,
  che la vostra miseria non mi tange,
  né fiamma d'esto 'ncendio non m'assale.   *93*
Donna è gentil nel ciel che si compiange
  di questo 'mpedimento ov' io ti mando,
  sì che duro giudicio là sù frange.   *96*
Questa chiese Lucia in suo dimando
  e disse: «Or ha bisogno il tuo fedele
  di te, e io a te lo raccomando.»   *99*
Lucia, nimica di ciascun crudele,
  si mosse, e venne al loco dov' i' era,
  che mi sedea con l'antica Rachele.   *102*
Disse: «Beatrice, loda di Dio vera,
  ché non soccorri quei che t'amò tanto,
  ch'uscì per te de la volgare schiera?   *105*
Non odi tu la pieta del suo pianto,
  non vedi tu la morte che 'l combatte
  su la fiumana ove 'l mar non ha vanto?»   *108*
Al mondo non fur mai persone ratte
  a far lor pro o a fuggir lor danno,
  com' io, dopo cotai parole fatte,   *111*
venni qua giù del mio beato scanno,
  fidandomi del tuo parlare onesto,
  ch'onora te e quei ch'udito l'hanno.'   *114*
Poscia che m'ebbe ragionato questo,
  li occhi lucenti lagrimando volse,
  per che mi fece del venir più presto.   *117*
E venni a te così com' ella volse:
  d'inanzi a quella fiera ti levai
  che del bel monte il corto andar ti tolse.   *120*
Dunque: che è? perché, perché restai,
  perché tanta viltà nel core allette,
  perché ardire e franchezza non hai,   *123*
poscia che tai tre donne benedette
  curan di te ne la corte del cielo,
  e 'l mio parlar tanto ben ti promette?"   *126*

'Since you so desire to learn the cause,'
She said in answer, 'I will tell you briefly
Why I am not afraid of entering here.   87
One has to be afraid of those things only
Which possess the power to do one harm;
Of others not, for they give no cause for fear.   90
I, of His mercy, have been made by God
Such that your wretchedness does not affect me,
Nor in this great fire does one flame assail me.   93
In heaven a gracious lady feels such pity
At this hindrance for which I send you out
That she is breaking a strict law on high.   96
This lady summoned Lucy to her bidding
And said: «One faithful to you now has need
Of you; and I entrust him to your care.»   99
Lucy, the enemy of all things cruel,
Arose and came to the place in which I was,
Where I was seated with venerable Rachel.   102
«Beatrice,» she said, «true praise of God,
Why do you not help him who loved you so
That for your sake he left the common herd?   105
Can you not hear the pity of his tears?
Can you not see the death contending with him
On the swollen river the sea itself can't best?»   108
Never were people in the world so prompt
To seek their profit or eschew their harm
As was I, after those words were spoken.   III
Down here I hurried from my blessèd seat,
Placing my faith in your fit and noble speech,
That honors you and all who have heeded it.'   114
When she had spoken to me to this effect
She turned her weeping, shining eyes aside,
So that I hastened all the more to come;   117
And I came to you, as she had asked me to:
I saved you from the beast that cut you off
From the short route up the lovely mountain.   120
So then, what is it? Why are you standing there?
Why harbor so much cowardice in your heart?
Why do you not have courage and conviction,   123
Seeing that three such blessèd ladies plead
In your favor in the high court of heaven
And my own words assure you of so much good?"   126

Quali fioretti dal notturno gelo
    chinati e chiusi, poi che 'l sol li 'mbianca,
    si drizzan tutti aperti in loro stelo,   *129*
tal mi fec' io di mia virtude stanca,
    e tanto buono ardire al cor mi corse,
    ch'i' cominciai come persona franca: *132*
"Oh pietosa colei che mi soccorse!
    e te cortese ch'ubidisti tosto
    a le vere parole che ti porse!   *135*
Tu m'hai con disiderio il cor disposto
    sì al venir con le parole tue,
    ch'i' son tornato nel primo proposto.   *138*
Or va, ch'un sol volere è d'ambedue:
    tu duca, tu segnore e tu maestro."
    Così li dissi; e poi che mosso fue,
intrai per lo cammino alto e silvestro.   *142*

As little flowers, by the frost of night
Bent down and closed, when the sun brightens them,
All straighten up and open on their stems,   129
So did I likewise with my flagging powers;
So much good ardor rushed into my heart
That I began, like a man set free: 132
"Compassionate was she who came to aid me!
Courteous were you, to have obeyed so swiftly
Those words of truth which she addressed to you!   135
With your own words you have so prepared my heart
With such desire to come
That I have now returned to my first resolve.   138
Go now, for a sole will is in us both:
You are my lord, my leader, and my teacher."
Thus I spoke to him; and when he set out
I started on the deep, wild way.   142

(translated by Patrick Creagh and Robert Hollander)

PREFACE

This study takes the tradition of the *Lectura Dantis* both as its model and its foil. Although our focus is on *Inferno* II, we have tried to avoid the tendency toward atomization characteristic of many traditional *lecturae* by analyzing both the canto's role in the poem as a whole and its relationship to other parts of the *Commedia*. We write on one canto out of a hundred, but we do so with the conviction that the whole poem is the first and best gloss on our canto and that the canto presents in part, or *in ombra*, many thematic and stylistic issues that are important for the whole poem.

Although the conventional *lectura* typically follows its canto's sequential presentation of material, we have chosen instead to organize this essay thematically, dividing our discussion into three related parts. The introductory chapter discusses and analyzes a pattern seen throughout the canto; it is at once a summary and a prelude, and it takes the form of an *explication de texte*. We consider various aspects of the canto's concern with language and with literature, arguing for its implicit metaliterary dimension. Questions of representation are central in the second chapter. We begin with an analysis of the role of the *tre donne benedette* considered first as a triad and then in terms of the specific attributes of each of the ladies. Our analysis of the nature of representation exemplified by Dante's figuration of these female figures leads to and culminates in a discussion of allegory. The third chapter explores Dante's diverse use of the canto's three major subtexts—Scripture, the *Aeneid*, and the *Consolation of Philosophy*. Throughout the *Commedia*, Dante's progressive poetic self-definition is in large part accomplished by his imaginative and strategic use of these texts. We examine their importance in Canto II to Dante's subsequent understanding of his vocation as the author of a "poema sacro." In both the second and third chapters we found it necessary to move from the immediate subject to its ultimate unfolding in the *Paradiso*; the central concerns of female mediation (Chapter 2) and of precedents for both the pilgrimage and the poem (Chapter 3) are first articulated in *Inferno*

II but later developed and recontextualized in the *Paradiso*. We came to conclude that the connections between this canto and the *Paradiso* were crucial and that, in fact, its uniqueness in the *Inferno* derives from its status as a foretaste (rather than a parodic inversion) of the final *cantica*.

Although we have dealt with several of the canto's hallowed cruces, we have done so only when we had something new to say about them or when the interpretive debate about them was itself instructive. Others we have passed by in silence, secure in the knowledge that Francesco Mazzoni's meticulous commentary on the canto would be available to any scholar who wished to learn more about them. Both the commentary tradition and the tradition of the *Lectura Dantis* tend to confer upon the crux a privileged status, as though its very existence determined the canto's interpretive trajectory or, tautologically, as though the history of interpretation itself endowed the crux with value. Within these traditions, there are several different kinds of issues that have gained such status. Canto II offers, for example, philological questions created by variant manuscript readings; thus the question of whether *mondo* or *moto* is the correct word in line 62 is a staple of the commentaries, as is the correct reading of line 108, which can be either "*ove* 'l mar non ha vanto" or "*onde* 'l mar non ha vanto." There are also questions about how we understand a phrase that may be read properly (from the grammatical point of view) in more than one way, questions such as whether *il chi e 'l quale* at line 18 refers to Aeneas or rather to the Empire, the "alto effetto / ch'uscir dovea di lui." Mazzoni's commentary consistently treats questions of this kind exhaustively, whereas we deal with them only when they are pertinent to our larger arguments. Thus we do, for example, take up such conventionally disputed issues as the meaning of the invocation to "alto ingegno," the significance of Beatrice's perplexing promise to praise Virgil to her Lord, and the interpretation of the *fiumana*. Because this is an essay rather than a commentary (even if, at times, the distinction between the two genres may be blurred), we have not limited ourselves to the problems consecrated by tradition but have tried to invent, as it were, our own sense of the true difficulties posed by the canto.

*　　*　　*

A project such as this one is imaginable at present only because of the extraordinary rethinking of Dante which has gone on in America in the past two generations. This essay is inevitably in many ways an *omaggio* to the late Charles S. Singleton, whose work laid the foundation on which so much that matters has been built. Singleton's first significant publications on Dante were on Canto II, and we have found those early articles, as well as Singleton's later work and his commentary, continually useful. There are many scholars we cite often, and our notes reflect a host of debts to scholars on both sides of the Atlantic. But we would like to express our special gratitude here to the two scholars who have taught us most about how to think about Dante: John Freccero and Robert Hollander. Their work, although quite different, helped us to see, to focus, and to formulate the issues that became central in our study. We would like to thank them as well for their personal support; the teaching of Dante all over America owes much to their inspiration and to their generosity. Jeffrey Schnapp, Kevin Brownlee, Nancy Vickers, and Ronald Herzman read earlier versions of the manuscript and helped us with specific suggestions and general encouragement. The four members of the editorial committee of the Dante Society (Robert Hollander, Joan Ferrante, Aldo Scaglione, and Anthony Pellegrini) read the manuscript with great care and gave us extraordinarily detailed and helpful suggestions; we are deeply grateful to all of them.

We would also like to express our gratitude to the library staffs of Wellesley College and the University of Vermont, as well as to the staffs of the Widener and Houghton Libraries of Harvard University and Princeton University's Index of Christian Art. The generosity of the Northeast Modern Language Association, the Mary Ingraham Bunting Institute of Radcliffe College, the National Endowment for the Humanities, and the Stanford Humanities Center helped us in various ways to bring this project to completion.

Publication of this book has been aided by grants from Wellesley College and the Dante Society of America.

CHAPTER I

The Canto of the Word

Inferno II is a liminal canto—at once proleptic and retrospective. In the course of its 142 lines, Dante offers a preliminary definition of the roles of the pilgrim, the poet, and the reader. Canto II serves as an introduction to the *Inferno* and anticipates *Paradiso*, even while providing expository information by recounting events that antedate those of the *Commedia*'s initial canto. It is the only canto in the first *cantica* set largely outside the *Inferno*, its action taking us out of the narrative sequence both in time and in space. Virgil's account of his meeting with Beatrice returns us to a time before the opening sequence of *Inferno* I, while his account of her description of the action of the three ladies in heaven advances us to a place and a perspective we will not reach until the very end of the poem, when the pilgrim himself enters the Empyrean. These shifts in time and space are necessary to establish the providential origin of the pilgrim's journey; in addition to inscribing that journey within the order of grace, the canto suggestively inaugurates the complex interplay of the poet's literary and spiritual imperatives. Finally, it creates for its readers a paradigm for responding to the poem whose inception they are simultaneously witnessing.

Inferno II is traditionally considered, together with Canto I, as the *Commedia*'s "Prologue Scene," with Canto I viewed as the proem to the whole poem and Canto II as the prologue to the *Inferno* itself; this perception is reinforced by the presence of the *cantica*'s invocation in *Inferno* II, rather than in its opening canto, as might be expected and as will be the case in both *Purgatorio* and *Paradiso*.[1] Furthermore, at the beginning of *Inferno* II the pilgrim has not yet entered into the topography of hell proper: he is still on the margin of the journey, thus lending to the two introductory cantos their "detached" quality and contributing to the startling effect of the words over the gate of hell which initiate the descent in Canto III.

I

The second canto, which marks a self-consciously transitional moment for the poet as much as for the pilgrim, is characterized by its "in-betweenness" in both geographical and representational terms— between the shadowy landscape of Canto I and the intensely mimetic specificity of Canto III (Freccero, 1984, pp. 772–773). The poet must move from the opening canto's allegorical conventions to the third canto's characteristically "figural realism," just as the pilgrim must move from one set of challenges (the *selva oscura* and the three beasts) to another (the gate of hell and all that Dante finds beyond it). [2] The canto opens with an unexplained temporal lacuna: Canto I is set at dawn, whereas Canto II begins in dusk, but with no account of what takes place between Virgil's arrival in the first canto (and the ensuing discussion between protagonist and guide) and the opening sequence of the second. There are obvious symbolic reasons for Dante to commence the actual journey into hell in darkness, [3] but this time gap also contributes, along with the presence of the invocation, to a sense that the poem is here beginning for a second time. The "missing" hours may find their equivalent in the "extra" twelve hours which Dante gains at the conclusion of the *Inferno* by crossing into the Southern Hemisphere. [4] In any case, Dante's elision of this period of time between the first and second cantos signals the primacy of symbolic concerns over sheer verisimilitude.

The structure of *Inferno*'s first two cantos is at once chiastic and parallel. Early in the first canto Dante glances optimistically to the sun with the "bene sperar" (I, 41) appropriate to "l'ora del tempo e la dolce stagione" (I, 43). He is driven back into despair, however, by the sequential appearance of the three beasts until Virgil's gratuitous appearance ("dinanzi a li occhi *mi si fu offerto*," I, 62). The pattern is reversed in the second canto, where, near its beginning, Dante is blocked by his own fears and is then freed from this impediment by Virgil's subsequent narration of the sequential intervention of the three ladies. [5] The chiastic aspect of the structure of these opening cantos also enacts in miniature a larger structural pattern of the *Commedia* as a whole; the negative version precedes what will turn out to be a positive reality just as the *Inferno* itself precedes and implies the inversions of the subsequent *cantiche*. [6]

Structurally, *Inferno* II may be divided into four units. [7] A nine-line prefatory section culminating in the invocation is followed by a tripartite sequence of action: Dante hesitates to undertake the journey (10–42); in response to that hesitation, Virgil offers encouragement (43–126); Dante accepts the encouragement and resumes the journey

(127–142). Dante's initial resistance temporarily reverses the conclusion of Canto I, where he had warmly embraced Virgil's guidance, beseeching the poet's aid ("Poeta, io ti richeggio") and appearing resolute in accepting it: "Allor si mosse, e io li tenni dietro." Dante undoes this resolution by invoking what at first appears to be his humility in the face of such an extraordinary adventure as Virgil has promised him. Unlike Aeneas and St. Paul, Dante says, he is unworthy of so great a courtesy, so that in going he would risk presumption: "temo che la venuta non sia folle."[8] Virgil responds to Dante's fear by recapitulating a series of dialogues in which he has been both participant and audience. He begins with Beatrice's journey to Limbo to solicit his good offices on Dante's behalf; in response to Virgil's query as to why she has left heaven to visit hell, Beatrice, through her report of a series of heavenly dialogues, recounts the prior concern of Mary and Lucy which prompted her own mission. In concluding, Virgil addresses Dante once again, this time in a hortatory mode, asking why he delays inasmuch as

> tre donne benedette
> curan di te ne la corte di cielo,
> e 'l mio parlar tanto ben ti promette.   (II, 124–126)

In the canto's closing lines, Dante demonstrates the efficacy of Virgil's speech by his response to it and by his decision to resume the journey: "e poi che mosso fue, / intrai per lo cammino alto e silvestro" (II, 141–142).

The closing line of Canto II is so close to that of Canto I[9] that the plot of *Inferno* seems to proceed directly from the end of the first canto to the opening of the third, from Dante's decision to undertake the journey to his confrontation of the gate of hell which signals its formal beginning.[10] Before we analyze the changes that do take place in Canto II, it is worth asking why Dante was not fully ready to undertake the journey on the basis of Virgil's speech in the first canto. Perhaps it is because Virgil initially responds to Dante's situation in ways that are not entirely apropos. In Canto I, Dante finds himself blocked by the three beasts, a situation which at first appears to figure externally an internal impediment to his progress. Virgil responds to what is imaged as a personal crisis by invoking a "public" and universal solution in his prophecy of the Veltro. However one reads this prophecy, it is clear that Virgil is talking about the salvation of "umile Italia" and not the pilgrim alone, understood as a particular man in a specific moral crisis. When Virgil moves from the prophecy of the Veltro to propose Dante's journey, he does so without linking the two subjects in any way. A logical connection between the prophecy and the necessity of the journey is announced (*"Ond'* io per lo tuo me' penso e discerno / che tu mi segui," I, 112–113) but never actually made. At the conclusion of the first canto, Dante still needs to know what the journey means for his own particular historicity and destiny.

The similarity between the concluding lines of the first two cantos forces us to probe the way the second canto recasts the enterprise in more personal and interior terms. Canto II has been called the "canto of stasis"[11] because the kind of motion that it entails is not immediately evident and because its emphasis on reported speech makes it appear less immediately vivid than the cantos that frame it. Yet the changes that occur between the beginning and the end of Canto II—changes in Dante's spiritual state, in his relationship to Virgil, to nature, and to himself—are so great that rather than being a canto of stasis, Canto II must in fact be characterized as a canto of motion. Dante calls attention to the changes that take place in the course of the canto by making its end echo the language of its opening. Some of the more self-evident of these echoes are part of a verbal pattern central to the canto's larger themes. For example, both the first and last lines of the canto use verbs of motion (with the day departing in line 1 and the two poets departing in lines 141–142), while Dante begins the canto doubting whether Virgil should entrust him to "l'alto passo" (II, 12) and sets off confidently at the end on the "cammino alto" (II, 142). Given the importance of motion at this point in the poem, these echoes must be programmatic, indicative of the canto's larger identification of language and action.[12]

Near the end of the canto, Dante describes the renewal which Virgil's words effect in him by means of a striking simile that transmutes the earlier terms of his indecisiveness. The canto had begun with Dante the poet separated from the other "animai" who leave "le fatiche loro" at the hour of dusk; he alone is refused such release and must prepare for the hard task at hand. The closing simile reverses these terms, with Dante's spirits reviving like flowers opening at dawn; "fioretti" replace "animai," dawn replaces dusk. Dante becomes one with the rhythms of nature instead of standing uniquely in opposition to them, and his initial sense of isolation ("io sol uno") gives way to an assertion of community ("un sol voler è d'ambedue"). He moves from doubt about whether "la mia virtù . . . è possente" to a reawakening of "mia virtude stanca," and from the vacillation that led him to "cangia[r] proposta" to the surety in which he has "tornato nel primo proposto."

These verbal repetitions highlight the dramatic realignment within Dante's psyche which takes place within the course of the canto.

This realignment comes about entirely through the medium of language. Although the primacy of sight for *Inferno* as a whole is established in the invocation's celebration of memory "che scrivesti ciò ch'io *vidi*," surprisingly little attention is paid within the canto to things seen; in comparing Canto II with either of its adjacent cantos, one becomes aware that the visual has yielded for the moment to the auditory. Although the canto consists primarily of dialogue, it is a drama with no real *mise en scène*. Rather than a vivid description of a given landscape or place, the canto describes motion from place to place— motion within heaven, from heaven to Limbo, from Limbo to earth, and, at its conclusion, on earth itself, as Virgil and Dante resume the interrupted journey. It has been clear from the opening lines of the *Commedia* that Dante's journey will be a spiritual one, a voyage within the self as well as within the universe: his destination is a new spiritual locus. In Canto II Dante reaffirms this commitment by linking physical motion to spiritual or affective motion. Characters move physically only *after* they have been moved spiritually, and it is words that move them. The exploration of the mediating role of language becomes the means by which Dante begins to define his role as poet. The relationship between speaker and auditor must be understood as a figure for the relationship between writer and reader.[13] Throughout the canto, language and motion are inextricably connected in ways that suggest Dante's evolving perception of the potential role of poetry, and in particular of his own poem.

Vocation: The Word as Action

The paradigm for the relationship of words to motion within the canto as a whole occurs at its exact center—the twenty-fourth of the canto's forty-seven *terzine*. This *terzina* is central not only numerically but thematically as well. In these lines Beatrice introduces herself by name to Virgil (and thereby to us) and explains with remarkable compression the reason for her presence:

> I' son Beatrice che ti faccio andare;
> vegno del loco ove tornar disio;
> amor mi mosse, che mi fa parlare.   (II, 70–72)

The emphasis in the verbs is on the life-and-death reality of the here and now, but both past and future are linked to the present moment; love moved her (past) to speak (present) so that Virgil will go (future) as she bids. These lines are the "kernel" of the canto and, in a sense, of the poem: the relationship between love and motion which is explicit here is played out repeatedly throughout the canto and will be recalled in cosmic terms in the poem's concluding line, when the pilgrim's desire and will are at one with "l'amor che move il sole e l'altre stelle" (*Paradiso* XXXIII, 145). In this central *terzina*, Beatrice explains to Virgil why she has come to him, but as the third line shows, the fundamental motion, the prior motion, was interior; she came to him only after love had first moved her. Her objective in speaking to Virgil is to create in him an analogous response—to move him emotionally so that he will move physically to rescue Dante, using his "parola ornata" to move Dante in turn. The parallel syntax of the first and third lines of the *terzina* insist on the interconnection of speech, love, and motion: "Beatrice che ti faccio andare" and "amor . . . che mi fa parlare."

The chain of *pietà* that brings Virgil to Dante dramatizes a sequential reenactment of this paradigm: compassion leads to motion, which leads to words; the speaker's words draw forth the listener's compassion, and the cycle is repeated. The prime mover in the chain of causality is Mary, the only character who responds directly to an event (Dante's distress) rather than to the words of another. Beatrice's description of Mary's compassionate intervention makes it the origin of all subsequent action in the canto and, by extension, in the entire poem. By narrating this "past" event in the present tense Beatrice suggests the ongoing importance of Mary's role even when it appears finished:

> Donna è gentil nel ciel che *si compiange*
>   di questo 'mpedimento ov'io ti mando,
>   sì che duro giudicio là sù *frange*.   (II, 94–96)

Mary's caring words to Lucy, the next stage in the drama, cause a comparable "double motion": as Beatrice represents Lucy's reaction, "si mosse, e venne al loco dov' i' era" (II, 101). "Si mosse, e venne" suggests a double motion; the reflexive form of the verb ("si mosse") points to Lucy's emotional response, to the motive for her subsequent motion. It is because she was moved by Mary's words that she came to Beatrice. Once again affective motion precedes and manifests itself in external motion.

Lucy's response is an animated plea to Beatrice:

Disse:—Beatrice, loda di Dio vera,
    ché non soccorri quei che t'amò tanto,
    ch'uscì per te de la volgare schiera?
Non odi tu la pieta del suo pianto,
    non vedi tu la morte che 'l combatte
    su la fiumana ove 'l mar non ha vanto—?   (II, 103–108)

Lucy's aggressive syntax—why don't you help, don't you hear, don't you see—suggests her surprise over Beatrice's failure to respond with the loving immediacy we come to see as normative; if she hears, why doesn't she feel, why doesn't she act? Beatrice's response to Lucy's words sets up the next verbal transaction; her response is to engage Virgil's emotions so that he will use his speech to move Dante:

Al mondo non fur mai persone ratte
    a far lor pro o a fuggir lor danno,
    com' io, dopo cotai parole fatte,
venni qua giù del mio beato scanno,
    fidandomi del tuo parlare onesto,
    ch'onora te e quei ch'udito l'hanno.   (II, 109–114)

Words and action are once again linked: it was specifically in response to Lucy's "cotai parole fatte" that Beatrice moved, and she did so to ask for verbal assistance, "parlare onesto." The conclusion of this speech restates Beatrice's earlier command to Virgil: "Or movi, e con la tua parola ornata . . . l'aiuta" (II, 67–69).

In his own summary exhortation, Virgil recapitulates the paradigm, urging Dante to resume the journey by underscoring the interrelationship of love and language, of the compassion of the *tre donne benedette* and his own words, "'l mio parlar [che] tanto ben ti promette" (II, 124 and 126). Dante concludes by responding to the entire narrative in exactly the terms in which Virgil had presented it:

Oh pietosa colei che mi soccorse!
    e te cortese ch'ubidisti tosto
    a le vere parole che ti porse!   (II, 133–135)

Virgil's obedient response to Beatrice's "vere parole" demonstrates both her compassion and his courtesy, his words finding their proper response in Dante's emotions and actions:

> Tu m'hai con desiderio il cor disposto
>   sì al venir con le parole tue,
>   ch'i' son tornato nel primo proposto.   (II, 136–138)

Virgil's words had "disposed" Dante's heart to resume the actual journey; Dante speaks of himself as "tornato," once again using a verb of
motion metaphorically.

The canto's verbal exchanges, taken together, suggest the positive
potential of language and imply an uncomplicated simultaneity of interpretation and of response to language, a celestial model, as it were,
of verbal interaction. To hear (*udire*) is to obey (*ubidire*): speech and
response are coordinate. There are, however, two moments in this
canto which render the question of interpretation problematic by
dramatizing the distinction between one character's words and another's understanding of them. When Dante protests that he is unworthy
of the journey, he invites Virgil to interpret his words: "Se' savio; intendi me' ch'i' non ragiono" (II, 36). Even though Dante's apparently
humble and self-deprecatory words had seemed entirely appropriate to
one in his condition, he ends by asking Virgil to understand them in a
way better than they were expressed, presumably by supplying details
and nuance which Dante, in his distress, might have overlooked. Dante
asks Virgil to be a creative interpreter of his words, and Virgil does just
that, repeating Dante's verb ("intendere") in responding, "S'i'ho ben la
parola tua intesa, / . . . l'anima tua è da viltade offesa" (II, 43, 45). We
should not lose sight of what a great surprise Virgil's response is. Dante
thought he had meant that he was not "degno" of an experience such
as Virgil had proposed; what Virgil hears in those words is that Dante
is a coward. There is an important distinction already "planted" in the
very language of Dante's speech—between Virgil who is "savio" and
Dante who "ragiona," between, that is, *sapientia* and *ratio*. Virgil's response, like that of all the actors in the celestial relay, comes at the level
of wisdom, a psychic process informed by a love capable of transcending the dead-end rationality with which Dante had persuaded himself
of his own inadequacy.

Since Virgil comprehends the unspoken significance of Dante's
words rather than the words alone, he is aware that they mean almost
the reverse of what Dante actually says. In the protestation of humility, Virgil hears a preoccupation with self—perhaps because Dante
repeats the pronoun "io" no fewer than five times in verses 31–34.
In denying that he deserves God's grace, Dante has missed the point.
The refusal of the gift of grace, however noble the alleged reason for
the refusal, is in fact an assertion of ego. Virgil's recognition of that

fact allows him to define Dante's reticence as cowardice rather than humility. His response is to show Dante how he can free himself from it:

> Da questa tema a ciò che tu ti solve,
> dirotti perch' io venni e quel ch'io 'ntesi
> nel primo punto che di te mi dolve.   (II, 49–51)

The reflexive form of *solversi* is the key here: Virgil will not be the one to liberate Dante from his fear, but he will provide an account of the concern of others so that Dante will be able to unbind himself. This emphasis on Dante's own participation in his psychic changes is confirmed in the repetition of the phrase "tal mi fec'io" (II, 40 and 130) to describe both Dante's undoing of his resolution and his recommitment, his ultimate reaction to Virgil's words.

In hearing Dante's words better than he intended, Virgil also provides Dante with a better model for understanding what he hears, a hermeneutic based not only on reason but also on the affections. Virgil's motivation, like that of all the agents in the canto, is based on loving compassion—"di te mi dolve"; in misunderstanding the nature of such gratuitous concern, Dante had discounted the mystery of human love as well as that of grace. Had he been aware of the chain of concern that led Virgil to him, Dante would have understood the continuity of *caritas* from heaven to earth and seen that the very power of love lies precisely in the fact that, though everyone needs it, no one can be said to deserve it. In protesting that he is unworthy of Virgil's offer, Dante assumes that he is being rewarded for some accomplishment or virtue; as Dante will learn in this canto, the concern of the *tre donne* is a response not to his strengths but to his weakness—not to what he deserves but to what he needs.

In "reading" Dante better than he intended, Virgil re-enacts the role which Beatrice had played with him in their earlier encounter in Limbo. For in Virgil's question about her presence in Limbo, Beatrice had immediately intuited the unspoken issue of fear. He asks her:

> Ma dimmi la cagion che non ti guardi
> de lo scender qua giuso in questo centro
> de l'ampio loco ove tornar tu ardi.   (II, 82–84)

Beatrice first explains "perch' i' non temo di venir qua entro," by recourse to an aphorism, in Mazzoni's words, "una solenne sentenza aristotelica:"[14]

Temer si dee di sole quelle cose
   c'hanno potenza di fare altrui male;
   de l'altre no, ché non son paurose.   (II, 88–90)

Virgil asks about self-protection, while Beatrice responds in terms of selflessness. Moving from a generic comment on fear to the particular conditions of her own descent, she responds that it was indeed fear that made it necessary for her to come—her fear for Dante, not for herself:

e temo che non sia già sì smarrito,
   ch'io mi sia tardi al soccorso levata,
   per quel ch'i'ho di lui nel cielo udito.   (II, 64–66)

Virgil shows that he has learned the lesson of Beatrice's words in his own subsequent speech to Dante: fear for one's own security can be debilitating, but acceptance of the concern of the other is empowering.

Invocation

Our analysis thus far has concentrated on what we earlier described as the last three of the canto's four narrative sections considered as a single, logically interrelated unit. We have focused on the ways the pilgrim's role is providentially grounded and articulated by means of a paradigm of words, emotion, and motion, a paradigm which dramatizes the salvific potential of language as seen in terms of the pilgrim's situation. Now we turn to the question of the poet's role as it is established by the canto's opening nine lines and to the more specifically literary issues raised by this "overture." In Dante's use of literary allusion as well as in the invocation, we can see him at once adopting and transforming the texts of tradition.

The canto opens on a particularly literary note. Its first six lines contain two recognizable Virgilian allusions. Dante, we remember, had greeted Virgil in *Inferno* I by avowing Virgil's importance to his prior literary career:

Tu se' lo mio maestro e 'l mio autore,
   tu se' solo colui da cu' io tolsi
   lo bello stilo che m'ha fatto onore.   (I, 85–87)

The opening lines of Canto II give evidence that not just Virgil's style but his very words are here in Dante's mind. The first *terzina* recalls a common Virgilian formula in which human isolation is set against the nightly repose of the remainder of the natural world.[15] Since this "nox erat" formula occurs four different times in four different situations in the *Aeneid* (III, 147; IV, 522–523; VIII, 26–27; IX, 224–225), it is not immediately obvious which particular echo Dante wishes to evoke, or whether the allusion is to be regarded instead as generically Virgilian. The first two of the Virgilian instances seem equally likely to be the allusion we are intended to hear, as Mazzoni, following Pietro di Dante, concludes (p. 165). Even though the artistic function of the one would be very different from the other—ironic, that is, as opposed to typological—either usage would be consonant with Dante's way of adapting Virgil elsewhere in the poem and indeed in this very canto.

The passage cited by most commentators is from Book IV of the *Aeneid*, the falling of the final night of Dido's life. The description of nightfall is followed by Dido's pained soliloquy and the description of Aeneas already at sea. If this is the intended allusion, then Dido's situation provides an ironic counterpoint to Dante's; she is about to lose her love and her life, while he is about to rediscover his love and gain eternal life. But if the allusion is meant to recall Book III, a different intertextual relationship obtains; the allusion would supply a thematic parallel to Dante's situation. The description of nightfall in that book is the setting for Aeneas's dream, in which his mission is clarified and redirected by the visionary appearance of the *penates*. Aeneas's landing at Crete, like Dante's initial attempt to climb the mountain unaided, has been a false start.[16] Like Virgil in Canto II, the *penates*, representatives of a transcendental wisdom, reframe Aeneas's mission, bringing the gods' perspective to bear for Aeneas, just as Virgil recounts the heavenly prehistory of Dante's mission. The allusion thus would identify Dante's situation with that of Aeneas and would place Virgil in the role of the messenger of the providential vision of the mission at hand. That either Virgilian allusion might be appropriate offers an early example of the complexity of Dante's use of the *Aeneid*: it can function as an ironic subtext whose presence underscores Dante's distance from his model, or it can enrich the specific context of Dante's text through significant parallelism. Both of these modalities are explored by Dante throughout the *Commedia*, though rarely with the ambiguity that makes it as difficult to decide between them.[17]

The second Virgilian allusion in the opening lines is, as Hermann Gmelin noticed, to the climactic moment in Book VI when Anchises greets his son in the Elysian Fields. Dante's "la guerra / sì del cammino e sì della pietate" rewrites Virgil's "uenisti tandem, tuaque exspectata parenti / uicit iter durum pietas?" (VI, 687–688) [Have you come at last,

and has the pious / love that your father waited for defeated / the difficulty of the journey?]. Robert Ball notes the importance of Dante's
allusion to the culmination of Aeneas's *pietas* at the moment when the
pilgrim is about to begin his own underworld descent. As Ball shows,
Dante's polysemous use of the word *pietà* undergoes "semantic complication" by association with classical, and in particular, Virgilian
pietas (pp. 60–61).[18] In this very canto, the only place in the poem
where the adjective *pietosa* is used of Beatrice, we can witness a shift in
the word's meaning—from anguish to compassion—a shift that mirrors the canto's larger concern. But the recall to the *Aeneid*'s "iter
durum" also glosses the nature of Dante's own journey; although Dante
does not undertake his descent in search of his father, it will be the
prelude to his own reunion with a transformed Anchises figure, Cacciaguida, who will in turn articulate Dante's mission. (In the largest
sense, of course, Dante's journey is to his spiritual father, God the Creator, Alpha and Omega.)

The Virgilian allusions, apart from their specific meanings, begin
to establish the literariness of the canto's opening, but the most overtly
and conventionally literary gesture is, of course, the invocation, which
comes as the conclusion to the opening nine lines. These lines are characterized by a complex interplay of verb tenses. The narrative voice
moves from the opening description of the pilgrim's situation rendered
in the imperfect ("se n'andava," "toglieva," "m'apparecchiava") through
an announcement of the poet's future relation to the pilgrim's experience ("che ritrarrà la mente") to the vocative present of the invocation
("or m'aiutate"). Both the first six lines and the subsequent *terzina* of
the invocation conclude with verbs in the future tense, words whose
sounds echo one another: "che *ritrarrà* la mente che non erra," and
"qui si *parrà* la tua nobilitade." The play of tenses in the opening nine
lines (imperfect, *passato remoto*, present, and future) mimes the complex interweaving of temporalities of the journey and its poetic counterpart: both future verbs anticipate during the present of writing the
effect of the future completion of an act that, in the narrative, has only
just begun.

This interlacing of temporalities opens up the question of the status
of the poet. For even if the poet has of necessity completed the pilgrim's
journey, as poet he is at the beginning of the journey of writing, and
thus fallible and open to error despite the lessons of the journey; the
fiction assumes that he has already completed the journey, but since he
has yet to experience the act of composing the poem inspired by that
journey, the act of composition must be projected into the future. Only

such a formulation can allow us to understand the complexity of the poet's own figure: the poet is *in via* as well as the pilgrim. Most of the time we are not aware of this fact, and Dante criticism traditionally promotes the distinction between a fallible pilgrim and an infallible poet—a pilgrim, to take the classic example, who faints at Francesca's speech and a poet-convert who retrospectively manifests a "corrected" relationship to that same speech. Perhaps we also need to think of a third "Dante" to differentiate the writer of the poem from both of his creations: from the figure of the poet created within the text of the *Commedia*, no less than from the pilgrim. Dante's assertions of personal salvation and the conventions of first-person conversion narratives should not blind us to the fact that the poem's persona, which alleges to be the poet's own voice, is as much a fictional creation as the voice of *Moby Dick*'s Ishmael or the voice of the *Canterbury Tales'* narrator. That the *Commedia*'s narrative voice is identical with Dante's own is "true" only insofar as it is the major premise of the poem's fiction.[19]

These considerations are relevant to the interpretive debate generated by Dante's first invocation.[20] The main questions are, first, whether the references to "muse," "alto ingegno," and "mente" are invocations to all three or only to the first two, and, second, what the precise nature of "alto ingegno" might be. As for the first question, the poem's syntax makes it clear that only the first two powers are called upon for assistance. As Hollander says, "*mente* is put forward as the power within him that records what *alto ingegno* makes available to it. It is not invoked" ("*Inferno* II: Canto of the Word"). In fact, *mente* is celebrated ("qui si parrà la tua nobilitate") rather than called upon.[21]

The relationship of "muse" to "alto ingegno" is, however, more difficult to specify. The majority of the commentators take "alto ingegno" to refer to Dante's own *ingegno*, many of them citing the use of "altezza d'ingegno" in Cavalcante's address to Dante in *Inferno* X. The dramatic situation of that canto, however, would call such a reading into question since the point of the interchange between Cavalcante and Dante is precisely to undercut any such claims for the unaided human intellect. The only way that one could maintain this reading would be to see the poet at the opening of the *Inferno* in an "infernal" stance analogous to the one Peter Hawkins suggests that he briefly takes on in *Inferno* XXV. Although this might at first seem farfetched, we have to remember that this invocation is only the first of nine. As Hollander has pointed out, these invocations are placed strategically and hierarchically across the *Commedia* (1980, pp. 31–38). It is possible that the first of them may be designed to reflect the limits of the poet at the beginning of his own formulation of the poem. If so, the very limits of the project open it up to subsequent redefinition and development, just as Dante will redefine the categories in which the poem may be seen. Dante reinvents generic terminology as the poem progresses so that what had been called a "comedìa" in the *Inferno* is ultimately seen as a "teodìa" (Barolini, pp. 271–279). The poem, that is, remains open to reformulation by the poet as he creates it—an effect which necessitates a retrospective reading of its poetic assumptions as well as of the pilgrim's experience. [22]

An alternate reading of the invocation insists on interpreting "alto ingegno" as a veiled reference to a divine source of power. Among the older commentators this position was taken by Castelvetro and Bennassuti, and it has recently been revived by Hollander: "I would propose that Dante first seeks the human skills of poetic expression from traditional sources ['Muse'] and then the power of the highest conceptualization from its sole and very source ['alto ingegno']. The raw daring of such a claim has kept our following wit at a nervous distance" ("*Inferno* II: Canto of the Word"). In this reading we must understand "alto ingegno" as a reference to God and thus as the equivalent of Dante's invocation to "buono Apollo" at the opening of *Paradiso*. Hollander proceeds from the assumption that Dante's narrative stance as poet is consistent from the poem's outset: since the poet has concluded the entire experience described in the poem before beginning to write about it, he must be invoking "alto ingegno" as a divine source for the entire literary enterprise.

In choosing to interpret "alto ingegno" conclusively as an address either to Dante's own powers or to a divine agency, one needs to suppress the ambiguity of the phrase, an ambiguity highlighted by the oscillation of the commentary tradition between these two readings. Mazzoni suggests another way into the problem by treating "muse" and "alto ingegno" as one of the poem's many "coppie sinonimiche: si tratterà piuttosto d'una dittologia o iterazione sinonimica, a indicare l'Arte poetica in generale; e dunque l'alto ingegno è il genio delle Muse ispiratrice di poesia e delle Arti" (p. 175). Mazzoni's formulation of "alto ingegno" as "poetic art in general" situates the source in an indeterminate space, neither inherent in the poet as practitioner of that art nor coterminous with God. Mazzoni's argument correctly places the emphasis on the *literary* nature of the enterprise. For most of the twenty-five times "ingegno" is used in the *Commedia*, the word has the sense of "genius," that is, of one's inborn capacity for conception or invention. [23] The pairing of "ingegno" and "arte," common in Virgil and other poets of antiquity, is frequent in Dante as well, where "ingegno" indicates one's given faculties and "arte" those which are acquired. Dante's invocation of the power of "alto ingegno" could thus, as Mazzoni implies, be to the faculty of poetic virtue in a generic sense since his own possession of it would be no merit of his own, but rather a gift. In this sense, he can both ask for it and have it. Dante himself provides support for just such a reading in the invocation to the Gemini in *Paradiso* XXII, a passage that resolves the possible contradictions of the earlier invocation:

> O gloriöse stelle, o lume pregno
> di gran virtù, dal quale io riconosco
> tutto, qual che si sia, il mio ingegno.
>
> (*Paradiso* XXII, 112–114)

Thus "ingegno," like "mente," is a faculty that inheres in the poet—and yet it is different in that it is a power which, in the last analysis, was given to him from outside.

* * *

In addition to its opening lines, there are other aspects of the canto which bring literary issues to the foreground. Although Dante's vocation as a poet will not be articulated in its entirety until the final *cantica*, the process of discovering and revealing the potential of his poem begins in Canto II. Accordingly, the canto contains a high quotient of language about language; it is, as Hollander has said, the canto of the word, the canto in which the word "parola" appears more than in any other. [24] The contrast established between Beatrice's speech ("soave e piana") and Virgil's "parola ornata," as Benvenuto was the first to argue, introduces the question of stylistic decorum at the outset. For Benvenuto, this contrast signals a more significant opposition between the humility of "sermo divinus" and the "altus et superbus . . . sermo Virgilii et poetarum" (p. 90). Erich Auerbach, and after him, Hollander and Giuseppe Mazzotta, develop Benvenuto's contrast between divine speech and the elevated and proud speech of Virgil and the other poets into a Christian critique of pagan stylistic categories and their moral implications. [25] The distinction may also imply a critique of Dante's own earlier artistic ideals as they were formulated in the *De vulgari eloquentia* and manifested in his earlier poetry; it points to one aspect of the shift from the poetics of the *Convivio* to the poetics of the *Commedia*, from the stylistic purity of the "bello stilo," not only to a Christian "sermo humilis," but also to the lexical and stylistic capaciousness Gianfranco Contini has aptly called the "plurilinguismo" of the *Commedia.*[26]

But the issue is more complicated than it appears, because the canto both articulates and violates traditional notions of decorum: Benvenuto's polarities do not take account of the inversion of expected diction in the speeches of Beatrice and Virgil. Mazzoni speaks of Beatrice's *sermo humilis* in contrast with "le più ricercate figure retoriche di Virgilio" (p. 156), but for a good part of their interchange, each of the two characters actually speaks in the other's idiom. Beatrice's speech is highly rhetorical, characterized by allusions to Scripture, to Aristotle, and to Virgil himself,[27] while Virgil's speech is replete with echoes of Dante's stilnovistic poetry. The stylistic register of the canto as a whole is complicated by its richly varied lexicon, which commingles stilnovistic, epic, biblical, philosophical, and theological diction. The precise valence of each of these components of the total register is not always clear at this stage of the poem, a fact which complicates the interpretation of certain key phrases.

How, for example, are we to read Beatrice's calling on Virgil with respect to "la tua parola ornata?" This certainly sounds like a positive attribution until we note that the next occurrence of the phrase comes in a description of Jason in the *bolgia* of the seducers ("Ivi con segni e con parole ornate / Isifile ingannò," *Inferno* XVIII, 91–92).[28] Since the word is elsewhere connected with the coronation of the great poets of antiquity,[29] it retains the complimentary sense that it has in *Inferno* II, while suggesting the problem of the potential seductiveness of highly wrought linguistic constructs. As it turns out, in *Inferno* II the one speaker who can be defined as using language in this way is actually Beatrice herself. When Beatrice promises Virgil that she will often sing his praises before God (II, 73–74), what can she possibly be promising?[30] The fiction of the poem everywhere insists on the impossibility of such an action taking place or of its having the slightest impact even if it could take place. Beatrice's promise cannot, that is, be understood as a truthful comment on the relationship of the saved to the damned. (Nor can her saying that she is worried that she will not reach Dante on time: this fear makes no sense given what we are later told about the way the blessed see in and through divine knowledge of all time, as *Paradiso* XVII makes clear.) Her promise, it would seem, is a rhetorical act in a good cause. It takes part of its meaning from the value of praise as a speech act as Dante had earlier defined it in the *Vita Nuova*, an act worthy without reference to any end outside of itself. The disinterested quality of praise which Dante had dramatized as the key insight of the

Vita Nuova is here enacted by Beatrice, who in this canto is called "loda di Dio vera."

The question of the "parola ornata" is ultimately a question about literary language and its potential for both truth and falsehood, part of the poem's ongoing interrogation of the relationship between rhetoric and truth. These questions are particularly acute in Dante's poem because of its unique conflation of literary and biblical models. However theological Dante's poem may be in its import and even in its aims, it remains a self-consciously literary artifact. The tension between the poem's eschatological imperatives and its literary ambitions is central to its construction and its effect. [31] The pilgrim's drama does not take precedence over the poet's, as Benvenuto suggests in his marvelous "misreading" of the line "Io non Aenea, io non Paolo sono." Where Dante seems to be invoking models appropriate to the pilgrim, Benvenuto (p. 78) reads this line as referring to the poet's sources:

> Examinabat enim autor intra se vires suas, et arguebat et objciebat contra se: Tu non es Homerus, tu non Virgilius; tu non attinges excellentiam famosorum poetarum, et per consequens opus tuum non erit diu in precio.

> [For the author was examining his powers within himself, arguing and objecting against himself: You are not Homer, you are not Virgil; you will not attain the excellence of the famous poets, and consequently your work will not long be valued.]

But of course Dante's models at this juncture are not merely the great poets of antiquity represented by Homer and Virgil. We would need to rewrite Benvenuto's version of the line to read, "You are not Virgil, you are not Scripture," which in turn might be read as "You are not fiction, you are not truth," since the *Commedia* claims to tell the truth and at the same time calls attention to its fictions. By following in the footsteps of both the great classical epics and Scripture, it invents for itself a new and unique status.

*   *   *

In this proemial canto, Dante dramatizes the inescapably intertwined value and riskiness of language and of literature. The opening lines establish the poet's persona and insist on the literariness of the poem, while the remainder of the canto places the pilgrim's journey under the sign of grace through the representation of a series of sequential mediations that repeat the paradigm of words-emotion-motion. The process dramatized here *in bono* is the reverse of the one we will encounter soon after in *Inferno* V. In that canto, compassion replicates passion; the multiple seductions of literature and speech set off a sequence of imitations *in malo*. Our capacity to evaluate this subsequent narrative owes much to our experience of its "inverse reflection" in *Inferno* II (Barolini, pp. 7, 10–12). Through a series of negative exempla (Francesca da Rimini, Pier della Vigna, Brunetto Latini, and Ulysses being among the most famous of them) the *Inferno* explores and attempts to exorcise the negative power of the word, its potential for destructive seminality— for schism, self-deception, and perversion. *Inferno* II's narration of sequential mediations posits a model that does not unfold until after the rest of the first *cantica* is completed. Canto II provides at the outset an emblematic model for the constructive and salvific possibilities of language and of literature, an ideal relation between emotion and motion, action and words, language and love. Castelvetro, commenting on the chain of grace in this canto, takes objection to its proliferation of mediations. "Non è verosimile," he argues, using a term dear to sixteenth-century literary discourse; the Virgin could surely have acted without the assistance of Lucy and Beatrice, or all three could have acted together at once (p. 44). Castelvetro's criticism has the advantage of calling our attention to Dante's deliberate emphasis on the *process* of mediation. It is precisely the multiplication of agents in the drama and the cumulative effect of multiple reenactment that establishes the paradigm as such.

This serial narrative structure is reminiscent of the sequence at the heart of another great exemplary narrative, Augustine's *Confessions*. The account of Augustine's conversion in Book VIII takes place as the climax of a series: stories of conversion in that book lead to the conversion of others, dramatizing the power of the written word to change the hearts of its readers. When Augustine passes the text of the Epistles of Paul to his friend, Alypius, thereby providing him with the text that has been the instrument of his own conversion, the gesture extends the process by instantly turning Augustine's own experience into an exemplum, a process the *Confessions* hopes to continue to effect in the souls of its ideal readers. [32] In Book VIII of the *Confessions*, as in *Inferno* II, the embedded narrative structure establishes a sequential rhythm whose conclusion draws the reader into the process he or she is witnessing. In *Inferno* II, no less than *Confessions* VIII, response to the speech of another is shown to be a creative and creating act as important as speech itself, since the salvific potential of speech can be enacted only with the proper response. *Inferno* II becomes in part the story of how one should respond to the story of another. Insofar as speech and response are equivalent to writing and reading, we are being shown at the very opening of Dante's poem what our role as readers is ideally supposed to be: the last step in the chain of compassionate causation initiated by Mary thus specifically writes the reader into the poem's metaliterary concerns. Just as the *Confessions* is both record and result of Augustine's conversion, the *Commedia* was intended, as the Letter to Cangrande asserts, "to remove those living in this life from the state of misery and to lead them to the state of happiness."[33] Mary speaks to Lucy, who speaks to Beatrice, who speaks to Virgil, who speaks to Dante, who speaks to us; this remarkable canto both reveals the origin of Dante's journey and points to its end.

CHAPTER II

Tre Donne Benedette

Problems in Interpretation

Prologue and Analogues

Virgil persuades Dante of the propriety and the providentiality of the journey by recounting its celestial origin in the sequential intervention of *tre donne benedette*. The importance of this scene may be inferred from its length: it lasts from line 52 to line 120, a total of 68 lines, or nearly one half the canto. Like a "play within a play" it crystallizes a number of the poem's major concerns. The immediate space-time setting established in the opening canto is temporarily replaced by other locations (the celestial rose and Limbo) and dissolved into a prior temporality.[1] We begin our analysis of this scene by considering its possible models.

Although it has become traditional to refer to this scene in terms of an epic topos as a "prologue in heaven" (Mazzoni, p. 151), commentators have not explored the exact implications of such a formula. Dante's specific model for such a prologue is his model for much else that takes place in the opening cantos of the *Inferno*, the *Aeneid*. Some years ago Robert Hollander argued that "the parallels between *Inferno* I and II and *Aeneid* I offer convincing proof that Dante consciously reflected Virgil's first book in the beginning of his book" (1969, p. 83); his detailed examination of Virgilian echoes in the *Commedia*'s opening cantos made clear the precision with which Dante uses the *Aeneid* as a constitutive subtext from the very opening of his narrative. What has not been noticed, however, is the double-edged nature of Dante's invocation of the Virgilian prologue in heaven: the differences between the two scenes are as significant as the similarities. As is often the case, the more visibly the *Commedia* recalls the *Aeneid*, the more Dante opens a space of differentiation between the two texts.

In both the *Aeneid* and the *Commedia* the prologue in heaven follows an opening scene of crisis *in medias res*; in both poems such a prologue reframes the action by placing it within a transcendental perspective. In the *Aeneid*, the prologue in heaven follows the opening sequence in which Aeneas is shipwrecked on the coast of Africa. Virgil stages an encounter between Aeneas's tearful mother, Venus, and Jupiter which culminates in Jupiter's promise of Aeneas's and Rome's ultimate triumph. Jupiter's promise/prophecy introduces the temporality of the future into the poem's action, supplying a transcendental telos for the action that follows. The prologue concludes with two "heavenly descents": [2] Mercury is dispatched to Carthage to make the Phoenicians receptive to Aeneas, and Venus appears to Aeneas to lay the groundwork for his encounter with Dido. Aeneas himself, however, never hears about Jupiter's promises; Jupiter's speech is given for Venus's benefit—and for the reader's—but the hero as yet receives no divine reassurance. Furthermore, Venus plays an ambiguous role, symbolized by her appearance in disguise. When she predisposes Aeneas to fall in love with Dido, she thinks she is doing so for his good, but, as we know from Book IV, this is a love that actually stands in the way of the very promises Jupiter has made to Venus in Book I; Aeneas must leave Dido and Carthage behind to fulfill the destiny Jupiter had foretold. He recognizes Venus's true identity only at the very end of their exchange as she is departing, a recognition which he expresses with a poignant cry:

> ille ubi matrem
> adgnouit, tali fugientem est uoce secutus:
> "quid natum totiens, crudelis tu quoque, falsis
> ludis imaginibus? cur dextrae iungere dextram
> non datur ac ueras audire et reddere uoces?"   (I, 405–409)

> [And when Aeneas recognized his mother,
> he followed her with these words as she fled:
> "Why do you mock your son—so often and
> so cruelly—with these lying apparitions?
> Why can't I ever join you, hand to hand,
> to hear, to answer you with honest words?"]

Aeneas's words to his fleeing mother are selectively echoed in *Inferno*

II: while Aeneas longs for "veras voces," Dante gives thanks to Virgil for Beatrice's "vere parole"; while Venus is called "crudelis" by her son, Lucy is "nemica di ciascun crudele." These verbal similarities become a means of ironically distancing the texts from one another, calling attention to the profound contrasts between them. [3]

In Canto II, all three female figures behave with unequivocal maternal solicitude toward Dante, and Virgil's narration of their intervention is designed precisely to reassure the pilgrim. But in the *Aeneid*, Aeneas's actual mother appears to her son in a disguise that associates her with Dido—she appears in a hunting outfit similar to the one Dido will later wear—whose love will prove destructive both to Aeneas and to herself; Venus's identity as well as her solicitude thus partake of complex dissimulation. Throughout the *Aeneid*, the female deities are shown to be destructive, disruptive, or ambiguous; moreover, the power of the gods in general is ambiguous in Virgil's poem, at least at the level of the characters' awareness of it. For Dante, this is an aspect of their limitations as pagan deities, as "dèi falsi e bugiardi" (*Inferno* I, 72). The ambiguity of pagan oracular knowledge, the "ambage" which are subject to human misinterpretation, will be contrasted by Dante with the "chiare parole" and "preciso latin" (*Paradiso* XVII, 34–35) with which he will finally be granted knowledge of his own future. The distinction between pagan and Christian prophetic speech is already suggested in Canto II by the contrast between the *Commedia*'s prologue in heaven and the *Aeneid*'s.

The comparison between Virgilian and Dantean, classical and Christian, perspectives is an ongoing stylistic and thematic dialectic of the *Commedia*. In an example such as the one we have been examining, there is an additional ironic distancing that occurs because Dante not only alludes to the *Aeneid* but also makes its author a character in the scene modeled on the Virgilian source; thus it is the character Virgil who participates in and reports on a scene derived from one contained in his own poem. In Dante's poem, Virgil replaces Venus as the "messenger" to the hero and provides exactly the comfort his own hero had been denied in a comparable moment.

Another implicit comparison is that between the ambivalent and often negative role of both the female and the feminine in Virgil and Dante's celebration of the potential power of female mediation. Virgil presents Aeneas's mother in her first appearance with suggestive erotic overtones, while Dante presents his beloved, Beatrice, as we shall see, in terms that "maternalize" her. These initial presentations prefigure subsequent divergences of major importance in the two poems.

The Virgilian prologue in heaven, despite its importance, is only one of several models for the scene. Another, as Edward Moore noticed (1896), is the encounter between Boethius and Lady Philosophy at the opening of the *Consolation of Philosophy* (pp. 282–288). As Pietro di Dante observed, Virgil's question to Beatrice about why she has descended to hell echoes Boethius's question to Lady Philosophy:

> "Et quid," inquam, "tu in has exilii nostri solitudines
> o omnium magistra uirtutum supero cardine delapsa
> uenisti?" (I. pr. iii, 6–8)

> ["Mistress of all virtues," I said, "why have you come, leaving
> the arc of heaven, to this lonely desert of our exile?"]

We shall have occasion to discuss this particular echo more fully later, but for now the important point is the Boethian paradigm. An awareness of its presence gives Beatrice's desire for consolation ("sì ch'i' ne sia consolata") special resonance; whereas Lady Philosophy *offers* consolation, Beatrice represents herself as *seeking* it from Virgil. (She is, of course, offering it to Dante by means of her request to Virgil, but her consolation will derive from consoling Dante.) The centrality of the word "consolation" to Dante's ongoing meditation on Boethius, and by implication on the role of philosophy in Dante's intellectual and moral development, is evident in the next occurrence of the word in the *Commedia* in the parallel canto, *Purgatorio* II, where, as Freccero (1973) and Hollander (1975) have shown, Dante stages a complex palinode to his earlier narrowly conceived Boethian allegiances and to the *Convivio*, the work that had celebrated them.

In a forthcoming essay on *Purgatorio* II, Hollander remarks that each of the three *cantiche* "begins hopefully and then moves to the experience of a troubling inadequacy of one kind or another; and then in each case aid or enlightenment comes down from above" ("*Purgatorio* II: The New Song and the Old"). The retrograde motion of each of the three Cantos II has yet another structural similarity; in each case Dante recalls the *Convivio* in specific ways to revise or correct an earlier stance he had taken there. This is most explicit, as Daniel Ransom has shown, in *Paradiso* II where Dante has Beatrice correct his earlier opinion on the cause of the moon spots. In *Purgatorio* II, the *Convivio* is present through Casella's singing of the canzone, "Amor che nella mente mi ragiona," from the third tractate of the *Convivio* in a context that, as Hollander and Freccero have argued, is a palinode to that poem and its Boethian ethos. In *Inferno* II the *Convivio* is present in more subtle forms, but here, too, we see Dante bringing it to mind so as to redefine and transcend its implications. As we shall see, this is clearest in Dante's reappropriation and polemical reattribution of the role played by the *Convivio*'s *donna gentile*. Dante's "rewriting" of the *Convivio*, like his "rewriting" of the *Aeneid*, is an intermittent but continuous aspect of the *Commedia*, for Dante is engaged in an ongoing revisionary reading of his own earlier poetry, and the dynamics of this process are analogous to those that govern his use of other poetic predecessors. Canto II provides several examples of this strategy which our essay will treat in context.

The Female Triad

That three ladies rather than one are instrumental in Dante's rescue may remind us of other places in Dante's earlier work in which the motif of a female triad is significant. The most important of these is the powerful exilic *canzone*, "Tre donne intorno al cor." The *tre donne* of this *canzone* are clearly allegorical figures, and most commentators follow Dante's son Pietro in seeing them as three aspects of Justice.[4] The ladies "generate" one another so that their relationship is seen as familial, each giving birth to the next, a sequential progression that seems faintly echoed in the relationship of the three ladies in Canto II. In the *canzone* the three ladies seek consolation from Love who is seated in Dante's heart, while in *Inferno* II it is the ladies who proffer aid to Dante. The motif of three ladies reappears in the *Convivio* (IV, xxii, 160ff.), where the figures are again to be read primarily in allegorical terms, as Dante makes explicit: the three Marys at the empty tomb are there interpreted as types of the three philosophical sects that seek beatitude in the active life. And in *Monarchia* II, iii, 7, Dante similarly analyzes the three wives of Aeneas in quasi-allegorical terms.

The recurrence of versions of the female triad suggests that Dante found it a congenial topos, and one that he associated naturally with schematic allegorical interpretation.[5] Most of the early commentators (and many of the modern ones) treat *Inferno* II's *tre donne benedette* as if Dante had similarly conceived them in terms of just such personification allegory, as if they were represented, for example, like the three ladies dancing at Beatrice's chariot in *Purgatorio* XXIX, 121–123. They have been glossed most frequently as manifestations of three types of grace (prevenient, illuminating, and cooperating) or as the three theological virtues.[6] As Giorgio Padoan commented ruefully, this mode of interpretation has not made much difference to the ultimate interpretive act: "Io credo che discussioni di questo tipo siano un po' oziose, perchè l'una o l'altra spiegazione non sposta di un millimetro la sostanza del discorso qui fatto dal poeta."[7] The tendency to think of the three ladies in abstract terms is also evident in the early illustrations that echo the preoccupations of the commentators. Peter Brieger notes that the arrangement of the three ladies echoes that of the three beasts in several illustrations, "proof that it is less the personal than the allegorical which is stressed."[8] It is also striking that none of the three ladies is illustrated with reference to any particular iconographic or consistent identifying attribute. Whether they are depicted on earth or in heaven, they are represented as a trio of equals.

In fact, the *tre donne* do share two important qualities which make them coordinate in their roles in the canto. Each of them is shown as manifesting *pietà* toward Dante, and each of them is a woman to whom Dante is, or was, "fedele."[9] Furthermore, the fact that Dante so closely associates Beatrice with the virgins Mary and Lucy is one of the ways in which he subtly occludes an important aspect of the "Beatrice storica."[10] As Jefferson B. Fletcher uniquely, but correctly, we think, observes, Dante is capable of a sleight of hand elsewhere in the poem on this very subject: "Mary, of course, was recognized as virgin of virgins, and martyr of martyrs, but it may seem incongruous for Dante to attribute, however poetically, the aureoles of virginity and martyrdom to his lady, married as she was and dying in her bed. Virgin he actually calls her, however" (1921, p. 111).[11] Fletcher is thinking of the moment in *Purgatorio* XXXIII where Beatrice is described as if she were a virgin: "Ma poi che l'altre vergini dier loco / a lei di dir" (vv. 7–8). If Beatrice is openly called "one of the other virgins" in the earthly paradise, in *Inferno* II she is subtly drawn into the typology of virginity by association with Mary and Lucy, Virgin-Mother and Virgin-Martyr. Needless to say, the historical Beatrice was neither virgin nor martyr, but in her role in the poem she appears to be both, at least with respect to Dante.

When we speak of the historical Beatrice, however, we need to remember that, whatever her actual historical status, all that we can know definitively is what Dante chooses to include in his representation of her. Beatrice's historicity in the *Commedia* is largely confined to the history of her relationship to Dante and to Dante's earlier poetry. If we compare Beatrice's introduction into the poem with Virgil's, it is strikingly lacking in what we ordinarily understand as historical specificity. Virgil locates himself in terms of his parentage, his moment in historical time and its ethos (I, 67–75), but Beatrice never speaks of herself in such language. In the places where Beatrice comes closest to describing herself (*Purgatorio* XXX, 121–138, XXXI, 49ff.), she is still speaking of herself *only* in relation to Dante. The most relevant aspect of Beatrice's pre-*Commedia* existence is her role in Dante's prior work. When one thinks of Dante's brilliant incorporation of historical detail elsewhere in the poem, it is clear that he has chosen to delimit this dimension of Beatrice's representation very carefully.

The tendency to discuss Beatrice in terms of personification allegory has been reinforced by such factors; we shall return to a fuller consideration of this issue later in this chapter, but first we wish to explore the literary and exegetical traditions that come into play in Dante's presentation of the *tre donne*. We shall discuss each of the ladies in turn, paying particular attention to possible specific reasons for Dante's choices. We begin with the obvious fact that, *pace* the early illustrators, the three ladies do differ from the three beasts in their ontological status: that is, Mary, Lucy, and Beatrice do have a historical and literal dimension independent of the poem that the lion, leopard, and wolf do not have. The questions we must ask are what is it that Dante knows about these particular women, and what is it that he tells us about them that allows us to understand the reasons they are the very ones to enact the relay of grace?

Mary

The tendency to think of the *tre donne* in terms of allegorical equivalents is due, perhaps, to Dante's refusal to name the first of them. Beatrice describes her with the words, "Donna è gentil nel ciel" (II, 94); the combination "donna" and "gentil" is a *hapax* in the *Commedia*, but it is, of course, a charged conjunction in Dante's prior work.[12] The *donna gentile* of the *Vita Nuova* is represented as a real woman whose compassion for the grieving Dante represents a twofold temptation: to excessive self-pity and to the substitution of a new love object for the memory of Beatrice. Great emphasis is placed on the *donna gentile's* capacity for pity; she is often called *pietosa*, and the first two sonnets Dante writes about her stress this aspect of her appeal to him: "Videro li occhi miei quanta pietate" and "Color d'amore e di pietà parea in lei accolta." In the *Convivio*, Dante again writes about the *donna gentile*, but there he insists on her solely allegorical meaning, namely, as *filosofia* (II, ii, 1–2; II, xii, 6; and II, xv, 1, 12 *et passim*). This retrospective rewriting of the earlier *donna gentile* episode into the story of Dante's discovery of philosophy as consolation and ultimately as beatitude violates the *Vita Nuova*'s version of the episode in a variety of ways. The incompatibilities between the two texts still vex Dante scholars and remain unresolvable.[13] For our purposes, the most important points are that the *donna gentile* of the *Convivio* is represented as an anti-Beatrice and is shown to have displaced Beatrice; moreover, Dante denies any historical meaning to her, insisting that she must be understood only in terms of "bella menzogna."

When Dante opens the *Commedia* by having Beatrice speak of a "donna" who is "gentil," he is recalling the earlier work dialectically. Mazzoni speaks of the transfer Dante makes between the two works as a "trasvalutazione del significato entro uno stesso significante" (p. 284), but without proposing that this transfer signals a shift in Dante's ideas about the source and instrumentality of beatitude. The effect of Beatrice's reappropriation of the terminology of the *donna gentile* to describe the initiator of Dante's rescue is analogous to Petrarch's invocation in the last poem of the *Canzoniere* to the Virgin as the "vera Beatrice," where Petrarch seems to be telling Dante who the one true source of beatitude is. In *Inferno* II Dante is telling *himself* who the true *donna gentile* is. And like Petrarch, he identifies her with the very archetype of female mediation, the Virgin. By making Beatrice the author of this revisionary reattribution, Dante suggests a narrative continuity between the three works in which both Beatrice and a *donna gentile* exist, even though in each of the three the *donna gentile* is seen as standing for a different referent. Furthermore, the energizing efficacy of the Virgin's compassion retrospectively comments on the narcissistic paralysis induced in Dante by the *donna gentile*'s pity in the *Vita Nuova*, making that text a prefiguration of Dante's dramatization of the way in which passion mirrors compasssion in *Inferno* V.

Although all modern commentaries identify the first of the three ladies as Mary, this consensus was reached relatively late in the commentary tradition.[14] The very anonymity of the lady was noted by some early commentaries and was treated as an attribute of the prevenient grace she was supposed to represent in the poem's allegory. Guido da Pisa, for example, says, "But since we do not know whence this grace comes, the first lady who is a sign of this grace, has no name."[15] The first to see the "donna gentile" as Mary was Castelvetro (ca. 1570), who simply made the identification without arguing the case; the next commentator to name Mary was Tommaseo (1865), who felt it necessary to argue the point.[16] By the early twentieth century this identification had become a commonplace, although Moore still felt obligated to acknowledge the prior controversy (1917, pp. 235–236). Like Tommaseo, many modern commentators note the congruence of Mary's action at the opening of the poem with St. Bernard's description of her in the prayer of the last canto of *Paradiso*:

> La tua benignità non pur soccorre
> a chi domanda, ma molte fiate
> liberamente al dimandar precorre. (vv. 16–18)

The role we see Mary fulfilling as mediatrix for all humanity, as communicator of grace and as merciful intercessor, is perfectly imaged in her actions on Dante's behalf in *Inferno* II. Furthermore, her demeanor, as several commentators note, suggests her role as queen of heaven in its courtly graciousness and delicate regality.[17] These qualities are consonant with language used about Mary in the *Paradiso*, where she is "*Regina celi*" (XXIII, 128), "la regina" (XXXI, 100 and 116), and "Agusta" (XXXII, 119). Mary speaks to Lucy in the tones of a queen informing a lady about her knight's distress:

> Questa chiese Lucia in suo dimando
> e disse: "—Or ha bisogno il tuo fedele
> di te, e io a te lo raccomando—." (II, 97–99)

Apart from the other reasons for which one assumes that Dante has Mary in mind here, Moore, following Tommaseo, cogently argues that since both Lucy and Beatrice are treated as though they have a historical as well as a figurative reality in the *Commedia*, it would be very strange if the third lady in the trio had a different ontological status.[18] Given the thematics of female mediation and gratuitous rescue, surely Mary has to be the source and type in mind.[19] One might think in this connection of the last minute salvation of Buonconte ("nel nome di Maria finì" [*Purgatorio* V, 101]). The importance of the "name of Mary" is reasserted in a key moment in *Paradiso* XXIII: Dante speaks of "Il nome del bel fior ch'io sempre invoco / e mane e sera" (XXIII, 88–89) exactly after he announces the inadequacy of the Muses to aid his poem any longer (55–63). The "noninvocation" of the Muses (Hollander, 1980, p. 37) is thus coordinate with the announcement of a daily invocation to Mary in a canto in which the "sweetest milk" of the Muses is played off against the "ubertà" of Mary's kingdom.

Furthermore, the poem and the journey can be seen to begin and end on Marian intercession, achieving thereby a circular completion. This circularity is present with respect to the other two ladies as well. The order in which they appear in the drama of Dante's rescue is Mary, Lucy, and Beatrice. The *Commedia* concludes with a farewell to Beatrice, a mention of Lucy, and a prayer to Mary (Cantos XXXI, XXXII, and XXXIIII, respectively). Moreover, when each of the three ladies is mentioned in the concluding cantos, the language specifically recalls the role each had taken in *Inferno* II—a symmetrical effect that cannot be accidental. At the beginning of the poem we see Mary's gracious intervention on Dante's behalf; at the end, we are reassured that such grace is universally available.

Mary's role as mediatrix determines the roles of Lucy and Beatrice as well. Female mediation is central to medieval Christian thought and to Dante's thought in particular; the positive power of such mediation forms part of Dante's critique of the *Aeneid*, where, as we have seen, the female deities are profoundly ambiguous. Robert Ball has argued that

> Dante transcends the repetitive cycle of fathers and sons, not only by passing through the series of father-imagos which have ruled his past by means of their potentially unlimited authority, but also by adhering to a principle of female mediation, rigorously excluded from the historical chain of origins and destinies in the *Aeneid* (where Juno and Venus are both disruptive forces), but recuperated by Dante as both a literary and a theological mode in the course of his journey. (p. 27)

In *Inferno* II, Dante explicitly dramatizes the centrality and efficacy of such mediation; Mary's canonical status in this respect determines the roles of Lucy and Beatrice, legitimizing all other salvific interventions by serving as their initial model. Mary's own role is, of course, an imitation of Christ's salvific mediation for all mankind, but the emphatic feminization of the process of mediation at the poem's opening predisposes the reader to accept the extraordinary claims Dante will later make for Beatrice.[20]

Lucy

If Mary is the universal mediatrix and Beatrice is Dante's personal intercessor, Lucy is halfway between the two—at once a public figure, drawn from the world of medieval hagiography, and a private one, with a special relation to Dante, who is called her "fedele." Lucy has a key role in *Inferno* II and again in *Purgatorio* IX, where she is the agent of Dante's "translation" to the gate of Purgatory. When she is last mentioned in *Paradiso* XXXII, however, Dante recalls *only* her role in *Inferno* II:

> e contro al maggior padre di famiglia
> siede Lucia, che mosse la tua donna
> quando chinavi, a rovinar, le ciglia.
>
> (*Paradiso* XXXII, 136–138)

Lucy is the only nonbiblical female saint mentioned by name in the heavenly seating plan (other than Beatrice herself) and the only such figure mentioned by name in the poem. (Dante does allude periphrastically to St. Clare in *Paradiso* III, 97–99; all of the female characters of *Paradiso* are by definition saints, but only Lucy is both named by Dante and canonized by the Church.) She is also the only nonbiblical figure of either gender who is named as occupying a place in the top rung of the celestial rose. The importance thus accorded to Lucy is extraordinary: why does Dante single her out for such attention?[21]

Moore, in an essay first published in 1917, commented, "The prominence given to Sta. Lucia in the *Divina Commedia*, both in the actions attributed to her and the exalted position assigned to her in Heaven, has scarcely, I think been sufficiently explained" (p. 235). Moore suggests that we think of her as Dante's patron saint and then explores several reasons why this might be the case. Any such explanations depend on a combination of biographical and hagiographical conjectures and assumptions; since many of these recur in the commentary tradition, it is useful to explore their limits before proceeding further:

First, Lucy was regarded as the patron of those with eye problems. Jacopo and Graziolo both suggest that Dante's devotion to her derives from this connection, and subsequent commentators point to the episodes in the *Vita Nuova* and the *Convivio* in which Dante speaks about his difficulties with his eyes. A careful look at these texts, however, calls this explanation into question. In the *Vita Nuova*, Dante's eye troubles are presented as a *contrapasso* for his prior defection from Beatrice in the period of his infatuation with the *donna gentile*. He calls the *donna gentile* "la vanitade de li occhi miei" [the vanity of my eyes] (XXXVII), and then speaks of his tears and the "martirio" they cause as follows:

> Onde appare che de la lor vanitade fuoro degnamente guiderdonati; sì che d'allora innanzi non potero mirare persona che li guardasse sì che loro potesse trarre a simile intendimento.
>
> (XXXIX)

[Thus it seems that they were justly rewarded for their inconstancy, so much so that from then onwards I could not look at anyone who might return my gaze in such a way as to cause my eyes to weep again.]

If Dante's eye troubles are seen as primarily symbolic in the *Vita Nuova*, in the *Convivio* they are entirely physiological, a result of studying too hard. The cure is effected in equally naturalistic terms: "E per lunga riposanza in luoghi oscuri e freddi, e con affreddare lo corpo de l'occhio con l'acqua chiara, rivinsi la vertù disgregata che tornai nel primo buono stato de la vista" (III, ix, 15) [And by long repose in dark and cool places, and cooling the body of the eye in clear water, I knit together again the disintegrated power, so as to return to my former good condition of sight]. The fact that prayer plays no role in either episode is not necessarily evidence that St. Lucy did not enter into Dante's understanding of them, but it certainly is no evidence that she did; if Dante had recourse to Lucy, neither text gives any hint of it. The reason for the persistence of this gloss is the assumption that the dominant attribute of Lucy is her relation to eyes, a connection made in a multitude of paintings, many of them by famous artists. But as far as we can tell, this connection formed no part of either her legend or her iconography in Dante's period. Although it may well have been part of folklore by that time, it was by no means her defining attribute.

A second possible biographical connection is that Beatrice's church after her marriage to Simone dei Bardi in 1286 would have been Sta. Lucia de' Magnoli.[22] This fact is noted by Scartazzini, Dean Plumptre, Moore, K. Witte (cited in Moore, IV, pp. 246ff.) and Silvio Pasquazi, all of whom express varying degrees of interest. For us, it is an intriguing possibility, because it suggests a connection between Lucy, Beatrice, and Dante's youth, a connection implicit in Canto II, where Lucy speaks to Beatrice with a certain familiarity and with an awareness of Dante's relation to Beatrice during Beatrice's lifetime. It is also suggestive, given the reappearance of Beatrice in *Purgatorio* XXX "oltre la riviera," that this church is located in the Via dei Bardi in the Oltrarno and that the married Beatrice would thus have been literally across the river from Dante.

A third possibility is noted by Scartazzini, Witte, Plumptre, and Moore, who mention the existence of a Florentine Sta. Lucia degli Ubaldini, sister of the Cardinal who appears in *Inferno* X. This Sta. Lucia was a nun in the Franciscan convent of Monticelli, the very one from which Piccarda Donati (*Paradiso* III) had been abducted. The

Florentine St. Lucy's feast day was May 30, which both Witte and Moore suggest could well have been Dante's birthday. Moore thinks Dante may have conflated iconographical and biographical details from both saints and venerated a "composite" St. Lucy, both the local saint on whose feast day he was born and the more famous fourth-century virgin-martyr.

Each of the above explanations for the special prominence given to Lucy is clearly conjectural, and each seems too "private" and too limited to explain her unique role in the poem. What can we learn about thirteenth-century "versions" of St. Lucy that may help us to see why Dante chooses her for the roles she plays in his poem? At this point it would be helpful to review the public or common knowledge about the saint that would have been available to Dante and his contemporaries.

First, St. Lucy's Day, December 13, coincided with the winter solstice in the pre-Gregorian calendar. It is hard to believe that this would not have been important for Dante, given his profound awareness of astronomical phenomena and their symbolic potential. The paradoxical fact that the day of least light commemorated a saint whose name was derived from the etymology of "light" made Lucy into an emblem of hope, of light in darkness. (This is a paradox John Donne explores in his beautiful "Nocturnal upon St. Lucy's Day," a meditation on "the year's midnight and the day's.") This liturgical-astronomical nexus recalls another one, the coincidence of the vernal equinox and the Passion, which is central to the *Commedia*'s structure. Even though the *Commedia* is set in the season of the vernal equinox, Dante may be calling to mind that other cardinal point of the sun's yearly cycle, the solstice, by means of his allusion to Lucy.

We have evidence for such associations in a fascinating and perplexing passage in the *Convivio*, where Dante discusses at some length the yearly passage of the sun along the ecliptic. [23] He speaks of the two poles that form the fixed points of the celestial equator and then imagines them as cities: "Imaginando adunque, per meglio vedere, in questo luogo ch'io dissi sia una cittade e abbia nome Maria" [Let us imagine, then, for our better understanding, that there be a city on that spot which I have named, and that it be called Maria], he says, describing the North Pole; the South Pole calls forth another naming: "E qui imaginiamo un'altra cittade, che abbia nome Lucia" (III, v, 10–11) [And here let us imagine another city and let it be called Lucia]. The designation of the fixed poles as cities is odd, and the choice of these two names has mystified commentators. [24] Since the major subject of the passage is the sun's annual revolution, and the areas of earth which are consequently light or dark given that revolution, Lucia would have the most sun at the moment when Maria had the least, exactly at the moment of the winter solstice in the northern hemisphere. That is, Dante's imaginary cities place Lucy in the inverse position from that which is in fact the case on her actual feast day, redoubling the paradox we have already seen associated with that day. On the winter solstice, the imaginary city of Lucia would have twenty-four hours of daylight. Another tantalizing connection is that the placement of Maria and Lucia opposite each other anticipates Dante's placement of them in *Paradiso* XXXII, where they are nearly in the same relationship, on the opposite sides of the heavenly rose, but with Lucy directly opposite Adam and Mary facing John the Baptist.[25]

Second, Lucy's legend, widely diffused in the Middle Ages, was contained in an apocryphal *Passio*, which was virtually repeated in a number of important texts such as Vincent of Beauvais's *Speculum hystoriale* and Jacobus de Voragine's *Legenda aurea*, as well as in portions of the proper of the mass said on her day.[26] Lucy's martyrdom is set in the time of Diocletian's persecutions and is thought to have taken place in 304. In its elemental form, her legend recounts her trip from her native Syracuse to Catania to pray at the shrine of St. Agatha for her mother's cure from hemorrhage. St. Agatha appears to Lucy, urging her to request her mother's healing on her own rather than through intercession and prophetically names her the patron of Syracuse. After her mother's cure, Lucy returns home, vows her perpetual virginity, and proceeds to give away her dowry to the poor. Her outraged betrothed reports her to Diocletian's consul, Paschasius, as a Christian, and he in turn sets up a series of tortures designed to break her will. He threatens to take her off to a brothel, but not even a team of oxen can move Lucy, so firm is her constancy. She survives flames, boiling oil, and other tortures, finally dying by a sword wound, in her final moments taking the Eucharist and prophesying the peace of the church.

The stories associated with her beautiful eyes (that she plucked them out when they were praised by her suitor or by Paschasius or that they were taken out by command) play no part in her original legend or in any version we can find of it in Dante's period.[27] The first iconographic evidence of the Lucy-eye connection, as we shall see, appears to be mid-fourteenth-century. What is most powerful in the legend is the constancy of Lucy's will, her fortitude. The antiphon of the mass said on her day makes it her central attribute: "Columna es immobilis, Lucia, sponsa Christi" [You are a pillar immovable, Lucy, bride of Christ]. Her martyrdom testifies to the qualities Dante praises in the first sphere in the *Paradiso* when the difference between the absolute and the conditional will is clarified by Beatrice's discourse:

> Per che, s'ella si piega assai o poco,
>   segue la forza; e così queste fero
>   possendo rifuggir nel santo loco.
> Se fosse stato lor volere intero,
>   come tenne Lorenzo in su la grada,
>   e fece Muzio a la sua man severo,
> così l'avria ripinte per la strada
>   ond' eran tratte, come fuoro sciolte;
>   ma così salda voglia è troppo rada.   (IV, 79–87)

Although Lucy's "salda voglia" is the central feature of her legend, no commentator before Pasquazi so much as mentions it. Pasquazi presents a series of texts which make it clear that in the Middle Ages Lucy was most characteristically praised as an emblem of fortitude.[28] Of the texts he cites, the most interesting are two sermons by Fra Giordano preached in Florence on St. Lucy's Day in 1304. Fra Giordano's first sermon opens with a theme relevant to Dante's concerns at the opening of the *Commedia*—a critique of philosophical definitions of beatitude "in questa vita" which insists that true beatitude "è posta in vita eterna" (p. 20). He goes on to the subject of Lucy, concentrating on the exemplarity of her virtue: "E puotesi recare in persona di questa beatissima Santa Lucia, in cui questa costanzia singolarmente si mostrò, che da mille paja di buoi non potè essere tratta. . . . [F]u colonna immobile, e monte fortissimo: e però Cristo ne' Santi suoi ci ha posto l'esemplo, che dovemo sequitar." Fra Giordano's discussion of the role of saints stresses their traditional functions as "amici di Dio" and as models whom we can more easily imitate than Christ himself. He praises fortitude as a virtue of the saints particularly with respect to the instability of the world, which "è modo d'una ruota," a turning wheel without any constancy. Only the firmness of individual will can counter the instability of the world.[29]

Fra Giordano praises Lucy not only for her exemplary firmness but also for her words: "e sue parole i Santi li ricolgono per pruova e per autorità ferme, come se l'avesse dette uno dottore grande, o uno grande filosofo: che quel maladetto le disse, che la farebbe corrompere al mal luogo per forza. Ed ella disse: Se tu mi farai sforzare, io non perderò mia verginità, nò; che ove l'anima non consente, non si perde merito; anzi avrò doppia corona, l'una del martirio, l'altra della pazienza in quella tribolazione" (p. 25). In the second sermon, preached in the church of Sta. Lucia de' Magnoli, Fra Giordano praises Lucy's firmness, humility, and charity, ascribing her virtues directly to her relationship to Christ: "La meditazione e la memoria di Cristo dà fortezza, e dà constanzia eternale, e fa essere immobile; imperocchè di ciò esce ogne dono, e ogne virtù, e ogni fortezza spirituale, ed ogne costanzia e severitade" (p. 29).

Although Pasquazi is the first to note the centrality of fortitude to Lucy's legend, he does not argue that this is the reason for her presence in *Inferno* II, but instead sees her as a figure of "the infused natural virtues" in general. [30] To us, the centrality of fortitude in her legend has a more compelling immediate relevance to the themes of this particular canto. Dante had begun the canto in a state of inconstancy, unwilling what he had willed, and is, as Virgil correctly says, "da viltade offesa." The pusillanimity he manifests here is underlined by the description of Virgil as "magnanimo" in the very next line. The canto concludes with a repetition of the terms "ardire" and "franchezza," which articulate Dante's new-found courage to undertake the journey. This constellation of key terms (pusillanimity, magnanimity, fear, boldness, inconstancy, courage) points to the larger rubric of fortitude and its opposite, fear, as they are delineated by St. Thomas. Vittorio Russo (1965) has shown that Thomas's discussion of fortitude in the *Summa Theologiae* deals with all the key terms involved in Dante's psychic state here. In the same context, Thomas also discusses martyrdom in relation to fortitude, and it is here that he cites St. Lucy's response to her torturer from the *Passio*, the very words which Fra Giordano described as worthy of "uno dottore grande o uno grande filosofo." [31] Lucy's emblematic courage makes her, then, a particularly fitting saint in this canto, considering Dante's own crisis of fortitude. [32]

Furthermore, the opposition of pusillanimity and magnanimity which Dante enacts in psychological terms in this canto actually constitutes a prolepsis of the action of the following two cantos in which Dante will encounter the souls of the pusillanimous (III) and the magnanimous (IV). [33] In retrospect we can see that Dante himself might have made a "gran rifiuto" if he had allowed "viltà" to prevent him from undertaking the "alta impresa," both of the journey and of the poem. [34] Fear is an issue here as it is in Canto I, which is often called "il canto della paura," but whereas Dante seems to fear external danger in Canto I (even if the dangers are actually dramatizations of aspects of an inner crisis), in Canto II Dante explicitly fears overstepping his own limits (Pasquazi, pp. 163–164). Virgil's account of the actions of the female mediators is designed to counter that inner fear of unworthiness and to reframe the terms on which Dante makes the journey. By the end of Canto II Dante is not merely fleeing danger, he is embarking on a divinely ordained mission. [35]

Although fortitude is the major theme of Lucy's legend, the connection of her name with the word for light led to another common attribute in representations of her. In the earliest known visual representations of Lucy she bears a martyr's crown and a palm and is not distinguished from other virgin martyrs by specific iconographic details; she is represented in this way in the mosaic of the virgin martyrs in the sixth-century San Apollinare Nuovo and in the apse fresco in the eighth- to eleventh-century San Sebastiano al Palatino. By the thirteenth century, however, she begins to be represented holding a lamp, a clear allusion to her name rather than to her legend as it was diffused in the *Passio*. (It is this association which seems to have led later to the elaboration of the Lucy-eye iconography and finally to the legend of her eyes having been plucked out.) Lucy is represented with a lamp in the thirteenth-century mosaic of Sta. Maria Maggiore, Rome, and in several other thirteenth-century depictions, as well as a painting attributed to Simone Martini in the Berenson collection. A painting by Pietro Lorenzetti (dated 1347) in the church of Sta. Lucia de' Magnoli combines the two motifs by showing Lucy carrying a lamp, inside of which two eyes are evident. The eyes show up in a number of fourteenth-century images of the saint, but all of them are dated mid- or late fourteenth century: in a reliquary cross in the Museo Nazionale in Florence, in a painting in the Walters Gallery attributed to Pietro Lorenzetti, in a Roman missal in the Bioblioteca Nazionale of Turin, and in an antiphonary of the Biblioteca Estense in Modena. In the mid-fourteenth century, thus, the Lucy-light connection is more evident in visual than in verbal representations (and *none* of the visual representations predates the *Commedia*). [36]

The only known written source is a very important one, Jacobus de Voragine's *Legenda Aurea*. Though it does not deal with the legend concerning her eyes, it opens with an excursus on the etymology of Lucy's name:

> Lucy means light. Light has beauty in its appearance for by its nature all grace is in it, as Ambrose writes. It has also an unblemished effulgence; for it pours its beams on unclean places and yet remains clean. It has a straight way without turning, and goes a long way without halting. By this we are to under-

stand that the virgin Lucy was endowed with a stainless purity
of life; that in her was an effusion of heavenly love without any
unclean desire; that she followed a straight way in her devotion
to God, and a long way in daily good works without weaken-
ing and without complaint. Or again, Lucy means *lucis via*, the
way of light. (p. 34)

It is easy to see how this set of associations became traditional; and it is
no doubt the Lucy-light connection that determines the frequency of
the early commentators' interpretations of Lucy as "illuminating grace."
Jacopo had spoken of her as "grazia di Dio," and Benvenuto, Buti, and
nearly all subsequent commentaries specifically mention "*gratia illuminans.*"[37] A secondary theme in the commentaries enters with Boccaccio's designation of Lucy as "divina clemenza, divina misericordia,"
which is echoed by Buti and combined with the more traditional gloss;
Buti speaks of "grazia illuminante, tutta piena di misericordia." "Lucia
nemica di ciascun crudele" certainly points to the quality of clemency
which, as several commentators note, is defined by Thomas as the opposite of cruelty.

Despite the problems of specific terminology there is no question
that Lucy, like Mary and like Beatrice in this canto, is a link in a relay
of grace and that all three are prismatic figures of the gratuitous and
transcendentally inspired phenomenon which is the opening act of
Dante's salvific journey. But, as we have seen, the sheer richness and
adaptability of the figure of Lucy in both the hagiographic and iconographic traditions make it difficult to pin down any one meaning that
fully accounts for her vital role here and again in *Purgatorio* IX. The
complexity and proliferation of visual representations of Lucy is un-
usual, and her role in Dante's poem, richly suggestive as it is on so many
levels, must be seen in a similarly wide frame. Maria Chiara Celletti's
entry in the *Biblioteca Sanctorum* calls attention to the suggestiveness of
the Lucy legend and its capacity to proliferate meanings:

Questo accumularsi di attributi e di simboli, che, tuttavia nelle
immagini più antiche è assai ridotto, lasciando alla figura della
santa un suo isolato splendore, testimonia effettivamente della
ricchezza di ispirazione suscitata dalla leggenda e dalla sugges-
tiva personalità della giovenetta siracusana. . . . La sua forza di
ispirazione è così profonda e varia che molte raffigurazioni
sfuggono agli schemi tradizionali. . . . È tutta una lussureg-
giante e poetica selva di immagini. (pp. 252–254)[38]

Dante's elevation of Lucy to such a special role in his poem may be partially explained by some of the factors we have explored here, but it seems unlikely that any one of them alone can provide a full explanation. Although we have found any literal connection between Dante's eye troubles and Lucy too limited and limiting a gloss, the associations with illumination remain powerful if one thinks of the spiritual blindness from which Dante was awakened. In a canto in which, as we shall see, the allusion to Paul's blindness and healing is so important, this seems to be the most relevant association. Although Beatrice will be Dante's Ananias in *Paradiso* XXVI, Lucy can play that role here. In fact, there is a pervasive overlap or slippage between the roles played by the female mediators: it is Beatrice rather than Lucy whose eyes are mentioned in Canto II, and yet when Lucy is described in *Purgatorio* IX, she echoes Beatrice's opening speech ("Io son Lucia" echoes "Io son Beatrice" in *Inferno* II), and her beautiful eyes are mentioned.[39] These verbal parallelisms reaffirm the similarities between Beatrice and Lucy, just as Dante's apostrophe to Beatrice as "pietosa" affirms the Beatrice-Mary linkage.[40]

Beatrice

Despite the importance of both Mary and Lucy, Beatrice is, of course, the "star" of Canto II. It is through her report that we learn of the words and actions of the other two, and the combined efficacy of all three women is subsumed by Beatrice, who, at the canto's conclusion, is apostrophized by Dante as "colei che mi soccorsi" (II, 133). Her cameo appearance in Canto II serves a double purpose: it both recalls the youthful Beatrice of the *Vita Nuova* and anticipates the transfigured Beatrice who will be Dante's guide from *Purgatorio* XXX on. Lucy suggests an earlier narrative prehistory by reminding Beatrice (and the reader) of "quei che t'amò tanto, / ch'uscì per te de la volgare schiera"; such a statement grants Beatrice a reality outside the poem and assumes a narrative continuity with the *Vita Nuova*.[41] Yet there are clear advances over the *Vita Nuova*'s version of Beatrice; Canto II reveals a Beatrice who initiates action and who speaks, unlike the distant figure of Dante's youthful "libello." Although Beatrice is never represented by means of direct quotation in the *Vita Nuova*, her first appearance in the *Commedia* grants her the largest speaking role in the canto. (Of the canto's 142 lines, 83 are Virgil's, but of those, 48 are his reporting of her direct speech.)

At the end of Canto I Virgil speaks of Beatrice without naming her as the "anima . . . più di me degna" who will replace him as Dante's guide to the "beate genti." This oblique reference gives way in Canto II to direct representation; Beatrice is to be not only a goal of the journey but one of its initiators. In his farewell address to Beatrice in *Paradiso* XXXI, Dante recalls the scene in *Inferno* II, praising Beatrice as the source of the entire experience:

> O donna in cui la mia speranza vige,
> e che soffristi per la mia salute
> in inferno lasciar le tue vestige,
> di tante cose quant' i' ho vedute,
> dal tuo podere e da la tua bontate
> riconosco la grazia e la virtute.   (XXXI, 79–84)

The scene in *Inferno* II in which she left these *vestige* in hell has two parts: in the first Virgil describes his encounter with Beatrice, and in the second she describes the events that led up to the encounter. Virgil's first words describing Beatrice are replete with generic stilnovistic lexical and stylistic echoes. Virgil speaks of the as yet unnamed Beatrice as "beata e bella," of her speech as "soave e piana," and of her "angelica voce." These phrases, as well as "Lucevan li occhi suoi più che la stella," rightly remind most commentators of Dante's early poetry and of his descriptions of Beatrice in the *Vita Nuova*. For some commentators, this reprise of stilnovism represents a backward movement for Dante, a sign of his dependency on prior poetic achievement rather than a step forward into a new inventiveness. [42] It is important, however, to see that Dante's reappropriation of earlier stylistic moments functions as a commentary on them from the point of view of the *Commedia*. This is a vital part of Dante's ongoing poetic experimentalism which Contini succinctly delineates as "quel suo degradare un'esperienza precedente, toglierle la sua finalità intrinseca, usufruirla come elemento dell'esperienza nuova" (1946, p. ix).

The time gap between the *Vita Nuova* and the *Commedia*, a gap filled among other things by Dante's redefinition of the *Vita Nuova* in the *Convivio*, is both abolished and redefined by the reappearance of stilnovistic terminology in this new context. Each time Dante reasserts the continuity of the *Commedia* and the *Vita Nuova* he implies a critique of the *Convivio* and a reversal of its negative judgment of his early work. This critique is clearest in the meeting with Bonagiunta in *Purgatorio* XXIV, when the older poet cites the first of the poems in praise of Beatrice, "Donne ch'avete intelletto d'amore," as the turning point in Dante's poetic vocation. [43] When Beatrice comes into the *Commedia*, through the medium of Virgil's words, she seems consonant with Dante's earlier presentation of her. But Dante immediately opens her characterization to the acquisition of other symbolic potential by a strategic enhancement of meaning. The complex configuration of subtexts that lies behind this canto helps us to see Dante subtly preparing for a figural reading of Beatrice which is consonant with her historical and poetic earlier identities even as it transcends them.

One of the ways Dante suggests larger meanings is through the presence of biblical paradigms that point to typological precedents or analogies for the roles Beatrice is shown enacting. Two major biblical figures underlie the presentation of Beatrice in this canto, both of which have been recognized only recently. Amilcare Iannucci has shown that Beatrice is present in this scene as a *figura Christi* insofar as her descent to Limbo on behalf of Dante reenacts Christ's harrowing of hell (esp. pp. 38–40). Dante clearly has this typology in mind in his farewell prayer to Beatrice, in which, as we have seen, he refers to her as having left her footprints in hell (*Paradiso* XXXI, 79–81). Beatrice's descent, like Christ's descent into Limbo, is a type of the "condescension" of the Word. In the *Paradiso*, Dante speaks of the language of accommodation, the condescension of the Word in Scripture, in the same terms as the Incarnation:

> Per questo la Scrittura *condescende*
> a vostra facultate, e piedi e mano
> attribuisce a Dio, e altro intende.   (*Paradiso* IV, 43–45)

> onde l'umana specie inferma giacque
> giù per secoli molti in grande errore,
> fin ch'al Verbo di Dio *discender* piacque.
> (*Paradiso* VII, 28–30)

The homology between these theological and linguistic notions, between descent and condescension, underlies the reciprocity of theology and poetics which the *Commedia* enacts.[44] Beatrice's Christological dimension will be more fully present in her appearance at the top of the mountain of Purgatory, but it is implied already by the dramatic action of *Inferno* II and perhaps even by Virgil's description of her at the end of Canto I ("anima più degna di me"), in which we may hear an echo of John the Baptist's words, "qui autem post me venturus est fortior me est" (Matt. 3:11) [he who is coming after me is mightier than I].[45]

The nature of Beatrice's mediation here recalls a second biblical *figura*. Beatrice concludes her plea to Virgil with tears in her eyes:

> Poscia che m'ebbe ragionato questo,
> li occhi lucenti lagrimando volse,
> per che mi fece del venir più presto.   (II, 115–117)

These lines have elicited passionate approval from Boccaccio to the present as a sign of Beatrice's "humanity"; it is almost a critical topos to expatiate on the beauty of the lines and their role in the characterization of Beatrice. Padoan praises Boccaccio's admiring comment on the tears as a sign of Boccaccio's sensitivity to the "umanità viva di Beatrice, solitamente ridotta dai commentatori trecenteschi a fredda e statica allegoria."[46] And subsequent commentators vie with the tradition in their own tributes to the "umanità viva" of Beatrice.[47]

Beatrice's tears do, of course, function on the level of characterization, but they also suggest her figural role. One literary precedent for them, as Hollander points out (1969, pp. 91–92), is Virgil's description of Venus's tears in a comparable mission of mercy in *Aeneid* I: "et lacrimis oculos suffusa nitentis" (I, 228) [her bright eyes dimmed and tearful]. But this literary source is conflated with a biblical one that gives Beatrice's tears a more precise typological resonance (Jacoff, 1982). Dante is recalling here the salvation oracle of Jeremiah in which the prophet describes the matriarch Rachel's posthumous and successful intervention on behalf of the Jews as they are on their way into Babylonian exile.

> Haec dicit Dominus:
> Vox in excelso audita est lamentationis,
> Luctus, et fletus Rachel plorantis filios suos,
> Et nolentis consolari super eis,
> Quia non sunt.
> Haec dicit Dominus:
> Quiescat vox tua a ploratu,
> Et oculi tui a lacrymis,
> Quia est merces operi tuo, ait Dominus,
> Et revertentur de terra inimici.   (Jer. 31:15–17)

[Thus saith the Lord: A voice was heard on high of lamentation, of mourning, and weeping, of Rachel weeping for her children, and refusing to be comforted for them, because they are not. Thus saith the Lord: Let thy voice cease from weeping, and thy eyes from tears: for there is a reward for thy work, saith the Lord: and they shall return out of the land of the enemy.]

In patristic exegesis, Rachel weeping for her children becomes a symbolic matriarch, a figure for *Mater Ecclesia*.[48] Beatrice, too, will be represented as a *figura ecclesiae* later in the poem,[49] but here the most important aspects of the biblical allusion actually are the literal ones: Rachel as mother, as seeking consolation, as posthumous intercessor, as occasioning God's extraordinary promise of forgiveness, return, and salvation. Each of these details has an obvious connection with the dramatic situation of *Inferno* II. Furthermore, the allusion to Jeremiah has particular importance, given Dante's use of Jeremiah in Canto I to establish the nature of his spiritual exile in the "selva oscura."[50] The first two cantos thus invoke both the apostasy narrative and the salvation oracle from Jeremiah, thereby suggesting both the problematic situation of the opening crisis and its promised resolution through divine intervention. Beatrice's tears are the very sign of her efficacy as *mediatrix* within the poem's governing typological structure, its exploration of exilic and Exodus typologies and the relationship between them.

It is probably because Beatrice weeping for Dante as she leaves Virgil is a partial refashioning of the typology of Rachel weeping for her children that Beatrice's place next to Rachel in the heavenly seating plan is mentioned in this canto.[51] Beatrice is seen from the very beginning of the poem as *mediatrix* both in the Christological and in the ecclesiological sense. Many commentators have noticed her quasi-maternal concern for Dante; the allusion to Rachel weeping for her children substantiates and deepens the meaning of this insight.[52] And like the biblical Rachel, Beatrice is dramatized both as beloved and as mother; Dante, in fact, reminds us of Rachel in her role as beloved in Canto IV when he identifies Israel (Jacob) by reference to "Rachele, per cui tanto fé." The duality of Beatrice's role, at once courtly and erotic, maternal and mediatory, necessitates the conflation of stilnovistic language and biblical resonance. It is characteristic of Dante's subsequent representation of Beatrice as well; the duality is there in her appearance at the top of the mountain of Purgatory, and her maternal nature becomes increasingly important in *Paradiso*, even as her beauty, "'l piacer santo" (*Paradiso* XIV, 138), is more and more celebrated.[53]

These typological resonances are crucial; they allow Dante to create a figural dimension in the characterization of Beatrice without calling into question her historical reality. The hostility to allegory we find implicit in nearly all commentaries that praise Beatrice's tears (and her humanity) as an alternative to her allegorical meaning depends on a notion of allegory which Dante's poem subverts by its deployment of typology. Beatrice is not reducible to a univocal allegorical correlative, as most of the early commentators tried to make her; but neither is she merely, as Mazzoni puts it, the Beatrice *storica*, "ben viva al cuore di Dante" (p. 284). By thinking of the multiplicity of typological roles she plays, depending on the context in which she is described, we can see that Dante's complex portrait of Beatrice includes a variety of consonant or congruent aspects all of which must all be taken into account. The conflation of stilnovistic, Boethian, and biblical resonances which contribute to her composite existence in this canto creates a textual density that takes the place of a historical identity understood simply in its literal sense.

The Question of Allegory

"Donna di virtù"

The polyvalence of the *Commedia*, or to use Dante's term from the Epistle to Cangrande, its polysemy, is acknowledged in theory by most scholars, but in the analysis of specific passages one often detects a desire to escape from the true complexity of polysemy, a desire to retreat to the comfort of a false duality that would read either allegorically or historically, figurally or literally. This is apparent in the ongoing debate over the meaning of Virgil's first words to Beatrice.

> O donna di virtù, sola per cui
>   l'umana spezie eccede ogne contento
>   di quel ciel c'ha minor li cerchi sui.   (II, 76–78)

The interpretation of these lines determines the very text read. The philological form of the question asks what is the antecedent of the relative pronoun "cui." Does humankind exceed all other sublunary creatures because of Beatrice or because of "virtù"? Ever since 1934, when Michele Barbi argued that Virgil could not be speaking of Beatrice here, but rather must be praising "virtù," and especially since Giorgio Petrocchi's decision to accept Barbi's reading and to encourage that reading by removing the comma after "virtù," the Italian text reproduced in all subsequent editions—with the exception of Mattalia's—omits the comma. In Italian editions of the *Commedia*, it is "virtù," not Beatrice, through which the human race "eccede ogne contento."

Despite Charles Singleton's vivid and well-argued protest in 1956 against Barbi's reading, the issue seemed closed in Italy until Anna Maria Chiavacci Leonardi reopened it in a recent essay (1984), noting that Singleton's "ben solido" argument "non ha trovato alcuna eco nei nostri studi" (p. 7).[54] Chiavacci Leonardi is, we believe, the first Italian critic to take into serious account Singleton's 1956 attack on the Barbi hypothesis that Beatrice, because she is presented as a historical person, cannot simultaneously be thought of allegorically here. Singleton reads the line as characterizing Virgil's own point of view; according to him, Virgil recognizes in Beatrice only what he is capable of recognizing, namely Contemplation or Lady Philosophy. Although Chiavacci Leonardi's reading differs from Singleton's in some important ways,[55] like Singleton's it assumes that the double focus of historical and allegorical meaning is fundamental to Dante's presentation of Beatrice.

The debate on the meaning of Virgil's address to Beatrice is closely tied to the debate on a second passage in this canto, Beatrice's opening description of Dante as "amico mio e non de la ventura." This line, as Mazzoni shows (pp. 256–277), has given rise to no fewer than seven interpretations. The dominant reading, which begins with Jacopo della Lana, Boccaccio, and l'Anonimo Fiorentino, takes the line as a description of Dante himself, so that it might be paraphrased as "Dante is *my* friend even if he is a victim of bad fortune." Boccaccio sees this as a strategy of Beatrice, part of her attempt to enlist Virgil's aid, a declaration of her concern for Dante, and her attempt to elicit Virgil's pity for his situation. One of the conventional arguments against this reading is that in 1300, the fictive date of the poem, Dante was not "unfortunate," at least not from any worldly point of view. He was then at the very top of Fortune's wheel and had some time to go before discovering himself on its downward track. (Whether this would have made Dante seem a friend of Fortune in the eyes of Boethius—or, for that matter, in the eyes of the *Commedia*'s author—is a question we will discuss in another context.) The second major interpretation, found in l'Ottimo, Guido da Pisa, and Buti, takes the line as a description of Dante's love for Beatrice as she is understood in her traditional allegorical role as Theology or Revelation. This reading is adopted by most of the sixteenth-century commentators. As Landino puts it, Dante is a lover of "dottrina" as an end in itself, rather than as a means to acquire earthly rewards, the goods of Fortune. A third reading, advanced by Benvenuto, takes the line to mean that Dante is the *true friend* of Beatrice, one whose love, unlike Fortune's, is not subject to change.

Mazzoni himself favors the reading of Mario Casella, who argued in 1943 that the line had to be read as a description of the *quality* of Dante's love for Beatrice, namely a wholly gratuitous and disinterested love of the kind Dante had described himself as discovering in the spiritual and poetic turning point of the *Vita Nuova*.[56] Although Padoan (1976) called Casella's argument "un grosso pasticcio," Mazzoni is not the only recent scholar to find it persuasive. Casella had invoked Abelard and Saint Augustine to gloss the contrast between those who love distinterestedly and those who are called "amici fortunae," and Mazzoni adds to Casella's glosses a series of apposite texts from St. Bernard and Aelred of Rievaulx. His acceptance of Casella's reading is consonant with, and perhaps even dependent upon, Domenico De Robertis's interpretation of the *Vita Nuova*: the double theme of disinterested love (growing out of classical literature on friendship and its developments in Christian discourse on spiritual friendship) and the poetry of praise (its literary counterpart) is the focus of De Robertis's learned and compelling study.

This is a coherent position, one with great merit because of the ways it links *Inferno* II with the *Vita Nuova*, with which it has important lexical and rhetorical connections. What is not immediately clear, however, is that this reading also functions within a scholarly tradition whose objective is to oppose allegorical interpretations of Beatrice, an objective made explicit by Mazzoni, who flatly states that "noi fermamente crediamo di dover rispingere ogni allegorizzazione astratta del personaggio di Beatrice, come di quello di Virgilio" (p. 275, and see also pp. 271 and 277–279). Despite this caveat, he himself comes close to just such a reading in his analysis of the *tre donne*, whom he ultimately delineates by analogy "come Misericordia (in Maria); come Giustizia (in Lucia, 'nemica di ciascun crudele'); come Carità, cioè Amore (in Beatrice)" (p. 73). Even if, in such an interpretation, abstractions do sneak back into the discourse, suggesting conventional personification allegory, there is still no attention to figural allegory; Mazzoni acknowledges Auerbach, Singleton, and Freccero, but their work does not affect his conclusions or his fundamental hostility to the idea of allegory as "forzatura interpretativa che nuoce alla poesia" (p. 277). For all his extraordinary erudition and philological acumen, Mazzoni is still, on this point, the heir of Benedetto Croce who, in 1921, declared, "L'allegoria non è . . . se non una sorte di criptografia. . . .

Nella poesia e nella storia della poesia le spiegazioni delle allegorie sono affatto inutili, e in quanto inutili, dannose. Nella poesia l'allegoria non ha mai luogo" (see pp. 13, 20, 28, and 64).[57]

However solid De Robertis's reading of the *Vita Nuova* may be, it cannot fully engage Beatrice's Christological dimension in that book, nor does it allow us to gloss fully the line "amico mio e non de la ventura." Although Mazzoni brings to bear a number of texts Dante was likely to have known in which the notion of the friend of Fortune occurs, he never mentions in this connection the one text most explicitly engaged with the idea of Fortune, Boethius's *Consolation of Philosophy*. Once we think of Boethius we begin to see that the line "amico mio e non de la ventura" cannot be understood apart from Virgil's response to it, his apostrophe to Beatrice as "donna di virtù, sola per cui." Singleton (1956) pointed out the close connection between Virgil's perception of Beatrice in this apostrophe and Beatrice's description of herself: "Indeed, may we not see that Virgil's 'point of view' or perspective is respected by Beatrice herself, when in speaking to him she refers to the man to be rescued as 'amico mio e non de la ventura?' . . . It is a language, a way of phrasing, which a Virgil could understand. In this way, Beatrice is already telling Virgil who she is."[58] Both lines are Boethian in their resonances, as Singleton, following Moore, understands. Singleton writes as if the Boethian provenance of the language adequately defines Beatrice's allegorical role here in relation to the *Convivio* figure of the *donna gentile* seen as Lady Philosophy. Mazzoni, on the other hand, is so committed to the "historical" Beatrice of the *Vita Nuova* that he ignores the Boethian resonances of Beatrice's words and discounts those of Virgil, insisting that "il riscontro boeziano addotto da E. Moore non vincola quanto all' interpretazione" (p. 278). Nor does he mention that the Boethian echoes in Virgil's speech were noticed long before Moore by Pietro di Dante (in all three redactions). For us, Beatrice as "donna di virtù" recalls both the Beatrice of the *Vita Nuova*, "regina de le vertudi" (X, 2) and the Boethian "magistra virtutum," Lady Philosophy, who is said to supplant Beatrice in the *Convivio*. The Beatrice of *Inferno* II subsumes both these figures in her new poetic incarnation. Earlier we argued that Dante had reappropriated the term *donna gentile* from the *Convivio* and transferred it to Mary, the "donna è gentil nel ciel" of this canto; another word closely associated in the *Vita Nuova* with the *donna gentile*, "pietosa," a *hapax* in the *Commedia*, is similarly reassigned, for at the end of Canto II it is Beatrice who is "pietosa."[59]

Although Singleton and Chiavacci Leonardi differ in important details in their arguments against Barbi's anti-allegorical reading of the "donna di virtù" passage, both scholars share a sense of the reductive-ness of vision out of which Barbi's choice is made. They rightly insist that any either-or choice between literal and symbolic dimensions is arbitrary. Singleton puts the argument in terms that wittily make the connection between Dante's poetics and his theology: "To see her so, to 'read' Beatrice so in the poem, has proved to be something of a major difficulty with the modern reader, and by modern I mean post-Renaissance. The difficulty seems to persist. It amounts, actually, to a reader's heresy (if we may conceive of such a thing, and with all due allowance made) not unlike one of the well-known heresies that denied one or the other of Christ's two natures" (1956, p. 34).[60] Singleton's hypothesis of the reader's heresy is a telling one, since Dante's concep-tion of Beatrice, as Singleton has himself so powerfully shown else-where (esp. 1958), is significantly Christological. What needs to be emphasized is the relationship between Dante's incarnational theology and the nature of representation in the poem.

Perhaps it would help to move to another field in which we can see the same concerns explored for comparable issues. In a provocative and fascinating study, *The Sexuality of Christ in Renaissance Art and in Mod-ern Oblivion*, Leo Steinberg approaches the issue of Renaissance natu-ralism as a theological rather than a purely aesthetic question, one that takes seriously the implications of incarnational theology. Steinberg de-scribes himself as writing to correct "the many who still habitually mis-take pictorial symbols in Renaissance art for descriptive naturalism" (p. 1). He explores the double valence of pictorial language in the Re-naissance: "The image, then, is both natural and mysterial, each term enabling the other. But this reciprocal franchise is peculiar to the Catholic West, where the growth of a Christward naturalism in painting is traceable from the mid-thirteenth century" (p. 11). Steinberg's lan-guage of "reciprocal franchise," like Auerbach's "figural realism" and Singleton's "double focus," points toward the doubleness of an aes-thetic of representation which finds its *raison d'être*, its origin and its correlative, in an incarnational theology: the Word becomes flesh, the divine takes on human form, thereby allowing the human to become an imitation or an intimation of the divine.

This premise helps explain how Dante was able to discover the figurative layers of his own experience, as well as, in both senses, the figure in his life who made him aware of the divine within the human: Beatrice, true bringer of beatitude, "loda di Dio vera," as she is called in this canto. The point may seem axiomatic to those trained in a post-Auerbachian world, but a glance at the most authoritative Dante criti-cism, as well as at Auerbach himself,[61] would suggest that the position is far from universally maintained. As we have seen, Mazzoni approves of Barbi's argument because of a profound distaste for the idea of the allegorical as abstraction; when he says that the depiction of Beatrice "has nothing of the allegorical and of the abstract" (p. 271), the implication is that these terms are equivalent. Dante had himself written such an either-or allegory in the *Convivio*, in which he is the first to insist that the *donna gentile* is "nothing but" an abstraction. The recuperation of stilnovistic language in Canto II's opening presentation of Beatrice is a rejection of this mode of discourse; Dante may be hyperbolic in his praise of Beatrice in the *Vita Nuova* and in the *Commedia*, but he insists on her "real presence," to use another term crucial to the theology of his time. Since it is the dualistic allegory of the *Convivio* that Dante rejects in the *Commedia*, it is a profound historical irony that so many of his critics continue to insist on it.

Rethinking the Question

The position we have been arguing, however, might seem to be contradicted by the debate concerning another of the canto's most vexed lines. In her description of Dante's state *in extremis*, Lucy cries out to Beatrice: "non vedi tu la morte che 'l combatte / su la fiumana ove 'l mar non ha vanto" (II, 107–108). The *Commedia*'s earliest commentators devised two different solutions to the meaning of this mysterious "fiumana" where death fights with Dante, and these two alternatives remained normative for centuries. Although some commentators see the *fiumana* as a literal river, usually the Acheron, which Dante will cross in Canto III,[62] they immediately gloss the river in symbolic terms. For example, Acheron, the "Joyless" River, is, in the words of Jacopo di Dante, "la viziosa e ignorante operazione del mondo" [the vicious and ignorant operation of the world], against which Lucy saw Dante struggling. Benvenuto draws a similar conclusion, stressing the metaphorical relationship between the instability of a flowing river and the instability of human life.[63] A second group of interpreters, following Boccaccio, looks backward to the "selva oscura" of *Inferno* I, seeing the two as alternative but equivalent symbols for the locus of the individual's moral struggle, the field on which a psychomachia is being fought.[64] Buti expresses this position with particular clarity, seeing the shore as an intermediate place for the pilgrim who has concluded one phase of the struggle only to confront another, the need to climb the mountain.[65] Whether one sees the river as a symbol of the world's vices or as the place where one would combat such vices, its interpretation is moral and allegorical in decidedly nonfigural ways, and as such its presence in this *terzina* raises an important question for those, like ourselves, who read Dante's poem typologically: to give the *fiumana* a "purely" symbolic status is to deny the literal sense of the narrative and thus the double focus for which we have been arguing.

There have recently been some reactions against these dominant readings. In 1959, Antonino Pagliaro presented a thoroughly literal reading of the line, insisting that Dante here is using a straightforward comparison drawn "dalla esperienza della navigazione fluviale, la quale rende in modo perfetto lo stato di impedimento e di pericolo di viandante."[66] Bruno Nardi argued for yet another way of reading the line literally, seeing it specifically as a description of the Arno, the "fiero fiume" which Dante will elaborately describe in *Purgatorio* XIV. Nardi's analysis of this line (1961) turns into a diatribe against all those who read allegorically and against any reading that attempts to see Dante as an everyman, a position he terms "ermeneutico qualunquismo." Mazzoni, at the conclusion of his lengthy and extremely useful excursus on the problems of this entire *terzina*, accepts the position argued by Singleton (1948), who relies on a widespread exegetical tradition whereby the river is to be equated with the sea, *Inferno* II's "fiumana" with *Inferno* I's "pelago" (I, 23), and both with the *fluctus concupiscentiae*, earlier represented by the "lupa" and the general situation of the opening canto.[67] In accepting Singleton's argument, Mazzoni rejects—rightly, it seems to us—what he sees as the unnecessarily narrow readings of Pagliaro and Nardi. Singleton's position, however, seems still to share with the earlier commentaries the tendency to assign to the *fiumana* a purely symbolic or emblematic function and so to make of the whole episode a *bella menzogna*: the river where Dante struggles still flows only through a moral landscape.

Freccero (1966) expanded Singleton's reading of the line by bringing to it a more specific set of exegetical glosses. Freccero questioned the Singleton-Mazzoni equation of the river with the sea, arguing that the specific verbal formulation, "ove 'l mar non ha vanto," requires that the river be superior to, and therefore other than, the sea, while still being on the same ontological level in Dante's fiction. Marshaling a series of classical and patristic texts, Freccero shows that the Jordan was identified with the circular cosmic river Oceanos, "the river of rivers," as Wallace Stevens was to call it,[68] the boundary between life and death in classical mythology; furthermore, the Jordan, primarily because of its association with the baptism of Christ, was seen in relation to the rivers of the earthly paradise and became a figure (tropologically) of the baptism of the spirit by which a convert crosses over into the life of grace. Freccero brings to Singleton's reading of the "fiumana" Singleton's own later insight that Exodus is the master structural principle of the poem. After outlining the three stages of the Exodus (crossing the Red Sea, wandering in the desert, and crossing the Jordan into the Promised Land), Freccero connects the "fiumana" of Canto II with the Jordan as figure of baptism of the spirit, the death of the Pauline old man and the birth of the new. Dante's situation is that of one who has crossed the sea (the Red Sea of Exodus typology) but who cannot make the final crossing over the river into the Promised Land until he makes a descent into humility, a descent that will be a death of the old self. Thus the river of death becomes a figure for the whole infernal journey that is to follow.[69]

This is a particularly convincing reading, in part because it uncovers Exodus typology in *Inferno* II, at the outset of the journey, exactly where one would expect to find it, given its centrality to Canto I and to the poem as a whole. Furthermore, Exodus typology here reinforces the exilic typology implicit in Beatrice's tears, which, as we have seen, suggest the figure of Rachel weeping for her children as they are entering exile. The relation between Exodus and exilic typology is, of course, fundamental both to the Hebrew Bible and to Christian exegesis; and during the course of the *Commedia*, Dante will come to perceive his own exile as an exodus. Freccero's essay broadens Canto II's field of reference to include this connection—so central to Dante's spiritual self-definition in the *Commedia*—seen *in ombra*, as it were, a shadowy and not yet fully intelligible promise of future renewal and restoration.

And yet, however persuasively Freccero demonstrates the *fiumana*'s relationship to conversion, the moral *sensus* of Exodus, his reading still leaves the *fiumana* short of being fully "figural" insofar as the literal sense remains absent. The defining characteristic of allegory of the theologians as opposed to allegory of the poets is the uncompromised historicity of the literal sense: whatever else the Exodus might mean, it never ceases to mean that the Jews really marched across a wilderness, out of bondage, and into the Promised Land. But surely we are not to believe that Dante is "really" in the Easter season of 1300 on the banks of the Jordan (nor, *pace* Nardi, or some of the early illuminators of the *Commedia*, is he at the shore of *any* literal river). Rather, as Freccero argues, the poem presents a double perspective at this point; what Lucy sees from the perspective of heaven as a "fiumana," Dante, who is still on the near side of the river, had seen in *Inferno* I as a "lupa." Either way, however, the "fiumana" or the "lupa" would seem to exist with a degree of "reality" radically different from that of, say, the three ladies and Virgil, whose incarnational status is dramatized. Freccero observes, while addressing Singleton's argument, that the river and the sea must belong to the same order of representation: would the same not be true of the river and of the ladies who perceive Dante struggling there?[70]

We will address this problem shortly, but first we need to think more about the specific language Dante uses to delineate the "fiumana." The notion of boasting that concludes the line "su la fiumana ove 'l mar non ha vanto"[71] recalls the language earlier in *Inferno* II when Dante speaks to Virgil about Aeneas's journey to the underworld: "per quest' andata onde li dai tu vanto" (II, 25). The word "vanto" occurs twice in this canto and nowhere else in the poem in quite the same sense:[72] the reason why it should twice appear here, as well as its specific meaning, remains unaddressed by commentators. (Translators often avoid the problem altogether in dealing with Aeneas's journey, opting for a general paraphrase such as "this journey in which you say. . . .") No one has remarked upon the important fact that both of these moments associated with boasting are also associated with rivers. The specific reference to Aeneas's journey "onde li dai tu vanto" is to his trip to the underworld, but in particular to that part of it that took place at the shore of the Lethe, where, in Dante's words, he heard from Anchises "cagione / di sua vittoria e del papale ammanto" (vv. 26–27). In this river, the souls of the dead are being cleansed of their former memories and are readied for rebirth as Aeneas's descendants, the future heroes of Rome. Aeneas hears about a future which he himself will never actually achieve; he does not cross the Lethe, any more than Virgil will cross it at the top of the mountain of Purgatory, for Dante's Lethe will divide Virgil's presence in the *Commedia* from his disappearance. Lethe is in fact the *terminus ad quem* of Virgil's participation in Dante's destiny.

We would propose the possibility that these two rivers, Jordan and Lethe, implicitly linked in Canto II by the peculiar repetition of the word *vanto* in the phrases "onde li dai tu *vanto*" and "ove 'l mar non ha *vanto*," are figurally related.[73] This proposition will require some explanation. Dante's combat with death at the shore of the *fiumana* surely must be a reference to his desperate situation in *Inferno* I, the circumstance there symbolized by the failed attempt to climb what Virgil calls "il dilettoso monte / ch'è principio e cagion di tutta gioia" (I, 77–78). Despite the problem of being a hemisphere removed, the mountain clearly "is," at least in a figurative sense, Mount Purgatory, for what else could the "dilettoso monte" be in Dante's cosmology but Purgatory, at whose peak he will find the Garden of Eden? As the original home to the parents of the human race and now, for Dante, the place from which the ascent to Paradise begins, Eden is both "principio e cagion di tutta gioia."[74] It is at the top of that mountain that Dante will cross over Lethe and Eunoe, the double barrier between Purgatory and Paradise.

The geographical details of Dante's Edenic rivers are somewhat confusing. Both rivers arise from a common source, an inexhaustible spring, although Dante must pass through the two branches in sequence, a double crossing reminiscent of the two baptisms—of water and of spirit—seen by the fathers as signifying, respectively, the remission of sins and the acquisition of grace. While Eunoe appears to encircle the top of the mountain, the waters of Lethe, as Matilda explains, flow from the plateau at the summit down the mountain:

> Da questa parte con virtù discende
> che toglie altrui memoria del peccato;
> da l'altra d'ogne ben fatto la rende.
>
> (*Purgatorio* XXVIII, 127–129)

These waters flow downward into the earth to the frozen lake, or dead sea, at its center, carrying the memory of sinfulness to be added to the waters of the infernal rivers. It is, therefore, to the effluent of this river that Cato must be referring when he challenges Dante and Virgil at the beginning of their ascent: "Chi siete voi che contro al cieco fiume / fuggita avete la pregione etterna" (*Purgatorio* I, 40–41). Cato marvels at their arrival by so unorthodox a route: he wonders whether the "laws of the abyss" have been broken or whether some new dispensation has been proclaimed (I, 46–48). No one, it would seem, makes the ascent out of hell against the current of this "fiume." For the wayfarers have arrived at the shore of Purgatory, not ferried by the angel boatman but by climbing from the center of the universe, concluding their ascent through the darkness by following the sound made by the mysterious *ruscelletto* in its descent toward the center (*Inferno* XXXIV, 127–134).

Rafaello Andreoli (1856) is the first commentator to have identified the *ruscelletto* of *Inferno* XXXIV and the *fiume* of *Purgatorio* I as the Lethe. Although some disagreement about this point remains, by the late nineteenth century it was sufficiently uncontroversial to Paget Toynbee that he included both citations in a list of references to "Letè" in his *Dictionary of Proper Names*, a reading passed on by C. H. Grandgent. Dante's Lethe, therefore, is a river that flows not into any body of water on the surface of the earth but to its very center, a kind of inverse spring that flows inexhaustibly into, rather than from, the earth's surface.[75] It is literally a "fiumana ove 'l mar non ha vanto," a point implied in *Purgatorio* I, where Dante eschews the readily available opportunity to have the "fiume" flow into the sea surrounding the base of the mountain. Dante's situation at the beginning of *Inferno*—at the foot of a mountain and at the shore both of a "*fiumana*" and of a "*pelago*"—thus anticipates the geography of *Purgatorio*'s opening scene, where the river at whose shore he finds himself is the Lethe. The ascent which he cannot make on his own initiative in *Inferno* I, what Freccero has called the "failed Exodus,"[76] he there resumes, having first descended in order to rise.

There are yet further connections between the Lethe and the Jordan. Dante's Lethe, as one of two streams that flow from a single source at the top of the mountain of Purgatory, inverts a major exegetical and iconographic tradition concerning the Jordan. From Jerome on, the Jordan is glossed as a river with a double source, the Jor and the Dan.[77] Isidore's formulation is typical:

> Jordanis Judae fluvius, a duobus fontibus nominatus, quorum alter vocatur Jor, alter Dan. His igitur procul a se distantibus in unum alveum foederatis, Jordanis deinceps appellatur. Nascitur autem sub Libano monte, et dividit Judaeam et Arabiam, qui per multos circuitus juxta Jericho in mare Mortuum influit.
>
> (*PL* 82:492)

> [The Jordan is a river of Judea, named from its two sources, one of which is called Jor, the other Dan. Because these are then joined at some distance along into one bed, it is thenceforth called Jordan. It is born at the foot of Mount Lebanon and divides Judea and Arabia, which after many circlings near Jericho flows into the Dead Sea.]

Dante's rivers, unlike the exegetes' Jordan, rise from a single source and then branch into two beds, but like the Jordan, the river at the foot of Dante's mountain flows into a dead sea, and at the top of the mountain, as Dante will learn, it figuratively divides the Promised Land from the desert. The Jordan's double source is frequently represented in visual art by the presence of two river gods, each of whom pours water from an urn, thereby creating a stream.[78] The two streams coalesce to form a single river, which, in many depictions, is shown to "turn backward," a reference to Psalm 113 (114–115) in which the line "the Jordan turned backward" celebrates the final episode of the Exodus, narrated in the Book of Joshua.[79] Dante's double stream, the Lethe-Eunoe, recalls the doubleness of the Jordan, both in *umbra* and in fulfillment, the biblical river of baptism. Furthermore, the Jordan-Oceanus connection noted by Freccero is recapitulated in the Eunoe, which, unlike Lethe, appears to encircle Eden. What Lucy sees as the boundary line of life and death in *Inferno* II prefigures the boundary line between purgation and beatitude; both instances engage the typology of baptism, and thus Jordan, which was traditionally associated with the rivers of Paradise. The struggle to cross the purgatorial rivers is anticipated in *Inferno* I, where Dante tries unsuccessfully to climb a mountain at whose base flows a river over which the sea has no vaunt. All that is missing, in that scene, is the literal sense: Dante is no more at the antipodes and therefore at the shore of the Lethe than he is at the shore of the Jordan. [80]

The Jordan, which, as we have seen, was associated both with the rivers of Paradise and with Oceanus, implies the double linear/circular form of the rivers of Purgatory, as well as the poem's other important *fiumana*, the river of light in *Paradiso* XXX, which "parve / di sua lunghezza divenuta tonda" as Dante drinks of it with his eyelids. The double river crossing of the top of Purgatory is refigured in this double vision of the river of light. The true fulfillment of the *fiumana* as Jordan-Lethe, [81] the *fiumana* as *limen* to a new level of spiritual experience, comes in the Empyrean, where Dante crosses the final threshold to the full and direct vision of the very world from which Beatrice had descended in the episode narrated in *Inferno* II. In *Paradiso* XXX, when Dante crosses over from the Primum Mobile into the "ciel ch'è pura luce," he is struck blind by its intensity; when his vision is restored, the first thing he sees is a river of light: "vidi lume in forma di rivera / fulvido di fulgore" (XXX, 61–62). From this river, this *fiumana*, as it is called at line 64, living sparks splash out upon the gemlike flowers along its banks. The river is presented as the poem's putative "final fiction," its final veil; for here at last, Dante, who has had to pursue the truth through mediations of language and image, is promised knowledge direct and uncompromised, an unmediated vision of truth itself. In a stunning literalization of the metaphor of the river of light, Beatrice instructs him to drink from it with his eyes, so that he will finally satisfy the metaphorical thirst for the truth:

> "L'alto disio che mo t'infiamma e urge,
>   d'aver notizia di ciò che tu vei,
>   tanto mi piace più quanto più turge;
> ma di quest' acqua convien che tu bei
>   prima che tanta sete in te si sazi."   (XXX, 70–74)

The *fiumana*, the flowers, the sparks, all are about to be transfigured from their appearance into their reality; all have been "di lor vero umbriferi prefazi" (XXX, 78), a consequence of Dante's imperfect vision rather than of any "difetto" of truth. It is the crossing of this *fiumana* that culminates in the threefold rhyme on "vidi" (XXX, 95, 97, 99), and it is what Dante "sees" in these final cantos that validates the entire poem, making "ciò ch'io vidi" mean infinitely more than we could have known when we first read in *Inferno* II the promise of its invocation to record faithfully its author's vision.

If the *fiumana* of *Inferno* II anticipates the liminal function of Lethe-Eunoe, it also must be seen as "umbrifero prefazio" of the *fiumana* of *Paradiso* XXX, itself a shadow of the truth it makes visible. The exodus that began when the *donne benedette* saw Dante struggling at the *fiumana* concludes in the crossing of this final *fiumana*, at once a simulacrum of the transition from time into eternity and the locus from which the ladies initiated the action the poem narrates. When this last river has been crossed, Beatrice will speak her final words, returning to the heavenly seat from which she had descended into Limbo; Dante addresses his valedictory to her (XXXI, 79–90) in words specifically recalling her salvific descent, as one who left her "*vestige*" in hell.

To return from the *fiumana* of light to the *fiumana* of *Inferno* II, the presence of multiple literary and exegetical subtexts contributes to the passage's richness of texture and meaning, but no matter how full a gloss one can give, our original question remains unanswered: what has become of the literal sense in *Inferno* II's reference to the *fiumana*? The answer must come in terms other than those we have been exploring, for the river is liminal in yet another way, defining the border, not only between life and death, but also between two different kinds of allegory and, as such, between two different epistemologies. *Inferno* II presents the first of four related moments, each doubly transitional—in plot for the character and in poetics for the author—and each marked by a river and an invocation. One such moment introduces each *cantica*, and the fourth marks the entry to the Empyrean; the first two take place at the shore of a river, and the last two involve crossings of rivers. The invocation at the beginning of the *Purgatorio* takes place when Dante is at the shore of the stream that had been called the *ruscelletto* in *Inferno* XXXIV and the *fiume* later in *Purgatorio* I, a stream that is really, as we have seen, Lethe. The conventional separation of Dante's text into three volumes obscures the fact that the invocation at the beginning of *Paradiso* follows immediately upon Dante's crossing of Eunoe in the closing lines of *Purgatorio* XXXIII. Finally, the "baptism" of Dante's eyes in the river of light in *Paradiso* XXX is immediately followed by an invocation asking the splendor of God for the power to tell of what he saw there.

We have argued for Dante's incarnational poetics in his conception of the *tre donne*, and indeed our sense is that *Inferno* II is radically different from *Inferno* I on precisely these grounds; the differences, that is, between the ontological status of the three ladies and that of the three beasts mark a shift in poetics. The moral geography of the first canto has a symbolic status independent of the literal sense (see Freccero, 1966). When Dante asserts at the beginning of *Inferno* II that he writes "ciò ch'io vidi," he informs us that this imagined reality has a status different from that of the generically allegorical actions and setting of the first canto. The *fiumana*, although it is mentioned in *Inferno* II, is a feature of the first canto's shadowy landscape; it exists in a temporal moment before Virgil's appearance to Dante, a moment Virgil now recalls to Dante in a "flashback." Therefore, it is no surprise that the *fiumana* returns us temporarily to the allegorical procedures of Canto I. Is Dante "really" at the Jordan? At Lethe? At the Acheron? At a *fluctus concupiscentiae*? He is, in *any* sense but the literal, at any of them, insofar as each can suggest some aspect of the typological significance of Dante's exodus experience. Seen from this point of view, Beatrice's descent into Limbo has poetic as well as moral significance; her return to Dante's life and his poetry is coordinate with both the primacy of the literal sense and the potential to perceive the various spiritual senses that are enfolded within it.

In fact, the fictive status of the *fiumana* of *Inferno* II is even less concrete than that of the components of the shadowy landscape in *Inferno* I: its status is wholly symbolic. In contrast, the rivers of the earthly paradise, however symbolic their implications, are nonetheless experienced and presented as literal rivers as well. The *fiumana* of *Paradiso* XXX is the fulfillment of both the infernal and purgatorial rivers; it is typological, but it is defined as such, and also as the gateway to the transcendence of figuration.[82] Each of these liminal rivers, finally, implies not only a moral transformation but a poetic one. Just as the first major turning point in the *Vita Nuova*, Dante's "conversion" to the poetry of praise, took place as he walked beside a "rivo," the *Commedia*'s rivers signal a change at once in the nature of the pilgrim's inner state and of the poet's powers.[83]

CHAPTER III

Pilgrim and Poet: Definition by Dialectic

The Pilgrim as Aeneas and Paul

At the opening of *Inferno* II, the frame is frozen, the poem's action suspended between the moment of intellectual conversion in which the pilgrim realizes that a change needs to be made and his affective and spiritual commitment to get on with the task.[1] Less obviously, perhaps, this canto is also transitional for the poet, presenting in dramatic fashion his emerging sense of the form as well as the function of literature. Throughout his literary career, Dante had defined himself in and through his writings, reinterpreting his past experiences and mythologizing his present situation so as to confer upon his life an emblematic or representative status. At the beginning of the *Commedia*, however, Dante's earlier intellectual and artistic accomplishments are simultaneously the essential preconditions for, and hindrances to, the poem's composition, for the *Commedia* makes it clear that it was at least in part through and because of those very accomplishments that he had found himself "smarrito."

In *Inferno* II, Dante introduces his readers to what will become one of the *Commedia*'s central strategies: he begins here to establish his identity, both as character and as author, by implicit comparison and contrast with other figures. Throughout the poem, each lover and each poet will shed light on Dante, as will each politician and each statesman, and especially each convert, the figures incrementally creating Dante's simultaneously unique and exemplary self-portrait. In *Inferno* II Dante begins this process, but not, as subsequently, through dialectical interchange with characters whom he encounters. (Because the journey is suspended in this canto, there *is* no one to meet.) Rather, he compares himself explicitly to Aeneas and Paul, two figures he has previously encountered only in texts, but with the specific details of that doubled comparison operating in a way analogous to the dramatized encounters to be found in the rest of the poem. These two figures provide, that is, an insight into the kind of pilgrim Dante is in process of becoming and the kind of poet he aspires to be.

Moreover, as is typical of a conversion narrative, the *Commedia* defines its hero's "present" by contrast with his past, though here with a particularly selective view of that past: namely, by contrast with the characterization of himself which Dante had presented in his own earlier writing, with his own earlier publicly presented self-definition. It is in this canto that the *Commedia*'s ongoing dialectical engagement of the *Convivio* (already implicit in *Inferno* I) begins to be made explicit,[2] and with it begins Dante's dramatization of his reevaluation of Boethius's life and work. The comparisons of Dante to these four figures—to Aeneas and Paul, as well as to Boethius and to his own earlier literary self-fashioning—are mutually reinforcing, and they illuminate a constellation of interrelated themes focusing on the notion of election. These themes are central to the *Commedia* as a whole, themes such as the relationship of Divine Providence to human freedom, of grace to merit, of suffering to deliverance, in addition to questions of the interpretation and the mediational function of language. For Dante, both as wayfarer and as author, these issues introduced in *Inferno* II are defining ones; the limits and liberation they imply will be explored throughout the *Commedia* and will ultimately be clarified, along with much else, in the encounter with Cacciaguida in the *Paradiso*.

"Io non Enëa, io non Paulo sono"

Although Dante protests to Virgil that he is not capable of undertaking this journey to the otherworld, his evaluation is clearly incorrect: since the journey being described in the poem's fiction must have been completed successfully for the poem's composition to be undertaken, the *Commedia*'s very existence gives the lie to the pilgrim's protest of inadequacy. The language in which the pilgrim frames his insecurity becomes part of the poet's self-definition:

> Ma io, perché venirvi? o chi 'l concede?
>   Io non Enëa, io non Paulo sono;
>   me degno a ciò né io né altri 'l crede.   (II, 31–33)

Clearly, one is to understand just the opposite of what the text here asserts, namely that in some way not clear to the pilgrim himself at this time of great personal anxiety, he really *is* like Aeneas and Paul. Mazzoni (pp. 231–233) is typical in describing these lines as a modesty topos of the type studied by Curtius, but the distinction between pilgrim and poet argues against reading Dante's hesitation in this way: the lines are dramatic rather than rhetorical, addressed not by the writer to his readers but spoken by the character in dialogue with Virgil. Although it may well be that the pilgrim's intent in these lines is to present himself as humble, Virgil, who acts in the canto with the authority of an ambassador from heaven, refuses to permit Dante this self-evaluation: he hears the words not as an expression of humility but as an unspoken admission of cowardice. Benvenuto, whose reading of this exchange is extremely sensitive, perceives the fallacy of Dante's objection and the corrective nature of Virgil's response:

> "Sum enim homo privatus quantum ad Eneam, et peccator quantum ad Paulum, et per consequens *me degno a ciò, né io né altri crede*, idest, nec ego, nec alius de me hoc credit. Sed certe Paulus erat peccator et persecutor istius fidei, quando fuit raptus ex gratia, et ita autor noster per gratiam fuit tractus ad istam contemplationem, sicut statim respondebit sibi Virgilius."
>
> (p. 85)

> ["For I am a private person compared to Aeneas, and I am a sinner compared to Paul, and consequently *me degno a ciò, né io, né altri crede*, that is, neither I nor any other believes this about me. And yet, Paul was a sinner and indeed a persecutor of the faith, at the time that he was rapt by grace, and likewise our author was drawn to this contemplative experience by grace, as Virgil will immediately respond to him."]

The remainder of *Inferno* II warns us to read ironically the dual precedents of Aeneas and Paul invoked at its beginning; had Dante properly understood his own allusions, he would have realized that the journeys of these two figures should encourage him to persist, not discourage him from continuing.

Readers should be careful not to see these lines about Aeneas and Paul simply as clues to Dante's "true" feelings about empire, papacy, and imperial-papal relations. The lines have often been detached from context and studied to determine what they reveal about Dante's Guelphism or about the continuity between his political thinking in *Inferno* II and his thinking in the *Monarchia* and the *Convivio*.[3] Valuable as such conjecture may be, we must not forget that Dante's reference to Aeneas and Paul is not a generalized evocation of the entire range of possible significations for the two figures in medieval Italian culture, nor even an evocation of Dante's idiosyncratic political or eschatological vision, but a set of specific allusions. The denial of the parallel to Aeneas and Paul in II, 31–33, concludes an eighteen-line description of these two figures and of their journeys—Aeneas's to Elysium and Paul's to the Empyrean.

> Tu dici che di Silvïo il parente,
>   corruttibile ancora, ad immortale
>   secolo andò, e fu sensibilmente.
> Però, se l'avversario d'ogne male
>   cortese i fu, pensando l'alto effetto
>   ch'uscir dovea di lui, e 'l chi e 'l quale
> non pare indegno ad omo d'intelletto;
>   ch'e' fu de l'alma Roma e di suo impero
>   ne l'empireo ciel per padre eletto:
> la quale e 'l quale, a voler dir lo vero,
>   fu stabilita per lo loco santo
>   u' siede il successor del maggior Piero.
> Per quest' andata onde li dai tu vanto,
>   intese cose che furon cagione
>   di sua vittoria e del papale ammanto.
> Andovvi poi lo Vas d'elezïone,
>   per recarne conforto a quella fede
>   ch'è principio a la via di salvazione.   (II, 13–30)

The specific texts to which these lines allude enable Dante to evoke in condensed fashion several interrelated notions about Aeneas and Paul applicable to himself at this critical moment in both the poem and the journey, especially the assertion that both figures were chosen by God for their missions: Aeneas is said to have been "ne l'empireo ciel per padre eletto" (II, 21), and Paul is identified as "Vas d'elezïone" (II, 28).[4] In addition to providing a clue to Dante's understanding of the vocations of Aeneas and Paul, these lines initiate the definition of his own analogous mission.

At first glance, the paired presentations in verses 13 to 30 seem to be decidedly nonparallel, given the great disparity between the number of lines devoted to Aeneas, fifteen, and the number given to Paul, just three. On closer examination, however, one finds that each of the two figures is described in just one *terzina*: Aeneas is described in the three lines that begin this passage, and Paul is described in the three that end it. The intervening twelve lines about Aeneas, which seem to grant to him so much more attention than is given to Paul, in fact tell us not about Aeneas but about Dante-Pilgrim, not about Virgil's account of his hero's journey but about Dante's analysis of that journey's significance. If we bracket those twelve lines of interpretation and examine only the two *terzine* that actually describe the figures, we find that the language is deliberately parallel: Aeneas "ad immortale secolo andò," and Paul "andovvi." If the twelve intervening lines were removed, the two parallel *terzine* would follow each other with no sense of discontinuity; indeed, the antecedent of the "vi" in "andovvi" would then be easier to locate, and the parallel presentation of the two figures would be more visible. As it is, only an acutely attentive reader would recall that the antecedent of "vi" in verse 28 is to be found back in verses 14 to 15, "ad immortale secolo." These twelve lines, however, are not arbitrarily inserted but are included to call attention to matters of literary and historical interpretation. We will analyze these intervening twelve lines closely, but first let us explore the syntactic and rhetorical parallelism of the two bracketing *terzine*. Both of them emphasize three points with implications for Dante: in them, Aeneas and Paul are identified not by name but by an epithet that constitutes a brief, but nonetheless precise, literary allusion; each *terzina* describes the nature of the trip taken; and each presents the journey's purpose.

Paul

The brief reference to Paul actually contains two separate allusions.[5] The term "Vas d'elezïone" recalls his conversion, the central event in his life as narrated in Chapter 9 of Acts of the Apostles.[6] There, in the conclusion of the drama that occurred on the road to Damascus, God reveals to Ananias the special purpose reserved for Saul, his "chosen vessel" (or "vas electionis" in the Vulgate's literal translation of this Hebraism):

Vade, quoniam vas electionis est mihi iste, ut portet nomen meum coram gentibus, et regibus, et filiis Israel. Ego enim ostendam illi quanta oporteat eum pro nomine meo pati.

(Acts 9:15–16)

[Go thy way; for this man is to me a vessel of election, to carry my name before the Gentiles, and kings, and the children of Israel. For I will show him how great things he must suffer for my name's sake.]

God links Paul's mission with the necessity of suffering, and Paul begins both proselytizing and suffering immediately after his baptism in Acts 9. His preaching of "the Way" arouses the suspicion of the Christian community he had formerly persecuted and the hatred of the Jewish authorities he had previously served, and he finally needs to be lowered from the walls of Damascus in a basket to escape the foul play that had been planned for him (Acts 9:20–25).

The opening word of the Pauline *terzina*, "Andovvi," introduces a second scriptural reference and raises a second question. Where is it that he went, and when? To what episode is Dante referring? Several commentators, including some of the earliest ones, saw these lines as referring to the folk tradition that Paul actually went to hell,[7] a journey such as the one described in the apocryphal *Visio Pauli*.[8] This reading became increasingly widespread in the nineteenth century, shortly after the discovery and publication of some hitherto unknown visions of journeys to the otherworld, but it was by and large put to rest by Francesco D'Ovidio, who argued persuasively that the tradition represented by the *Visio* seems to have afforded only a vague inspiration to Dante. Rather, it was Paul's own canonical account of his spiritual ecstasy that influenced the *Commedia* in a profound way.[9] In II Corinthians 12:2–4, Paul speaks of himself periphrastically:

Scio hominem in Christo ante annos quatuordecim, sive in corpore nescio sive extra corpus nescio, Deus scit, raptum huiusmodi usque ad tertium caelum. Et scio huiusmodi hominem sive in corpore sive extra corpus nescio, Deus scit: quoniam raptus est in paradisum: et audivit arcana verba, quae non licet homini loqui.

[I know a man in Christ above fourteen years ago (whether in the body I know not, or out of the body, I know not; God knoweth), such a one caught up to the third heaven. And I know such a man (whether in the body, or out of the body, I know not: God knoweth): That was caught up into paradise, and heard secret words, which it is not granted to man to utter.]

The unidentified "man in Christ," the "certain man" who was taken to the third heaven and to Paradise, is, of course, Paul himself.[10]

The proper context within which to read Paul's report of his rapture actually consists of the entire conclusion of the Epistle, Chapters 10–13, where Paul defends himself from the slanders of false apostles in Corinth who have accused him of weakness and boasting. The account in Chapter 12 of his *raptus* is the climax of this self-defense, a demonstration of the power working through him despite his weakness; as an undeserved gift, it is something of which he refuses to boast. The context of II Corinthians also supplies the answer to the third question which Dante's *terzina* raises, namely the purpose for Paul's journey: "andovvi," we are told, he went there, "per recarne conforto a quella fede / ch' è principio a la via di salvazione" (II, 29–30).[11] Paul's account of his rapture provided reassurance for those believers in the Corinthian *ecclesia* whose faith had been shaken by the preaching and *invidia* of the false apostles at work in the city. In a wider sense, circulation of the letter also allows Paul to address other believers removed in time and space from first-century Corinth, bringing potential comfort to all the faithful by means of his writing.

The Pauline model for Dante's experiences in the *Paradiso* is widely recognized. Paul is referred to in *Paradiso* XXI, 127–128, in an elaboration of the epithet of Acts 9, as "il gran vasello / de lo spirito santo," and the third *cantica* begins by explicitly evoking both of *Inferno* II's Pauline passages. In *Paradiso* I's invocation to "buono Apollo," Dante asks that he himself be made "del tuo valor . . . *vaso*" (I, 14); later in the canto, Dante echoes II Corinthians in wondering whether he made his journey in spirit only or in his body as well, even to the point of recalling Paul's "Deus scit" with his "tu 'l sai" (I, 75). In the Epistle to Cangrande, moreover, Dante glosses the opening lines of the first canto of the *Paradiso* (I, 4–6) by citing the description of Paul's rapture in II Corinthians.[12] Later in *Paradiso*, at moments of transition to more intense levels of vision, Dante will once again recall the moment of Paul's conversion: in XXVI, 12, Beatrice's eyes are said to possess the power of Ananias's hand; and in XXX, 46–51, Dante says "così mi circunfulse luce viva," recalling the verb associated with the Damascus vision later in Acts ("circumfulsit" in 22:6 and "circumfulsisse" in 26:13).

Since it is so clear, therefore, that Dante sees Paul's experience as a model for his own, it is important to determine what experience Dante believed Paul had. The question of whether Paul actually saw God in his "essence and nature," or only through some accommodation appropriate to human perception, was crucial in patristic and medieval exegetical sources, where the passage from II Corinthians was a critical text in arguments about the way creatures can acquire knowledge of the Creator. In this tradition, Paul was regularly linked with Moses as one of only two figures in history given direct revelation of God's presence, even though the exact nature of that revelation continued to be disputed.[13] Some scriptural commentators believed, with St. Gregory, that no one still in the flesh could see God directly, so that the visions of Paul and Moses were mediated *per speculum* and were thus something less than the beatific vision; others followed St. Augustine in believing that both were given this privilege of seeing God in essence.[14] Joseph A. Mazzeo argues from examination of numerous passages in the *Paradiso* that Dante inclined toward this latter position concerning Paul's vision, making it all the more daring that he should perceive his own experience as parallel.[15] Mazzeo concludes: "Thus Dante's analogy between St. Paul and himself is intensely charged, and any theologically sophisticated reader of his time would have grasped the immensity of Dante's claim" (p. 99).[16]

In linking St. Paul with Aeneas, Dante establishes a typological relation of both comparison and contrast. Like both of them, Dante is about to be granted a privileged vision and to embark upon a mission of universal scope; however, the relationship to Aeneas remains a qualified one compared to the Pauline parallel. Aeneas, in his *descensus ad Elysium*, becomes the type fulfilled in Paul's *ascensus in Paradisum* and reenacted in Dante's experience in the *Commedia*.[17] Although Mazzoni is too severe in his distinction between Aeneas's thoroughly natural experience and Paul's supernatural one,[18] it remains true that the *Aeneid* presents a partial and flawed model that needs to be qualified if it is to be useful to the pilgrim.

Aeneas

The first *terzina* in this passage, the one referring to Aeneas, raises the same three points we have noted about Paul—the identification of the character by epithet, the nature of the journey, and its purpose—but in this case with only one allusion. It is, of course, in *Aeneid* VI that Aeneas makes his journey, "corruttibile ancora," to the otherworld, but our attention is focused more narrowly upon a precise moment within that book by the identification of Aeneas as "di Silvïo il parente." At the shore of Lethe, Anchises shows Aeneas the souls of his unborn descendants, thereby reassuring his son of the fame that awaits them, of the destiny they will fulfill. Anchises' revelation of the succession of future Romans will culminate in the poignant description of the early death of Augustus's adopted son Marcellus; it begins with his presentation of Aeneas's posthumous son Silvius:[19]

ille, uides, pura iuuenis qui nititur hasta,
proxima sorte tenet lucis loca, primus ad auras
aetherias Italo commixtus sanguine surget,
Siluius, Albanum nomen, tua postuma proles,
quem tibi longaeuo serum Lauinia coniunx
educet siluis regem regumque parentem,
unde genus Longa nostrum dominabitur Alba.

(VI, 760–766)

       [The youth
you see there, leaning on his headless spear,
by lot is nearest to the light; and he
will be the first to reach the upper air
and mingle with Italian blood; an Alban,
his name is Silvius, your last born son.
For late in your old age Lavinia,
your wife, will bear him for you in the forest;
and he will be a king and father kings;
through him our race will rule in Alba Longa.]

Glosses on *Inferno* II's description of Aeneas as "di Silvïo il parente" invariably refer the reader to this scene in *Aeneid* VI, often with the additional information that, by making Silvius the son of Aeneas, Dante follows the tradition of Virgil rather than that of Livy, for whom Silvius was the son of Ascanius and therefore Aeneas's grandson.[20] In the speech that begins with this reference to Silvius, Anchises foretells, from the "immortale secolo," the development of Roman history up to its fulfillment in Virgil's own lifetime with the establishment of the empire and of the Julian line. Given its position, spoken from the center of the poem and from the depths of eternity, Anchises' address offers an ideal vision of Rome's special mission, her universal vocation:[21]

tu regere imperio populos, Romane, memento
(hae tibi erunt artes), pacique imponere morem,
parcere subiectis et debellare superbos.   (VI, 851–853)

[but yours will be the rulership of nations,
remember, Roman, these will be your arts:
to teach the ways of peace to those you conquer,
to spare defeated peoples, tame the proud.]

Anchises announces this imperial destiny at the conclusion of the speech begun with the reference to Silvius: as the son of Aeneas in whom Trojan and Italic blood is first mingled, Silvius leads the file of unborn Roman heroes. [22]

Like the reference to Paul, therefore, the epithet that identifies Aeneas also identifies the moment in the source text in which the character's "election" is revealed; unlike the reference to Paul, however, the significance of that election is, for Dante, only partially understood within its own narrative. In *Inferno* II, it is Virgil's interpretation of Aeneas's journey that is advanced, but Virgil's limitation of vision had already been introduced into the poem in his own opening speech in which he had described himself as one who "vissi a Roma sotto 'l buono Augusto / nel tempo de li dèi falsi e bugiardi" (*Inferno* I, 71–72). At this moment in *Inferno* II, therefore, as has often been noted, Dante expects his readers to be aware of the disparity between the *Aeneid*'s problematical authority and the unqualified authority of the Pauline Epistles, a distinction suggested by the words with which Dante introduces each figure. In saying of Paul "Andovvi," he leaves no doubt about the credibility—or end—of a journey attested to by scriptural authority, but by prefacing his reference to Aeneas's journey with the qualification "tu dici che," he calls attention to the relative limitation of the *Aeneid*'s "merely" literary, as opposed to scriptural, authority. [23] This is not to deny that Dante saw the *Aeneid* as historical narrative. On the contrary, it is precisely because of its historical nature that it is subject to reinterpretation on the basis of subsequent events. Dante's reinterpretation is based not on literary but on historiographical grounds: Virgil's imperial teleology is inadequate to interpret properly the final significance of the events he was narrating. This limitation of Virgil's perception is the basis for the additional twelve lines introduced by the contrastive "Però, se"; from Dante's point of view, Virgil's text does not reveal Aeneas's true mission, and these additional lines, reinterpreting the *Aeneid*, are needed for its actual purpose to be grasped. [24]

In reading this passage, commentators have tended to overlook the distinction between the first three lines, which restate the *Aeneid*'s narrative, and the subsequent twelve, which consist of Dante's interpretation of Virgil's text. In the poem's fiction this interpretation is presented, not to the reader, but as part of a dramatic interchange which the reader is permitted to overhear: Aeneas's true historical significance is revealed directly to the author of the *Aeneid* himself. The alleged rhetorical purpose of the pilgrim in this context is to demonstrate his own unworthiness for the undertaking; but if this were the poet's sole objective he would have needed only the first seven of these fifteen lines (13–19), lines which might then be paraphrased, "You say that Aeneas went to the otherworld in the flesh, and this courtesy seems an appropriate one to people of understanding." Had Dante stopped at this point and omitted the next eight lines, the contrast of his own situation with the circumstances of Aeneas and Paul would have been even more emphatically presented. The analysis of Aeneas's precedent would then have been immediately followed by the *terzina* presenting Paul's parallel experience and then by the one in which Dante protests his own unworthiness: "Aeneas went there and he deserved it. . . . Paul then went there. . . . But I, why would I go there and by whose permission?" Presented this way, the sacredness of Rome's imperial mission would have been proffered as sufficient justification of Aeneas's journey. But it is in the eight additional lines (20–27) that Dante actively redefines Aeneas's enterprise, reinforcing his point by the uncommon emphasis with which each of the next three *terzine* concludes: verses 21, 24, and 27 refer not to Rome's imperial destiny but to Aeneas's unforeseeable function in Christian history.

Virgil would have agreed with Dante's assertion that the *Aeneid* showed its hero as "de l'alma Roma e di suo impero . . . padre," but, given his historical and religious limitations, he was of necessity ignorant of the assertions made in verses 21 and 24: that his hero's selection as father of the race took place "ne l'empireo ciel" and that the true purpose for which both Rome and her empire were established was to secure the future site of the Holy See.[25] By offering this reinterpretation "a voler dir lo vero," Dante underscores the notion that in these eight lines he corrects an error, that without such correction "lo vero" would be in jeopardy. It is important to recall, therefore, that *Inferno* II's premise is that Dante here does not correct the potential misapprehension of some anonymous and impersonal "reader"; rather, the pilgrim is providing this radical reinterpretation of the central moment of the *Aeneid* to the work's author. Throughout Dante's poem, the *Aeneid* is shown to be in need of completion by a Christian hermeneutic. Both Roman history and the great poem of its ethos are repeatedly brought into the orbit of Christian history and the *Commedia*'s poetics by such reinterpretation. At this early moment in the *Commedia*, Dante's interpretive gesture entirely alters what would otherwise have been the significance of those previous seven lines; the mission proclaimed by Anchises and understood as teleological by Virgil turns out to be only intermediate and instrumental. The final three lines about Aeneas (25–27), which summarize the relationship of the journey to its purpose, again emphasize the gap between Virgil's intention and his poem's ultimate meaning and as such provide a fitting conclusion to this revisionist reading of the *Aeneid*'s historical significance. Virgil may have boasted about the journey ("onde li dai tu vanto"), but he understood only half of the historical function revealed there: the "vittoria" but not the "papale ammanto."[26]

This allusion to the *Aeneid* sets up a series of reciprocal dramatic ironies. Dante concludes his protestation of inadequacy by calling upon Virgil to understand his words better than he has explained; this he does immediately after having himself performed an analogous act in his interpretation of Virgil's words about Aeneas: he has understood them better than Virgil had intended. There is an additional level of irony in that the pilgrim, even though he understands Aeneas's historical destiny better than Virgil intended, misunderstands his own typological relationship to Aeneas; "io non Enëa," he insists, when clearly there is a sense in which he is. Like Virgil's Aeneas, he is led toward discovery of his destiny and mission by means of intermediaries. The Sibyl leads Aeneas to Anchises, who reveals the future significance of Aeneas's mission in imperial history. Dante's Christian understanding of Aeneas's role adds an additional tier to the levels of mediation by subordinating Roman history to redemption history; the hand of Providence would seem to have been invisibly at work, directing the Sibyl to direct Aeneas to Anchises for purposes whose ultimate significance was of necessity obscure to her, to him, and to Virgil himself.[27] At the beginning of *Inferno* II, Dante, like Virgil's Aeneas, is being led toward an encounter in a Christian version of Elysium, but he still thinks, as in *Inferno* I, that he is simply following Virgil (perhaps as he had been doing during the composition of the *Convivio*'s fourth tractate).[28] In the canto's subsequent revelation of the concerns and intervention of the three ladies, however, we learn that Dante's Virgil, no less than Virgil's Sibyl, is himself the instrument of larger providential forces. The ironic complexity here is reciprocal: Dante has a broader historical vision than Virgil, but Virgil, whose insight has been informed by Beatrice's report from the Empyrean, has specific knowledge relative to his situation of which Dante is unaware. The pilgrim's interpretation is needed, therefore, to supplement Virgil's limited understanding of Aeneas's historical mission, and Virgil's analogously larger understanding is needed to correct the pilgrim's misunderstanding of his own vocation.[29]

The Pilgrim's Election

To speak of election in a Christian poem is inevitably to invoke questions of human freedom and divine grace. Indeed, it is probably because of the central importance of divine favor in *Inferno* II that so many commentators from the fourteenth century to the present have interpreted the *tre donne benedette* as three types of grace: this conventional allegorical reading responds in a systematic way to the significance of the canto's most important episode.[30] The pilgrim, in groping for an explanation for supernatural events, argues that Aeneas and Paul must have been permitted their journeys to the eternal realms because of deeds which he cannot presume to match. The gap here between the pilgrim's inference and the evidence dramatizes the *Commedia*'s retrospective structure. It is inherent in the way Dante presents souls in eternity that their lives are to be seen from the point of view of their endings.[31] *Inferno* II presents a paradoxical dichotomy in this regard. The pilgrim, who is himself *in via*,[32] invokes Aeneas and Paul as "finished products," as figures whose reputations render them so forbiddingly remote and whose accomplishments are so intimidating as to threaten to cut short his own spiritual journey. Examined more closely, however, the specific allusions to these two figures focus on them at moments when they, too, were *in via*, at moments of doubt and pain, of transition and spiritual redefinition. As such, Aeneas and Paul are not precedents whose accomplishments and reputations render them unreachably heroic but models of behavior appropriate to Dante and accessible to him.

The pilgrim cites Aeneas and Paul to demonstrate that he is unworthy of the enterprise to which Virgil has called him, but the specific allusions, combined with Dante's own situation in the *selva oscura*, reinforce the doctrinal commonplace that grace is granted unexpectedly, its undeserved nature underscoring the inscrutability of Providence.[33] Aeneas's paradoxical role in history is implied in the double negative of the pilgrim, who says that Aeneas was "not unworthy" of his descent to Elysium, not that he deserved it. Aeneas's privilege is warranted because of the deeds of his unborn descendants, and at that not of those who would later found the Roman Imperium;[34] from the *Commedia*'s point of view, the gift is granted to Aeneas because Rome's grandeur reaches its true fulfillment in Christian salvation history. In the case of Paul, it is even clearer that divine favor was not a reward for prior behavior. Rather, when God commands Ananias to restore vision to the blinded Saul, Ananias protests against being required to heal one who is so well known as an opponent of "the Way." Clearly Paul was not chosen because of his previous behavior, and if retrospect makes Paul seem the inevitable choice for his mission, Acts stresses the reluctance of Ananias and the initial mistrust of the Damascus community as evidence that the choice was a baffling one to first-generation Christians. In II Corinthians, in fact, Paul insists that his celestial rapture was a gift he did *not* deserve, that his ecstasy demonstrates, rather, the power of God mysteriously working through him despite his weakness. When Dante protests, therefore, that he is not worthy of a gift analogous to Paul's, he misses the point: Paul's purpose—in the very passage to which Dante here alludes—had been to assure his readers that *no one* deserves the gift which grace, by definition, entails. [35]

The experiences of Aeneas and Paul also reveal the inextricable connection between mission and suffering, [36] positing suffering as a necessary precondition, as well as a consequence, of commitment. [37] Aeneas, who had already endured a succession of hardships before Book VI, learns from the Sybil at the start of that book of the sufferings still in store: "o tandem magnis pelagi defuncte periclis / (sed terrae grauiora manent)" (VI, 83–84) [O you who are done, at last, with those great dangers / that lie upon the sea—worse wait on land], and she goes on to foretell an additional round of hardships, with the immediate future holding in store another foreign bride, another war, another Achilles. At the end of Book VI, therefore, when Anchises prophesies Aeneas's triumph, we know that his mission will be fulfilled only at the conclusion of yet more anguish.

Similarly, the two allusions to Paul point to the suffering he endures, and they do so precisely where the passages were seen to overlap. The Dante commentary tradition has not noted that the two passages conflated in *Inferno* II were already connected to each other in the scriptural exegetical tradition because they both refer to Paul's suffering. In Acts 9, God had said that he would show his chosen vessel "how great things he must suffer for my name's sake," and within a few verses the new apostle needs to be smuggled out of Damascus to avoid assassination. At the conclusion of II Corinthians 11, where Paul lists several of the occasions on which he had been called upon to suffer for his faith, he ends with a reference to this escape from Damascus. The opening words of Chapter 12 were sometimes seen, therefore, as referring to the series of hardships cataloged at the end of the previous chapter and particularly its concluding one. "Si gloriori oportet" would then be read as a reference to Paul's refusal to boast for his escape from the religious or civil authorities in Damascus, the episode narrated in Acts 9. [38] In II Corinthians, Paul goes so far as to argue that his suffering for God's sake is in actuality a sign of the grace necessary for the mystical journey: Paul will boast only in his infirmities (12:5); the "stimulus carnis," the thorn in the flesh, was given to him precisely to avert self-exaltation (12:7); and this is said to demonstrate the relationship between suffering, grace, and "virtus," a word whose primary meaning is "power," but which here also implies something like the modern English "virtue" (12:8–10). [39] Paul reports God's words to him, "Sufficit tibi gratia mea, nam virtus in infirmitate perficitur" [My grace is sufficient for thee, for *virtus* is made perfect in infirmity], leading Paul to rejoice in his oppression as a token of grace: "Cum enim infirmor, tunc potens sum" [For when I am weak, then am I powerful]. [40]

Dante, the character in the fictional time of 1300, may say he is not Aeneas or Paul, but the poet looking back over the development of his life—a life filled with moments of hardship, suffering, despair and alienation—knows the opposite. For Dante reveals during the course of the *Commedia* that he, too, has learned to see his suffering as paradoxical evidence of divine favor. What *Inferno* II dramatizes in the paired analogies of Aeneas and Paul is Dante's incipient sense of vocation. During his descent to Hades, Dante says, Aeneas heard things ("intese cose") important for his and his people's future: that his suffering is historically significant, that its telos is of universal import, that his apparent defeats and frustrations will in the end be purposive, and that his contributions are indispensible if that history is to be fulfilled. In Acts 9, Paul is also given his particular calling by Ananias, who serves as mediator of God's will, and here, too, the emphasis is on the interrelationship of vocation and suffering. [41] The difference, in fact, between *Inferno* I and *Inferno* II, between conversion and vocation, is the difference between Paul, blinded by the truth on the road to Damascus but as yet directionless, and Paul after Ananias sends him forth healed, as the "vas electionis": at that moment, "ceciderunt ab oculis eius, tanquam squamae" (Acts 9:18) [something like scales fell from his eyes]. Once Dante's calling is revealed to him and he can see well—in fact, *because* his vision, like Paul's, has been healed—he is ready to begin to serve, in his turn, as intermediary for his readers of "ciò ch'io vidi."

The Pilgrim still needs to live through the *Inferno* and *Purgatorio*, as well as half of the *Paradiso*, inferring his calling along the way, before Cacciaguida will clarify what has been hinted at. To borrow a schema from St. Thomas, Dante has at the beginning of *Inferno* II experienced only the first of the five effects of grace, "the healing of the soul." The rest of the poem is required to reveal what begins during the course of *Inferno* II, Thomas's second effect, "the willing of the good"; in Dante's case, this good involves the Poet's commitment to write about that spiritual healing in a prophetic way. [42] As with the other characters in the *Commedia*, the view from the end is confirmed by a retrospective examination of Dante's life. Paul had unwittingly been preparing for his vocation throughout his preconversion life. (This is perhaps, to borrow a more familiar truism from Thomas, to say that grace builds on nature, rather than obliterates it.) It is clear from the outset that these two are models for the journey; it becomes clear later in the *Commedia* that they serve also as models for the writing of the poem.

The Poet's New Mission

Dante's opening and closing addresses to Virgil in this canto have very different implications. The first speech begins, "Poeta che mi guidi," and the last, "tu duca, tu segnore, tu maestro" (II, 140). The second address to Virgil is not a mere paraphrase of the first, but represents a change of attitude about the function of poetry that responds directly to Virgil's intervening speech on the *tre donne benedette*, for Dante learns from Virgil in this canto that his previous ideas about the value of poetry were limited. In the address to Virgil at the beginning of Canto II, Dante seems still to be thinking of poetry as he had when he appealed for Virgil's aid in Canto I:

> O de li altri poeti onore e lume,
>   vagliami 'l lungo studio e 'l grande amore
>   che m'ha fatto cercar lo tuo volume.
> Tu se' lo mio maestro e' l mio autore,
>   tu se' solo colui da cu' io tolsi
>   lo bello stilo che m'ha fatto onore.   (I, 82–87)

The instinctive desire to join with Dante in this tribute to Virgil can easily keep us from noticing that its presuppositions are, from the *Commedia*'s perspective, fundamentally misguided. Dante's hope that his long study of and great love for Virgil's poem would somehow deliver him from his spiritual wilderness is touching and moving, but it is also, in terms of a rhetoric of conversion, patently vain: philology and literary affiliation may be important human activities, but they cannot on their own terms fill Dante's spiritual void. His praise of Virgil as the sole source of his own honor as a poet shows in retrospect how imperfectly he understands at the poem's beginning what he will come to learn during its course: the true nature of honor and of poetry, as well as the transformed role Virgil will come to play in his life and his writing. One of the main objectives of Virgil's speech in *Inferno* II is to correct this misperception: Virgil did not come to rescue Dante as a reward for philological study or because his literary influence can somehow "justify" Dante, but as an instrument of divine grace.

In fact, back in *Inferno* I, Virgil's response to Dante's request for assistance against the *lupa* may already have suggested a repudiation of the attitude toward poetry which Dante expressed there. Recalling the canto's controlling metaphor of the spiritual journey, Virgil responds to Dante's fears by warning that he will need to pursue another route if he is to escape the wilderness:

> "A te convien tenere altro viaggio,"
>   rispuose, poi che lagrimar mi vide,
> "se vuo' campar d'esto loco selvaggio."   (I, 91–93)

The "viaggio" which Virgil here rejects must mean more than just the literal road; it also means the spiritual path Dante has just implicitly proposed, namely *via* mastery of literary style. When Dante calls Virgil "poeta che mi guidi" at the beginning of *Inferno* II, he is still thinking of secular poetry and knowledge as the path to salvation.

Virgil's response, in presupposing a relationship between grace and poetry, initiates a redefinition of the vocation of poet and thereby of the basis of poetic excellence. In his account of the exchanges among the celestial ladies, as well as in the fact of his own mission, he emphasizes the intercessory function of language. Virgil's ability to serve such a mediational, instrumental function for his readers is attested to in his encounter with Statius, who, like Dante, was converted through Virgil's texts not only to poetry but, more important, to morality and to Christianity.[43] Just as Aeneas's true, though unforeseen, mission will be fulfilled in the Christian dispensation, the true, though unforeseen, end of Virgil's poetry is—for the *Commedia*—to be found in Dante's conversion. In *Inferno* II, Virgil sets up the preliminary terms of Dante's intermediary role as Christian poet: no less than Statius, Dante responds to the salvific power of Virgil's word, but unlike that "chiuso cristian"—and like Paul—Dante will openly proclaim the truth to others in his writing.[44]

There are many ways in which Paul may be seen as Dante's model: because of his journey to the otherworld and because of his conversion, but also as a model of the writer Dante hopes to become.[45] The postconversion Saul of Tarsus, combining his knowledge of Jewish law with what the Middle Ages saw as his rhetorical skill in gentile language, was uniquely qualified for his calling. Similarly, the converted Dante, with his combination of humanist learning and rhetorical facility in the vulgar tongue, had unique qualifications: no one else could have done what he is about to do. If Paul synthesized the Jewish within the Christian tradition, Dante did the same for the secular literary tradition. L'Anonimo Fiorentino apparently recognized this similarity, for in his gloss on "Andovvi poi lo Vaso" l'Anonimo describes Paul in ways reminiscent of Dante: "Et qui è da sapere che santo Paulo fue pagano, et grandissimo persecutore de' Cristiani. . . . Fue chiamato Saulo, grandissimo scienziato, et essendo grande rettorico, scrisse molte pistole a Seneca morale. . . . [Et] andando verso Damasco, venne per divino miracolo uno splendore grandissimo da cielo sopra santo Paulo, di tanta chiarezza che santo Paulo, vinto, smarrito et cieco degli occhi, cadde in terra" (p. 39). L'Anonimo speaks of Paul as a converted rhetorician, as though he were Victorinus or a zealous Statius; [46] more precisely, in speaking of Saul as a "grandissimo scienzato, et grandissimo rettorico," whose experience on the road to Damascus left him "smarrito," he recasts Paul as a type of Dante at the beginning of the *Commedia*. [47]

The "Fioretti" and the *Convivio*

In *Inferno* II, Dante begins to define the artistic no less than the personal realities mandated by his conversion; if he is now *novus homo*, who had he been—poetically speaking—as *vetus homo* and what was wrong with that artistic stance? The answer must be sought in the way the *Commedia* dramatizes Dante's perception of the *Convivio*: for in abandoning the project on which he had earlier staked his literary reputation, he reflects an altered attitude about himself and his craft. The dialectical relationship between the two texts is clear already in *Inferno* II with its emphasis on the necessity of mediation, both through personal intercession and through the medium of language. Mediation, evident in the actions of the *tre donne benedette* as well as of Virgil and implied by the allusions to Aeneas and Paul, functions simultaneously as cause and effect in the canto's dynamics, as both inspiration and obligation, as Dante's calling and his mission. Dante has been rescued through the care of others, and his role as poet is to serve as mediator of that event for his readers. In accepting this role, Dante rejects the *Convivio*'s fundamental assumptions about purely intellectual and literary goals and accomplishment, a rejection begun in explicit fashion in *Inferno* II. [48]

The Aristotelian axiom cited in the *Convivio*'s opening words asserts that philosophy is the privileged route to both truth and happiness: "Sì come dice lo Filosofo nel principio de la Prima Filosofia, tutti li uomini naturalmente desiderano di sapere" (*Convivio* I, i, 1). All things seek their own perfection, Dante continues, and since knowledge is the final perfection of the human soul, in that alone does one's true happiness consist. The remainder of the *Convivio*'s first chapter explores the consequent obligations for Dante as author, with respect both to his subject matter and to his readers. Since most people, he argues, lack the ability, the temperament, or the freedom to take up the pursuit of knowledge, they are unable to achieve happiness on their own. He positions himself as one of the happy few permitted to eat the "bread of the angels" (I, i, 7); he wishes to share with those who metaphorically eat like beasts the crumbs he has gathered at the table of the learned, and it is to feed the intellectually malnourished that he offers his *canzoni*, along with the learned interpretations he has newly composed for them (I, i, 8–9), as an intellectual banquet. Shifting his imagery from eating to drinking, he figures "those who know" as a living fountain at which the many may slake their innate thirst for knowledge (I, i, 9). The metaphor of an intellectual hunger and thirst to be satisfied through intellectual feasting and drinking continues throughout the work.

These introductory premises are generous and idealistic in context, but they are reevaluated and rejected in the *Commedia*, so much so that the situation in which Dante finds himself in *Inferno* I, lost in the *selva oscura*, is now widely read as Dante's subsequent perception that the attitudes expressed so optimistically in the *Convivio* should rather be seen as symptoms of spiritual crisis.[49] Although Nardi (1960) gives a lucid and valuable interpretation of the differences between the *Convivio* and the *Commedia*, he does not deal with the way the *Commedia* can be said to rewrite the *Convivio*. For him, the *Convivio* includes theological issues but subordinates them to philosophical concerns, while the *Commedia* is altogether another project, one centrally informed by its commitment to theological notions of beatitude. Nardi's sense of the break between the two works (and of the central role played by Dante's reading of the *Aeneid* in effecting it) is congruent with ours. What he does not discuss, however, is the way Dante returns to and reappropriates the specific language of the *Convivio* even as he moves beyond it. This dialectical dimension of the *Commedia*'s reading of the *Convivio* is of central importance.

By staging, in *Inferno* I, his inability to climb the mountain through his own power, Dante represents the failure of the rational, philosophic pursuit in which he had so confidently placed faith and hope earlier in his life.[50] On several occasions in the *Commedia*, Dante seems to perceive his earlier work—and to ask his readers to perceive it—from precisely this perspective: the *Convivio* was a false path which he repents having taken and from which he must "convert." We do well to be wary of accepting as our own Dante's unqualified rejection of his earlier work, for our retrospective position is surely more objective than Dante's own had been.[51] We, more than Dante, are likely to see the *Convivio*, to borrow a happy term from Barolini's analysis (pp. 25–26), as a "necessary detour" in Dante's development, since so many of the intellectual and social commitments he therein espouses will continue to be central to the *Commedia*'s final synthesis. Indeed, we need to distinguish between our evaluation of the *Convivio*'s role in Dante's intellectual and artistic development and the rhetorical function of Dante's own judgment upon that earlier role expressed in the *Commedia*, where his palinodic instinct leads him frequently to stage an absolute rejection of his earlier work, to recant the *Convivio* as, in retrospect, a sinful distraction.[52]

This self-evaluation, which is dramatized implicitly throughout *Inferno* II, is presented explicitly through a direct allusion to the *Convivio* at the canto's end. Dante there compares his reaction to Virgil's spiritually renovating words with a flower's response to the warmth of the sun:

> Quali fioretti dal notturno gelo
> chinati e chiusi, poi che 'l sol li 'mbianca,
> si drizzan tutti aperti in loro stelo,
> tal mi fec' io di mia virtude stanca,
> e tanto buono ardire al cor mi corse,
> ch'i cominciai come persona franca. (II, 127–132)

The simile has been admired for the beauty of its conception ever since the fourteenth century, but since it has not been seen as an allusion to the *Convivio*, its full thematic significance has never been recognized.[53] In the *Convivio*'s fourth tractate, Dante offers as his reason for addressing the question of "nobilitade" his desire to help bring those with misguided ideas about the topic back to the truth: "proposi di gridare a la gente, che per mal cammino andavano, acciò che per diritto calle si dirizzasse" (IV, i, 9) [I purposed to cry aloud to the folk who were going on the wrong path, in order that they might direct themselves on the right way]. He expresses some urgency about this task because he perceives that these people, in their intellectual illness, are hastening to a metaphorical death (IV, i, 10). In *Inferno* II, it will be Virgil's account of the words of Beatrice that serves as Dante's figurative sun, but here in the *Convivio*, in a similar figure of speech, the analogous role is played by Beatrice's rival, Philosophy.[54]

Dante identifies the lady of the fourth tractate's *canzone*: "per mia donna intendo sempre quella che ne la precedente ragione è ragionata, cioè quella luce virtuosissima, Filosofia, li cui raggi fanno li fiori rifronzire e fruttificare la verace de li uomini nobilitade" (II, i, 11) [by my lady I still understand the same, of whom I discoursed in the preceding ode, to wit, that most virtuous light, philosophy, whose rays make the flowers bud, and bear as fruit that true nobility of man, concerning which the ode before us purposes to speak in full]. The image is brilliant but, given its context, self-serving: the punning on *ragionare* and *raggi* makes it clear that the flowers and fruit to be ripened through the *virtù* of this sun will be those that are cultivated in the mind and that the power of this *luce* will be mediated through Dante himself. At the end of *Inferno* II, the situation is reversed: Dante is himself like the flower in need of nurture, rather than the great hope of those who otherwise would be helpless.[55] The elitism and exclusivity of the *Convivio*, whose intellectual light shines only on the few (and then largely as mediated through Dante), has given way to a sun that shines, at least potentially, on all.[56]

Boethius Misread

A question arises at this point with respect to Dante's conversion as it is represented in the *Commedia*. If Dante seems there so often to distance himself from the intellectual posture he had assumed in the *Convivio*, how did it happen that earlier in his life he enthusiastically adopted a position he would later reject with such finality? The answer Dante himself provides at two emphatic moments in the *Convivio* is that he thought he was following the lead of Boethius.[57] The parallels between the two figures are compelling: like Dante, Boethius was a poet-intellectual who decided to dedicate his talents to public service, claimed to have been unjustly condemned by the government he had served, and wrote about his experiences during his exile in a quasi-autobiographical work.[58] In the *Convivio*, however, Dante's misreading of the *Consolation of Philosophy* turns it into an inadvertent intellectual "Galeotto," the instrument of his anticonversion from Beatrice to Lady Philosophy. If the *Convivio* demonstrates, on the *Commedia*'s terms, Dante's error as writer, the *Convivio*'s depiction of Boethius shows his error as reader.

Dante brings the Boethian model to the foreground in two places in the *Convivio*. The first of these passages occurs in Dante's discussion of his shift in allegiance from Beatrice to Philosophy in his allegorical interpretation of the canzone, "Voi ch' intendendo il terzo ciel movete" (II, xiii).[59] Nothing could help him overcome his depression after Beatrice's death save for Boethius's work, "nel quale, cattivo e discacciato, consolato s'avea" (II, xii, 2). In a remarkable act of self-projection, the Dante of the *Convivio*, feeling himself in his grief "cattivo e discacciato" from his spiritual homeland, creates a Boethius in his own image and likeness, attributing to Boethius a rational self-sufficiency similar to his own. The reflexive verb *consolarsi*, with its implication that Boethius devised his work as a fiction with which to console himself, calls into question the *Consolation*'s very premise. It is, of course, just such self-sufficiency that makes the *Convivio* later seem to be fundamentally "wrong"—the mountain of *Inferno* I cannot be climbed simply by one's deciding to do so.[60]

The supplanting of Beatrice by Lady Philosophy in Dante's affections is so central to his life, and for our purposes so central to the events of *Inferno* II, that the moment of conversion warrants being recalled in some detail:

E sì come essere suole che l'uomo va cercando argento e fuori de la 'ntenzione truova oro, lo quale occulta cagione presenta, non forse sanza divino imperio; io, che cercava di consolarme, trovai non solamente a le mie lagrime rimedio, ma vocabuli d'autori e di scienze e di libri: li quali, considerando, giudicava bene che la filosofia, che era donna di questi autori, di queste scienze, e di questi libri, fosse somma cosa. E imaginava lei fatta come una donna gentile, e non la poteva imaginare in atto alcuno, se non misericordioso. . . . Sì che in picciol tempo, forse di trenta mesi, cominciai tanto a sentire de la sua dolcezza, che lo suo amore cacciava e distruggeva ogni altro pensiero. Per che io, sentendomi levare dal pensiero del primo amore a la virtù di questo, quasi maravigliandomi apersi la bocca nel parlare de la proposta canzone, mostrando la mia condizione sotto figura d'altre cose.   (II, xii, 5–8)

[And as it happens that a man goes in search of silver and beyond his purpose finds gold, the which some hidden cause presents, not, I take it, without divine command; so I, who was seeking to console myself, found not only a cure for my tears, but the words of authors, and sciences, and books, pondering upon which I judged that Philosophy, who was the lady of these authors, of these sciences, and of these books, was a thing supreme; and I conceived her after the fashion of a gentle lady and I could not conceive her in any attitude save that of compassion. . . . So that in a short time, I suppose some thirty months, I began to feel so much of her sweetness that the love of her expelled and destroyed every other thought. Wherefore, feeling myself raised from the thought of that first love even to the virtue of this, as though in amazement I opened my mouth in the utterance of the ode before us, expressing my state under the figure of other things. . . .]

The assertion that Dante composed "Voi ch'intendendo" in spontaneous emotional reaction to this moment of conversion makes of that poem's conflict between the two ladies a celebration of the victory of Philosophy, whose love "cacciava," banished, thoughts of Beatrice. [61]

As the opening words of this passage from the *Convivio* suggest, Dante has inverted the familiar Augustinian dynamic of reading pagan texts in salvific ways, not using gold of the Egyptians to support himself in the wilderness but transforming Boethius's potentially salvific work into a kind of fool's gold that actually leads him into the wilderness. [62] The process Dante describes is structurally similar to the paradigm of words-emotion-action which we have uncovered in the successive mediations of *Inferno* II. Boethius's words had moved Dante affectively to such an extent that he committed himself to Boethius's beloved Lady Philosophy and then wrote his *Convivio* in response. [63] The difference between this passage and the pattern of *Inferno* II is crucial, however, because it underscores the difference between Dante's preconversion and postconversion poetics. In writing the *Convivio*, Dante seems concerned not so much as he is in *Inferno* II to move his readers to an analogous response, as to show off his learning, to touch their minds rather than their hearts. [64]

The other passage from the *Convivio* which attests to Boethius's importance concerns the current situation of Dante as exiled writer. In direct address to his readers, at the very beginning of the *Convivio*, Dante confronts a fundamental literary question: should he name himself in his work? Writers have felt free to name themselves, he says, when an account of personal experiences would prove morally instructive to others; for this, Dante cites as his precedent the model of Augustine's *Confessions*. [65] One may also name oneself to defend one's reputation against unjust accusation:

E questa necessitate mosse Boezio di se medesimo a parlare,
acciò che sotto pretesto di consolazione escusasse la perpetuale
infamia del suo essilio, mostrando quello essere ingiusto, poi
che altro escusatore non si levava.   (*Convivio* I, ii, 13)

[And this necessity moved Boethius to speak of himself, so that
under cover of consolation he might ward off the perpetual
infamy of the exile, showing that it was unjust; since no other
arose to ward it off.]

No *ex post facto* recantation is needed for a reader familiar with the
Consolation to recognize that this is a shocking misinterpretation of
Boethius's text: it seems to accept the "preconsoled" Boethius of Book I
as normative and to claim that the entire *Consolation* is a mere "pretext"
for self-justification against "the perpetual infamy of his exile."

The passage, of course, tells us a good deal more about Dante's
bitterness over his own political exile at the time than it does about
Boethius, and Dante's attitude toward Boethius is, as we shall see, a
barometer of his developing responses toward his own exile. Dante
claims that the infamy against which he needs to justify himself is
literary—his earlier, apparently amatory, poems have been read in a
literal way, rather than as allegorical considerations of philosophical
topics[66]—but Dante's concerns here are clearly political as well as literary. In addition to providing Dante with a means of entry to the self-
allegoresis to which he will later subject his *canzoni*, Boethius seemed
also to have served him as a model for his self-defense against political
slander, given that what immediately follows this passage from *Convivio*
I, ii is written in the mode of an exile's *planctus*. According to what he
perceives as Boethian precedent, Dante laments his situation: victim-
ized by the infidelity of others, he suffers unjustly from what he calls
the "pena . . . d'essilio e di povertate" (I, iii, 3), and as an exile from
Florence, he refers to himself as an unwilling and bitter pilgrim ("peregrino, quasi mendicando, sono andato," I, iii, 4). Words such as *essilio*
and *peregrino* are charged with aesthetic and spiritual connotations in
the *Commedia*, as is the subsequent nautical metaphor comparing life
or literary composition to a sea voyage,[67] but here in the *Convivio*, they
lack the full resonance they would later acquire. Throughout this protestation of innocence in the face of ill fortune, Dante sounds like the
persona in Book I of the *Consolation*, the Boethius who has yet to be
reminded of the true nature of fortune and of happiness.[68]

If we may borrow for our discussion of the *Consolation* the familiar

Dantean distinction, the *Convivio* seems to ignore the difference between Boethius the pilgrim and Boethius the poet, between the con-
fused character that we meet at the work's beginning, in need of
Philosophy's graduated series of "cures," and the author whose eventual
clarity of self-vision enables him to dramatize the development of his
former into his present self. From this point of view, the dichotomy
Dante establishes at the beginning of the *Convivio* between Boethius
and Augustine is specious; both are in reality models of conversion,
and both may be said to combine aspects of Aeneas and Paul, of Ro-
manitas and Christianitas.[69] In the opening canto of the *Commedia*,
Dante is like the Boethius of the *Consolation*, Book I, no less than like
the Augustine of the *Confessions*, Book VII: he has not previously understood the true nature of his exile.

One need only read to the end of the *Consolation*'s first book to
discover, through the attitude of Lady Philosophy, what must have
been the stance of Boethius the author to his character's self-pity. In
response to the exile's lament over his ill fortune, Philosophy explains
that he has misunderstood the true nature of his banishment: "Sed tu
quam procul a patria non quidem pulsus es sed aberrasti; ac si te pulsum
existimari mauis, te potius ipse pepulisti. Nam id quidem de te num-
quam cuiquam fas fuisset" (I, pr. 5, 1–8) [You have not been driven out
of your homeland; you have willfully wandered away. Or, if you prefer
to think that you have been driven into exile, you yourself have done
the driving, since no one else could do it]. Much of the narrative focus
of the *Consolation* centers on Boethius's growing ability to accept the
implications of this revelation: that his true exile is spiritual, not political, and that, rather than being the victim of an unjust and jealous court
or of an unjust and indifferent Providence, his exile is self-imposed,
self-willed.[70]

In the *Commedia*, Dante adopts a similar attitude toward his own
situation. In the *Convivio*, he had presented his exile in terms akin to
those of Boethius in Book I of the *Consolation*, cursing his bad fortune,
his poverty, his loss of power and reputation, and the injustice that had
brought all this to pass. In the fiction of the *Commedia*, Dante is less
concerned with the exile of November 1301 (as the *Convivio* had been)
than with the one into which he had already wandered by the Easter
season of 1300, the exile out of which Virgil, as agent of the *tre donne
benedette*, was already leading him.[71] Like Boethius, Dante claims eventually to see political exile as instrumental precisely *because* it left him
"peregrinando, quasi mendicando": as a powerless mendicant, Dante
was able to return from the exile into which he had driven himself and

which his previous, apparently good, fortune had prevented him from perceiving.[72] Banishment from the city of his birth becomes the precondition for a more significant homecoming.

Paradiso X and *Inferno* II

Dante seems to acknowledge his former misreading of Boethius in exactly the terms we have been discussing in *Paradiso* X. In the heaven of the sun, as eighth luminary in the circle of philosopher saints, Boethius is identified in a way that "corrects" the *Convivio*'s reading and shows the grounds on which he ought to serve Dante as model:

> Per vedere ogne ben dentro vi gode
> l'anima santa che 'l mondo fallace
> fa manifesto a chi di lei ben ode.
> Lo corpo ond' ella fu cacciata giace
> giuso in Cieldauro; ed essa da martiro
> e da essilio venne a questa pace.   (*Paradiso* X, 124–129)

The third line in this passage makes its point in a peculiarly qualified way: Boethius makes the false world manifest—to one who hears him well. By raising in so unexpected and apparently unnecessary a way the possibility of "mishearing" Boethius (a possibility not specified for any of the other twenty-three souls of the two circles described in Cantos X and XII), Dante suggests that he had himself not always "heard" Boethius as well as he now does. (As in *Inferno* II, hearing, one's response to the spoken word, is a way of figuring the analogous act of reading, one's response to the written word.) This generalized warning against the possibility of mishearing Boethius seems to acknowledge just such a misreading by the pilgrim earlier in his life and by the poet in his earlier work.

The two *terzine* on Boethius in *Paradiso* X, besides warning against misreading, provide in compressed and precise fashion a "correct" reading of the *Consolation*, balancing three lines about the deceptions of this world with three celebrating the peace of the next.[73] While the first *terzina* balances Boethius's earthly life with his situation in the afterlife, the second contrasts the post-mortem state of his body with that of his soul. The first *terzina* makes two interrelated assertions: that Boethius is "the holy soul who made the false world manifest to whoever hears him well," and that he rejoices in heaven "through seeing every good." Dante here recalls the thematic center of the *Consolation*, the very heart of Philosophy's pedagogy, for after showing him that the goods of fortune are deceptive (in Book II), she comes (in Book III) to her greatest truth: that the true end of happiness ("beatitudinis finem") is the highest good, which contains all lesser goods within itself ("omnium summum bonorum cunctaque intra se bona continens" III, pr. ii, 7–8). This insight is capped by the great neoplatonic hymn "O qui perpetua" at the center of the poem (III, m. 9), in which Philosophy shows Boethius that the form of the *summum bonum* exists in God, as source of all creation and goal of human happiness.

The second of *Paradiso* X's *terzine*, in contrasting the state of Boethius's body and soul, implies a salvific, though inverse, relationship between political and spiritual exile. Dante's fundamental misunderstanding of Boethius's point about exile in the *Convivio* is here opposed by a view of it presented *sub specie aeternitatis*. The soul of Boethius is said to have been driven (*cacciata*) from his body by the power of the state that had betrayed him, but this earthly banishment figures the soul's anagogical return from its suffering and exile in the "region of unlikeness."[74] To speak paradoxically, what Boethius eventually came to know (and surely Dante came to know it about himself, as well) is that without his political exile, he might never have needed to confront his spiritual alienation.

Dante makes this Boethian meditation explicit in the Epistle to Cangrande,[75] in which his postconversion argument for the function of literature focuses on the relationship of happiness and rhetoric. The Aristotelian premise of the *Convivio*, that happiness derives from the pursuit of knowledge, is superseded in the Epistle by the Boethian notion that secular knowledge must be subordinated to the true source of happiness, contemplative union with God. Along with his understanding of "felicitas" as the end of human existence, Dante's sense of "literary teleology" is altered as well: his acknowledged purpose is now salvific, namely, "removere viventes in hac vita de statu miserie et perducere ad statum felicitatis" (paragraph 15) [to remove those living in this life from the state of misery and to lead them to the state of happiness].[76] In the Epistle's conclusion, Dante explores what was always in some form one of his central concerns, the relationship of knowledge and rhetoric. In the Epistle's last paragraph, Dante clarifies this relationship, speaking of the souls to be encountered in the *Paradiso*:[77]

> vera illa beatitudo in sentiendo veritatis principium consistit; ut patet per Iohannem ibi: 'Haec est vera beatitudo, ut cognoscant te Deum verum,' etc. [17:3]; et per Boetium in tertio *de Consolatione*: 'Te cernere finis' [III, m. 9].

[their true blessedness consists in their perception of the Origin of Truth. This is clear from the book of John, which says, "Now this is eternal life: that they may know thee, the only true God," and so forth; and from the third book of the *Consolation* of Boethius, where it says, "To behold thee is the end."]

Dante's "last word" on the meaning of the *Commedia* confirms the sense that his own experiences are parallel to those of Boethius, that is, to those of Boethius when he is "well heard," when he is properly read. The words, "te cernere finis" [to behold thee is the end] come from the end of the *Consolation*'s central poem, "O qui perpetua," where Boethius prays that his soul may rise to the divine throne, see the fountain of good, fix upon the divine light, burn off earthly fogs and clouds, and shine forth in all its splendor. The poem concludes with this neoplatonic doxology: "Tu namque serenum, / Tu requies tranquilla piis, te cernere finis, / Principium, uector, dux, semita, terminus idem" (III, m. 9, 26–28) [For Thou art the serenity, the tranquil peace of virtuous men. The sight of Thee is beginning and end; one guide, leader, path, and goal].[78] It is a long climb from the misguided attitudes of the pilgrim in *Inferno* I to this conclusion.

In *Inferno* II, Dante's Boethian recollections demonstrate his rejection of his earlier misreading. In addressing Beatrice as "O donna di virtù," Virgil recalls the words Boethius addressed to Philosophy in Book I when she identified herself to him. In the *Convivio*, Dante had turned to the *donna gentile*—allegorized as Philosophy—for consolation during his exile; *Inferno* II begins the process of reestablishing Beatrice's primacy in Dante's poetic life and of reconceptualizing the opposition between Beatrice and the *donna gentile*. In the *Vita Nuova*, it was the *donna gentile*'s compassion that had led Dante to self-pity, and in the *Convivio*, it was the reinterpreted *donna gentile*'s emblematic *pietà* that had led Dante to his intellectual commitment, but in *Inferno* II the compassion of Mary, the true *donna gentile*, produces entirely and unambiguously positive results. When she weeps, "si compiange," divine judgment "breaks" (II, 94–96), setting into motion the chain of mediation that brings Lucy to Beatrice with the question:

> ché non soccorri quei che t'amò tanto,
> ch'uscì per te de la volgare schiera?   (II, 104–105)

Lucy's question encapsulates the history of Dante's fictional relationship with Beatrice, and her careful control of verb tenses in this question—why do you not help him now inasmuch as he did love you then—implies a rejection of the values expressed at the beginning of the *Convivio*, where Dante had cast himself as victim in an unjust universe. In a perfectly just universe, the salvific events narrated in *Inferno* II could never have occurred. Had Beatrice responded in justice, her answer to Lucy's question would be dictated by the question's very language: Lucy's use of the *passato remoto* calls attention to the historical separation between Dante's present crisis and the alienation of affection from his former love; it is precisely because of the pastness of Dante's love for her that Beatrice "should" refuse to help. When Lucy concludes her rhetorical question by saying that Beatrice had led Dante to abandon the "volgare schiera," she recalls the *Vita Nuova*, where Beatrice served this function for the youthful poet, but she also recalls the opening chapters of the *Convivio*, where, in celebrating his apostasy from Beatrice, Dante credits the *donna gentile* as his inspiration for having departed from the vulgar herd ("fuggito de la pastura del vulgo") to feed at the banquet of knowledge. The "sacra conversazione" of Mary, Lucy, and Beatrice shows the limits of the *Convivio*'s earthly aspirations. Mary's compassion moves out beyond the limits of justice and breaks it, and Beatrice responds in unbroken love despite Dante's earlier apostasy from her.[79]

The other Boethian echo in *Inferno* II, Beatrice's reference to Dante as "amico mio e non de la ventura," also needs to be reexamined. The most straightforward meaning of the phrase—that Dante is Beatrice's friend even though he is the victim of fortune—has been called into question because Dante's fortune was still "good" in the poem's fictional time of 1300. Such a judgment errs, however, in accepting as normative the values of the *Convivio*'s Dante or of the "preconsoled" Boethius we find in Book I of the *Consolation*. Book II, the first phase in Boethius's healing, both begins and ends with discussions of the relationship between fortune and friendship. At the beginning of Book II, Philosophy tells Boethius: "Intellego multiformes illius prodigii fucos et eo usque cum his quos eludere nititur blandissimam familiaritatem, dum intolerabili dolore confundat quos insperata reliquerit" (II, pr. i, 6–9) [I am well acquainted with the many deceptions of that monster, Fortune. She pretends to be friendly to those she intends to cheat, and disappoints those she unexpectedly leaves with intolerable sorrow]. The personified Fortune is thus introduced into the *Consolation* with a warning against the deceptiveness of her apparent friendship. At the end of Book II, after the inadequacies of Fortune's various gifts have been exposed, Philosophy acknowledges that there remains one time when Fortune is not deceptive, namely when she is adverse. Good fortune deceives, bad fortune instructs; good fortune binds, bad fortune looses. At the end of Book II, Philosophy's concluding argument about the paradoxical and pedagogical value of adversity once again focuses on friendship: Boethius's false friends have departed with his good fortune, leaving his true friends behind. Philosophy concludes, "Nunc et amissas opes querere; quod pretiosissimum diuitiarum genus est amicos inuenisti" (II, pr, viii, 24–26) [Now you complain of lost riches; but you have found your friends, and that is the most precious kind of wealth].

This paradox may help explain Beatrice's reference to Dante as "amico mio e non de la ventura." For in the Easter season of 1300, all of the gifts of fortune discussed in Book II of the *Consolation*—wealth, honor, power, fame—were his, in promise if not in possession. The whole world would have assumed that Dante, soon to be elected prior of his commune, was Fortune's friend, but retrospect shows that he was in fact—and this is the given of the opening two cantos of *Inferno*—her victim, exiled in the *selva oscura* but blinded from self-knowledge by the "good" fortune he was enduring. In his self-deception, he attributed what he thought was his good fortune to the conquest of Beatrice in his affections by her rival Philosophy, and yet through it all, *Inferno* II asserts, Beatrice's love remains unbroken. This must be the significance of Beatrice's reassuring characterization of him as "amico mio e non de la ventura." What one might have taken to have been his good fortune proves only that at that time, despite appearances, he was not in reality Fortune's friend.

There may also be a subtle palinode of the *Convivio* in *Inferno* II's allusion to Paul's journey to the third heaven. In the *Convivio*, in his allegorizing of "Voi che 'ntendendo il terzo ciel movete," Dante had interpreted the nine heavens as various branches of knowledge, with the third heaven seen as Rhetoric, third of the seven liberal arts (III, xiv). Dante identifies the intelligences who move this heaven as rhetoricians, such as Boethius and Cicero, in whose fellowship he hopes to be included. The *Commedia*'s model of Paul's journey to the third heaven, presents a radically transformed value system:[80] the difference between the *Convivio*'s intellectually imposed, private interpretation of the third heaven and the *Commedia*'s acceptance of the conventional theological understanding of Paul's journey thus suggests in yet another way Dante's movement in the *Commedia* away from intellectual self-sufficiency toward spiritual communion, away from seeing himself as one who gathers crumbs from the table of the learned to one who gathers what falls from the table of the "Sodalizio eletto a la cena / del benedetto Agnello" (*Paradiso* XXIV, 1–2).[81]

Cacciaguida and Dante's Mission

The ultimate gloss on *Inferno* II comes at the center of *Paradiso*; Virgil had announced in *Inferno* II that Dante was summoned to undertake an "impresa," but not until the meeting with Cacciaguida does Dante learn the exact nature of his vocation. This encounter is linked to *Inferno* II by Cacciaguida's first and last words in *Paradiso* XV, two passages which recall all three of the figures of *Inferno* II whom we have been discussing—Aeneas, Paul, and Boethius.[82] When Dante first arrives in the heaven of Mars, his ancestor hastens to greet him with words that recall the meeting of Aeneas and Anchises at Lethe:

> sì pïa l'ombra d'Anchise si porse,
>   se fede merta nostra maggior musa,
>   quando in Eliso del figlio s'accorse.   (*Paradiso* XV, 25–27)[83]

Like Anchises, Cacciaguida will reveal details of his descendant's future.[84] In the subsequent lines, the first words he speaks to his great-great-grandson, Cacciaguida recalls Paul as well as Aeneas:[85]

> '*O sanguis meus, o superinfusa*
>   *gratïa Deï, sicut tibi cui*
>   *bis unquam celi ianüa reclusa?*'   (*Paradiso* XV, 28–30)

> ['O my blood, o grace of God abundantly poured down, to whom as to you was heaven's gate ever opened twice?']

In words spoken in Latin, the language of Aeneas's descendants, Cacciaguida marvels at Dante's journey, which he sees as evidence of divine election (the point that is so central thematically in *Inferno* II). Furthermore, although Cacciaguida's question seems to be rhetorical and therefore to invite the response that the privilege here described belongs uniquely to his descendant, the real answer to his question, of course, is that on at least one previous occasion the gate of heaven was unlocked twice—to Paul.[86] Finally, just as Aeneas and Paul are evoked near the beginning of the canto, the third of the major figures of *Inferno* II is recalled at its end. For Cacciaguida speaks of his own martyrdom in language that directly echoes the description of Boethius a few cantos earlier:

> Quivi fu' io da quella gente turpa
> disviluppato dal mondo fallace,
> lo cui amor molt'anime deturpa;
> e venni dal martiro a questa pace. (*Paradiso* XV, 145–148)

Several of these phrases are identical to those used of Boethius in *Paradiso* X, and in emphatic rhyming positions: Boethius revealed the "mondo fallace," and he, too, "da martiro . . . venne a questo pace." Cacciaguida is, as it were, rhymed with Boethius.

Dante's mission, as Cacciaguida finally clarifies it, is analogous to the promise and charge Anchises offered to Aeneas and which Ananias offered to Paul: like Aeneas (and like Cacciaguida), Dante will require a warrior's fortitude, and like Paul he must be a prophet who speaks the truth without compromise. First he must transcend the inescapable pain of exile, his private "stimulus carnis," the arrow that can be anticipated but not avoided (*Paradiso* XVII, 27). This figure of speech is identical to one used in St. Thomas's consideration of the question, "Is courage concerned chiefly with emergencies" (*ST* II–ii, q. 123, a. 9), where he quotes the following words of Gregory: "jacula quae praevidentur minus feriunt, et nos mala mundi facilius ferimus, si contra ea clypeo praescientiae praemunimur" [darts when anticipated have less impact; and we endure more easily the evils of the world, if we are protected against them by the shield of foreknowledge].[87] *Paradiso* XVII splits these two metaphors apart, with each half of Thomas's sentence making its appearance in a different speech of Dante's. Early in the canto, Dante seeks details of his forthcoming exile "che saetta previsa vien più lenta"; in his final speech, with his fears of exile confirmed, he asks how he should respond to the unavoidable grief in store, "per che di provedenza è buon che m' armi" (XVII, 109). It is specifically in response to this latter request that Cacciaguida admonishes Dante not to compromise his vision, even if this means that Dante must suffer temporal misfortune for telling the truth.

Paradiso XVII's recall and reworking of this passage from the *Summa Theologiae* also helps to illuminate *Inferno* II. For immediately after this discussion of fortitude, Thomas takes up the question of martyrdom,[88] and then the question of fear (fortitude's antithesis, as he argues, *ST* II–ii, q. 125, a. 2), a point implied by Virgil's response to Dante's pusillanimity in *Inferno* II. The vocation that was already implied in *Inferno* II and that is spelled out in *Paradiso* XVII, "né per ambage . . . ma per chiare parole e con preciso / latin" (vv. 31–35), is presented in both cantos in a constellation of motifs also found together in Thomas: Dante must move from fear to fortitude;[89] in the process he must, like Aeneas, Paul, and Boethius, transcend suffering; and he must, like Paul and Boethius, bear witness to the truth he discovers through his writing.[90]

The Cacciaguida episode manifests the overall architectonics of the *Commedia*, for its climactic dramatization of Dante's prophetic calling reengages themes, motifs, and allusions from *Inferno* II. Dante is once again seen as akin to Aeneas and Paul, is once again hesitant about how decisively he should proceed and needs the reassurance of his guide, is once again reassured by Boethian insights and is once again given a model of fortitude. Cacciaguida's reassurance about the forthcoming exile comes straight out of Boethius's distinction between the contingency of human vision and the simplicity of God's.[91] The effect, as in *Inferno* II, is to recall the paradox that misfortune is a blessing: it inspires self-knowledge instead of deception, and it reveals the identity of one's true friends. In *Inferno* II, it was Dante's celestial "friends" who remained faithful in his time of spiritual alienation, while Cacciaguida praises the friends he will come to depend upon during his future political exile.[92]

AFTERWORD

Our study of *Inferno* II has concentrated on both the paradigmatic and unique aspects of the canto. The canto is paradigmatic in its concern with language and literature, in its heightened awareness of the word, both uttered and heard. It enunciates several themes that will unfold across the *Commedia*, themes such as the importance of female mediation, the nature of poetic vocation, the relationship between biblical and literary models and between celestial and earthly perspectives. Dante shapes his poem by continuous incorporation and rewriting of earlier models, dialectically engaging biblical, patristic, and classical texts; his own earlier works, the *Vita Nuova* and the *Convivio*, also enter into the canto and are retrospectively revalued by their quasi-emblematic status within the *Commedia*.

The canto's uniqueness derives in part from its proemial function in the narrative; it sets up the poem's subsequent action, but it does so by establishing its prior conditions (temporally prior, that is, to the opening of the poem). The canto introduces at the beginning of the *Inferno* a number of anti-infernal modalities, thereby giving us a way of evaluating the parodic value of the episodes that follow. The true role of *pietà*, for example, is dramatized in the action of the *tre donne benedette*, whose cumulative compassion leads to Dante's rescue, while the negative possibilities of compassion as complicity will be seen in a variety of subsequent infernal encounters. The seminality of the word, its salvific instrumentality, is, as we have seen, the major issue in Canto II; throughout the *Inferno*, however, we encounter over and over again manifestations of the dangerous possibilities of language, its instrumentality in the service of deceit, division, and delusion. Canto II is unique insofar as it proleptically suggests a universe of discourse and of feeling which is characteristic, not of the *Inferno*, but of the two subsequent *cantiche*.

Canto II deals overtly with the pilgrim's situation at the beginning of the journey, since it is his hesitancy that occasions Virgil's narrative of the journey's prehistory. We have argued, however, that the terms of

that narrative also set up the conditions of the poet's ultimate understanding of his own vocation, a vocation at once tied to the terms of
the journey and yet transcending it as well. What is most extraordinary
is that Dante also builds into this canto the implied role of the reader.
The chain of grace which is enacted in the canto is, as we have seen,
also a relay of feeling and of language. By the canto's end the pilgrim is
ready to undertake the journey, the poet is ready to undertake the
poem, and the reader has been cued to the terms on which he or she
should undertake the reading of the poem, which thus becomes both
Dante's journey and our own.

ABBREVIATIONS

We have used the following abbreviations for references to frequently cited texts and periodicals:

ARDS	*Annual Report of the Dante Society*
DS	*Dante Studies*
ED	*Enciclopedia dantesca*
PL	Migne, *Patrologia Latina*
SD	*Studi danteschi*
SIR	*Stanford Italian Review*
ST	*Summa Theologiae*

For biblical citations we have used the text of the *Biblia Vulgata* published in Madrid by the Biblioteca de Autores Cristianos (1953), and for our translations we have closely adapted the Douay-Reims translation of the Vulgate. For Boethius's *Consolation of Philosophy* we have cited E. K. Rand's text in the Loeb Classical Edition, and Richard Green's translation (Indianapolis: Bobbs-Merrill, 1962). For Dante's *Convivio*, we have used Maria Simonelli's edition (Bologna: Pàtron, 1966) and Philip Wicksteed's translation (London: Dent, 1924). For Thomas's *Summa Theologiae*, we have cited Latin text and English translation in the Oxford Blackfriars' edition. Finally, for the *Aeneid*, we have cited R. A. B. Mynors's edition in the *Scriptorum Classicorum Biblioteca Oxoniensis* (Oxford: Clarendon, 1969), and Alan Mandelbaum's translation (Berkeley: University of California Press, 1981).

NOTES

CHAPTER ONE: The Canto of the Word

1. Mazzoni's commentary on *Inferno* II opens on this point: "Questo canto, secondo una formula invalsa, è il 'prologo al cielo' dell' opera . . . ; ma è pur anche—sul piano strutturale—il prologo alla prima cantica (come il precedente lo era a tutta l'opera)" (p. 151). Pasquazi makes a similar distinction between Canto I as a "proemio generale" to the *Commedia* and Canto II as "prologo" to the *Inferno* (1974, p. 163). This double prologue was recognized as early as Benvenuto da Imola: "nunc consequenter in isto secundo capitulo similiter pro-hemiali more poetico facit suam invocationem" (p. 73) [now following in this second similarly proemial chapter he makes his invocation according to poetic custom]. In a recent article, Freccero groups the first two cantos together: "Until we come to the entrance of Hell, things seem to exist in a double focus, suffused with moral and allegorical intent so that their substantiality seems totally compromised" (1984, pp. 772–773). For Freccero, Dante's "mimetic fiction" begins only in Canto III. See also Freccero, 1966a, and Singleton, 1957, esp. pp. 7–13.

2. We are indebted in this aspect of our analysis to the pioneering work of Auerbach, both in his first great essay on the topic ("Figura," written in 1944, translated in 1959) and in his subsequent writings.

3. Mazzoni discusses the symbolic value of the nocturnal placement of the descent as an image of the pilgrim's distance from God (pp. 166–170). It is customary to note that the infernal descent begins at nightfall, while *Purgatorio* begins at dawn and *Paradiso* at noon. Aeneas's entry into the underworld actually takes place at dawn (VI, 255), but Virgil nevertheless emphasizes the nocturnal nature of the underworld.

4. On the "extra" twelve hours, see Nohrnberg: "By crossing what is the International Date Line, Dante also regains twelve lapsed hours, and can thus rise with the sun on Easter, forty-eight hours after he entered Hell. Like his prototype, the Christ who harrowed Hell, Dante has kept the Jewish Sabbath in the tomb" (1977, p. 101).

5. Pasquazi argues that fear causes Dante to follow Virgil in Canto I but that the motivation shifts in Canto II: "Ma quando, riflettendo, gli vengono alla mente le figure di Enea e di Paolo, egli mostra di aver compreso, o almeno di avere virtualmente intuito che quel viaggio non è soltanto un *fuggire quel male*

e peggio, bensì è anche, e soprattutto, una vocazione positiva" (1974, pp. 163–164). See also Sanguineti, pp. 1–24.

6. Lansing analyzes the chiastic relationship of similes in the first two cantos (pp. 128–131).

7. The practice of some of the Trecento commentators in organizing their discussions according to the narrative structure of the canto under consideration frequently strikes the modern reader as reductive and uninspired, but the method seems to suit *Inferno* II particularly well. The early commentators divided and subdivided in different ways, coming up with anywhere from three parts (Pietro in the Nannucci edition) to five (Buti) or even six (Boccaccio and l'Anonimo Fiorentino) for the canto. Our reading of the canto's structure coincides with that of Benvenuto: "dividitur istud capitulum in quatuor partes generales; in prima quarum describit horam temporis, scilicet finem diei, et facit suam invocationem. In secunda movet dubium Virgilio de insufficientia sua ibi: *Io cominciai.* In tertia Virgilius removet dubium ibi: *S'io ho ben la tua parola.* In quarta autor ponit effectum et regraciatur Virgilio, et commendat qui misit eum ibi: *qual i fioretti*" (p. 73) [This chapter is divided into four general parts: in the first of these he describes the time, that is, the end of the day, and makes his invocation. In the second he advances a doubt to Virgil about his insufficiency, beginning *Io cominciai.* In the third, Virgil removes the doubt, beginning *S'io ho ben la tua parola.* In the fourth the author reacts and thanks Virgil and commends the one who sent him, beginning *Qual i fioretti*].

8. The adjective "folle" acquires extraordinary resonance from its subsequent usage in the poem, where it becomes emblematic of the "folle volo" of Ulysses, the negative double of Dante and Aeneas (see Thompson). Whereas Aeneas in a comparable moment in Book VI of the *Aeneid* had invoked precedents as a justification for making his own privileged journey, Dante cites them as a reason for refusing it. Aeneas urges the Sibyl's assistance, reminding her of the others—Orpheus, Pollux, Theseus, Hercules—who have been granted what he himself requests (VI, 119–123). Pietro cites this Virgilian passage as a parallel for Dante's protestation; but unlike Aeneas in this sequence, Dante's relationship to precedents as models is complex and indirect, an issue we shall discuss more fully in our final chapter.

9. Despite the similarities of the closing lines, it is significant that Dante sees himself as a follower at the end of Canto I, whereas at the close of Canto II his own volition is stressed in the emphatic "intrai."

10. As Pasquazi puts it, "il lettore potrebbe passare dal I al III senza avvertire, sul piano puramente narrativo, cronachistico, alcuna discontinuità" (p. 188). On the parallel endings of Cantos I and II, see Mazzoni, p. 157. The ending of the *Commedia* offers a structural similarity: at the conclusion of Canto XXXI, Dante is looking at Mary, and so one might logically proceed directly to Canto XXXIII and the prayer to her. Canto XXXII places Dante's vision within the whole of salvation history, but it does not advance the narrative any more than *Inferno* II does. While *Inferno* II looks back to a time before the poem's action, *Paradiso* XXXII points to its fulfillment in the end of time.

11. Ballerini discusses this canto as a *stasi*. This article, which we have not been able to see, is summarized in *Year's Work in Modern Language Studies* (1965), p. 306.

12. The diction of this canto is dominated by words associated with motion (*movi* 67, *mosse* 72, *mosse* 101, *mosso* 141); whether of going (*se n'andava* 1, *andò* 15, *andata* 25, *Andovvi* 28, *andare* 70, *andar* 120, *va* 139, as well as *cammino* 5, *cammin* 63, *cominciar* 39 and 42, *guidi* 10, *passo* 12, *via* 30, *scender* 83, *uscì* 105, *rivolve* 47, and *volse* 116) or of coming (*venirvi* 31, *venire* 34, *venuta* 35, *venni* 50, *vegno* 71, *venir* 87, *venne* 101, *venni* 112, *venir* 117, *venir* 137, as well as *tornar* 71, and *tornato* 138); and in addition, words implying impediments to motion or aberrations of motion (*erra* 6, *ingombra* 46, *impedito* 62, *impedimento* 95, and *smarrito* 64). Stability of place is an attribute of the papacy (Rome "fu *stabilita* per lo *loco* santo / *u' siede* il successor del maggior Piero," 23–24) or, more properly, of the Empyrean (*loco* 71 and 101, *sedea* 102, *scanno* 112, *nel ciel* 94, *ne la corte del cielo* 125). The celestial ladies temporarily renounce this stability on Dante's behalf, moving *qua giuso* 83, *qua entro* 87, *là sù* 96, *qua giù* 112. They relinquish the resting place they have won to help Dante remember his need to remain *in via*. His paralysis is inappropriate, and thus the horror over his being "*su* la fiumana *ove* 'l mar non ha vanto," and Virgil's unanswerable charge: given all this motion for your benefit by those who deserve to rest in God's presence, "perché tanta viltà nel cor *allette*," 121–122? This semantic field makes the verb of the canto's final line seem triumphant: "*intrai* per lo cammino alto e silvestro," 142.

13. Once this canto's focus on reading, understood in its broadest sense, is clear, so too is its concentration on hearing and response. Virgil emphasizes what he heard when Beatrice came to him in Limbo, "quel ch'io 'ntesi / nel primo punto che di te mi dolse" (II, 50–51), and Beatrice's emphasis is similar in describing her fear that she may have come to Limbo too late to be of assistance to Dante in his peril, "per quel ch'i'ho di lui nel cielo udito" (II, 66).

14. As Mazzoni notes, this allusion to Aristotle's *Ethics* III.ix.349 has been recognized since Boccaccio (p. 282).

15. This is an epic topos which had a lyric *fortuna*. It became a staple of the lyric tradition from Petrarch on, and both sixteenth-century and modern commentators (such as Casini-Barbi, Momigliano, and Sapegno) think of it as such. A recent commentary by Carlo Salinari, Sergio Romagnoli, and Antonio Lanza (1980) invokes the Provençal *Natureingang* topos, the spring opening in which the poet's situation is frequently at odds with the natural scene.

16. The Trojan refugees had misinterpreted the oracle's instruction to return to the ancestral homeland as a command to go to Crete and there set up an imitation of the Trojan civilization they had known. Aeneas's dream summons him from this narrow-minded nostalgia to pursuit of a more radical renewal for his people. It seems appropriate that a canto in which the interrelationship of word and action is so central should begin with an allusion to a moment of "misreading" in the midst of the *Aeneid*'s "exilic book," the book of Aeneas's "erring."

17. The two allusions (as well as the one in Book VIII) may be even more similar than we, or the tradition, have shown. Dido's soliloquy is followed by a scene in which Aeneas has a "vision" of Mercury (IV, 557), and the description of nightfall in VIII, 26–27, is followed by the appearance of the "deus loci," Tiberinus. Thus, after each of the first three allusions to nightfall, Aeneas receives visionary confirmation of his mission.

18. Ball cites Gmelin but develops an argument about the meaning of the allusion which is nowhere in Gmelin. He rightly sees the canto as a significant locus for the semantic complication his article analyzes.

19. Even though Dante usually maintains this premise, the *Commedia* at times contains moments that suggest the poet's fallibility. Hawkins argues persuasively that in *Inferno* XXV Dante shows himself (stages himself, we might say) as losing control; his virtuoso performance and boast in that canto show him temporarily capable of succumbing to infernal temptations *qua* poet. The ambiguous status of Dante's own "ingegno" is dramatized with relation to his role as pilgrim (in Canto X and Canto XXVI) but also in relation to his role as poet (in Canto XXV and at the opening of Canto XXVI, where he explicitly states it as such).

20. See Mazzoni, pp. 173–178, and Hollander's forthcoming essay, "*Inferno* II: The Canto of the Word." We are grateful to have read this essay in manuscript.

21. Chaucer's parody of these lines in *The Hous of Fame* makes this distinction very clearly, following his invocation to the Muses: "O Thoght, that wrot al that I mette, / And in the tresorye hyt shette / Of my brayn, now shal men se / If any vertu in the be / To telle al my drem aryght. / Now kythe [show] thyn engyn and thy myght!" (*Hous of Fame*, 520–528). Chaucer seems to imply that *ingegno* and *virtù*, "engyn and myght," are attributes of the poet's own mind. Chaucer continues to have *Inferno* II in mind a bit later in this passage, in the playful overkill with which he rewrites another famous line from this canto: "I neyther am Ennok, ne Elye, / Ne Romulus, ne Ganymede, / That was ybore up, as men rede, / To hevene with daun Jupiter . . . " (*Hous of Fame*, 588–591). Chaucer substitutes Romulus for Dante's Aeneas, Enoch and Elijah for Paul; the *Metamorphoses* replaces the *Aeneid*, the Old Testament the New. Chaucer's ironic Pilgrim-Narrator, "Geffrey," speaks these lines in parody of *Inferno* II while hanging from the claws of an eagle which is a comic distortion of the eagle of *Purgatorio* IX. The allusion to Ganymede, therefore, might also suggest Chaucer's awareness of the connections between *Inferno* II and *Purgatorio* IX, where Dante is borne aloft by Lucy/eagle as Ganymede had been by Jupiter's eagle.

22. Curtius regards the invocation of one's own powers as a topos not uncommon in late classical and medieval literature, citing examples from Ovid, Propertius, Prudentius, and others (pp. 233–239). Curtius's examples, however, seem closer to Dante's address to "mente," where he clearly celebrates his own powers. Mazzoni argues against reading *ritrarrà* as a reference to painting or drawing, providing several citations in which the term carries the sense of *ri-*

dire. Given the focus on the identity of vision and language in the subsequent apostrophe to "mente che scrivesti ciò ch'io vidi," the distinction seems unnecessary. Whether the reference is to Dante's own memory or to a quality of memory in general has long been in dispute. For Boccaccio, Dante's reference to the unerring quality of memory is specific, a tribute to his own prodigious memory: "*la mente*, cioè la potenza memorativa, *che non erra*, e questo dice, per ciò che si conosceva avere tenace memoria, per la qual cosa non temeva di dover errare né nella quantità né nella qualità" (p. 96). Several commentators note the similar formulation at *Inferno* XXVIII, 12, where Dante says, "come Livio scrive, che non erra," a puzzling statement, given the probability that Dante never actually read Livy.

23. See Vincenzo Valente's *voce* on "ingegno" in *ED*. On the complexity of the concept of *ingegno* in other comparable literary contexts, see Myerowitz, pp. 94–97, 177–178, and Hanning, esp. pp. 12–13, 105–107, *et passim*. In their forthcoming *Time and the Crystal: Studies in Dante's "Rime petrose,"* Robert M. Durling and Ronald L. Martinez discuss Dante's notion of *ingegno*: "Dante regarded his *ingegno* as something *bodily*, not intellectual in the strict sense, but depending on such faculties as memory, imagination, quickness of association, all of which—like dexterity or keenness of vision, for that matter—are vital to the practice of art, must be seen as constituents of *ingegno*, and have *bodily organs* that are created by nature before the intellectual soul is directly infused by God."

24. Hollander contrasts this with the insistent use of "paura" in Canto I; each word appears five times in its canto (*Inferno* II: "Canto of the Word").

25. Auerbach, 1965, pp. 25–66, esp. pp. 65–66; Mazzotta, 1979, pp. 157–158; and Hollander, "*Inferno* II: Canto of the Word," and 1980, pp. 217–218.

26. See the Introduction to Contini's edition of Petrarch's *Canzoniere*, p. x. Contini's brilliant and succinct characterization of Dante here complements Auerbach's meditation on the consequences of "sermo humilis" for Christian poetry and for Dante in particular (see note 25).

27. Mazzotta notes that Beatrice's speech "exhibits rhetorical lures through the extended *captatio benevolentiae*." Her speech echoes the words of Aeneas to Dido and his promise of enduring praise in *Aeneid* I, 605ff.: "semper honos nomenque tuum laudesque manebunt" (I, 609) [ever your name and praise and honor shall last], a promise which is both ironic and tragic in context (1979, p. 158).

28. See Hollander (1985) for the argument that the poem's later use of "parola ornata" retrospectively undercuts the positive implications of the phrase when used about Virgil in *Inferno* II.

29. Statius speaks of himself, "mertai le tempie *ornar* di mirto" (*Purgatorio* XXI, 90), and Virgil speaks of those Greek poets "che già di lauro *ornar* la fronte" (*Purgatorio* XXII, 108). The blessed are described as having "atti ornati di tutte onestadi" (*Paradiso* XXXI, 51), a line which combines the two words ("ornata" and "onesto") used to describe Virgil's "parlar" in *Inferno* II.

30. Barolini reviews the history of the commentary response to this puzzling

question (p. 9, n. 8). She connects this moment, as do we, to the issues raised by the complexity of its associations with "parola ornata" (p. 280). Dante has Virgil himself express a comparable view of the importance of earthly achievements of the virtuous non-Christians at *Inferno* IV, 76–78: "L'onrata nominanza / che di lor suona su ne la tua vita, / grazia acquista in ciel che sì li avanza."

31. Cf. Padoan for a discussion of the "continuo intrecciarsi dialettico e— perchè no?—anche le contraddizioni" of these conflicting energies within the poem (1977, p. 27).

32. The structure of sequential conversion in the *Confessions* is brilliantly analyzed in Durling (1974), pp. 7–28, esp. pp. 17–20. On Augustine's purposes in writing the work, see *Confessions*, X, 3.

33. This effect is also suggested at several points in the *Commedia*. See, for example, *Purgatorio* XXXII, 103–105, and XXXIII, 52–54.

CHAPTER TWO: *Tre Donne Benedette*

1. Just how much earlier is the time of the Virgil-Beatrice encounter? Iannucci makes the attractive suggestion that it occurs just before the moment of Virgil's arrival in Canto I, about noon on Good Friday: "Since Virgil appears to Dante moments after noon, it follows that Beatrice descends into Limbo at noon Jerusalem time on Good Friday, 1300 A.D. What all of this means is that there is a complete temporal and spatial correspondence between Beatrice's descent into hell and Christ's" (p. 38). Iannuccci's analysis might be amplified by taking into account the ways in which Dante's own journey is in part patterned on the typology of the harrowing of hell. See also "*Inferno* I, 63: 'Chi per lungo silenzio parea fioco' e la tradizione esegetica," Chapter 1 in Hollander (1983a), pp. 23–80.

2. In his examination of this topos, Greene surprisingly denies its relevance to Dante: "The basic reason for its absence from the *Commedia* is that Dante never thought of imitating Virgil in so precise a way, even though he was bent on emulating him" (p. 105). Quint's discussion of Dante's attempt to dramatize "extratextual significance" is more useful, although Quint limits himself to analyzing the descent of the "messo dal ciel" of *Inferno* IX (1975, pp. 201–207).

3. The phrase "vere parole," associated here with Beatrice, is played off against Virgil's "parola ornata."

4. On the problems of interpretation of the canzone itself, see Foster and Boyde, Vol. II, pp. 280–293. Paasinen discusses the relation between "Tre donne" and the *Commedia*.

5. We have begun to wonder if the most famous topos of a female triad, the three graces, might have been present in any form here. The extraordinary development of this topos in the Renaissance shows its potential for allegoresis. There are two aspects of the later allegorization of the three graces that seem particularly pertinent. In several Renaissance texts the three graces are conflated with the three theological virtues. Nohrnberg suggests that the three theologi-

cal virtues who attend Beatrice's triumphal chariot are actually represented in accordance with conventional language about the three graces, citing Landino's preface in which Landino "digresses" on the subject of the three graces after explaining the *tre donne* in terms of the three orders of grace (1976, p. 725). A second tantalizing Renaissance association is the relation of the three graces to the nine Muses. They are spoken of together in Plato's *Laws* III, 682a, Pindar's *Olympian* 14, and Horace's *Odes* III, 19; this association was known in the Renaissance and visibly incarnated in the famous frontispiece to Gafurius's *De harmonia musicorum instrumentorum* (1518). (The frontispiece is analyzed by Wind, pp. 265–269 and by Nohrnberg, 1976, pp. 729ff.) One might say that Dante opens the canto calling upon the nine Muses and is aided by the "three graces," understood as either the three theological virtues or the three kinds of grace in the most traditional glosses of the three ladies. On medieval representations of the three graces, see Seznec, pp. 167ff., pp. 208–209. The Graces are mentioned by Boccaccio (*De Gen. Deorum*, V, 35) and Petrarch (*Africa*, III, vv. 266–268), both following a description found originally in Servius.

6. The earliest and still an excellent summary of the notion that the ladies represent three orders of grace is in Buti (1385–95); Torraca (1905), who gives the best case for the three ladies as representing the three theological virtues, is seconded by Del Lungo (1926), Giglio (1973), and Padoan (1976). Scartazzini's commentary gives a useful sampler of the commentary tradition on this subject.

7. Padoan adds, "Le lunghe diatribe dei dantisti al proposito hanno pare un loro significato: e cioè indicano implicitamente come questi significati extraletterali siano qui una sovrapposizione un po' forzata, che non trova immediata rispondenza nell'arte del poeta" (1976, p. 54). Cf. Sapegno's demurrer: "L'allegoria rimane oscura, e molti dei particolari rapporti tra la funzione rappresentativa e il significato interno ci sfuggono" (p. 25).

8. "Pictorial Commentaries to the *Commedia*," in Brieger, Meiss, and Singleton, Vol. I, p. 94. The illustrations for this canto are in Vol. II, pp. 47–52.

9. In addition to the description of Dante as Lucy's "fedele" here, we might think of Dante's reference to Mary as "Il nome del bel fior ch'io sempre invoco / e man e sera" (*Paradiso* XXIII, 88–89). Dante is called "il fedele" of Beatrice by the three theological virtues in *Purgatorio* XXXI, 134. Beatrice laments Dante's infidelity in that very canto, but in the deepest sense, or from the perspective of the end, his fidelity is the governing motif of his life and poem, as he asserts in *Paradiso* XXX, 28–30: "Dal primo giorno ch'i' vidi il suo viso / in questa vita, infino a questa vista, / non m'è il seguire al mio cantar preciso." For Sarolli, "fedele" as it is used of Dante in Canto II makes Lucy a figure of faith and of the second person of the Trinity: "Il vocabolo 'fedele,' dunque, è la virtù teologale dalla fede di cui Santa Lucia è 'attributo *Trinitatis*'" (p. 165). Lucy is discussed as "attributo della Fede" on p. 164.

10. For an excellent survey of the problem of the "Beatrice storica," see Aldo Vallone's *voce*, "Beatrice," in *ED*. The earliest commentators, of course, did not think in terms of Beatrice Portinari; the specific historical identification comes in Boccaccio and in Pietro's third redaction. Like most modern commentators,

we proceed as if it were accurate. For a spirited argument against this position, see Curtius, pp. 372–378.

11. The question of whether Mary can be considered under the rubric of martyrdom is dealt with by St. Thomas, *ST* 2a 2ae.124.4, who cites Jerome's Epistle 8, 14: "Recte dicerim quod Dei Genetrix virgo et martyr fuit, quamvis in pace vitam finierit" [I should be right to claim that the Mother of God was both virgin and martyr, though she ended her days peacefully]. Thomas explains that this is to speak of martyrdom figuratively. Beatrice, we would say, is treated figuratively as a virgin throughout the *Commedia*.

12. Cf. Petrocchi's *voce*, "donna gentile" in *ED*. He sees no relation between the language used here about Mary and the earlier *donna gentile*. And cf. the *voce* of Gioachino Paparelli, "gentile."

13. Foster and Boyde give a thorough account of the biographical problems raised by the contradictions between the *Vita Nuova* and the *Convivio* (Vol. II, 34–362).

14. In the third and latest edition of his commentary (1985), Sapegno says, "Probabilmente la Vergine" (p. 25). D'Andria, takes issue with the consensus position, arguing that the *donna gentile* of Canto II is in fact the *donna gentile* of the *Convivio*, "la donna gentile—Filosofia: quella che—come già per Boezio—era stata di consolazione a Dante al tempo del suo sviamento dalla Poesia, e che ora in ciel si compiange dell'impedimento frappostogli nel tentativo di riprendere, uscendo dalla selva la smarrita diritta via" (p. 157). However wrongheaded this argument is, its very confusion shows that the terminology does lend itself to a consideration of the two works in relation to each other.

15. We quote from the translation by Cioffari, p. 20.

16. Tommaseo's commentary on *Inferno* II is followed by an excursus called "le donne del poema," a rich and interesting gloss. Tommaseo cites the early commentaries and then says, "Ma forse la Donna gentile è la Vergine, alla quale nel XXXIII del *Paradiso*," citing St. Bernard's prayer, which describes the qualities she is shown enacting in *Inferno* II. The whole discussion is pursued tentatively.

17. Palmenta speaks of "la divina Castellana" (p. 22). Sapegno is alert to the feudal tonality of the Beatrice-Virgil exchange as well, calling attention to her "istintiva gentilezza di donna, e quasi di regina che si piega a richiedere d'un favore il suo vassallo." The courtliness of the scene is one aspect of the focus on "cortesia," a word that shows up as an adjective three times in the canto (vv. 17, 58, and 134). Virgil had already introduced the notion of heaven as an imperial court in Canto I, 124–129. See also Barolini's analysis of Virgil's demeanor before Beatrice as an echo of the pose, conventional in chivalric romance, of the loyal knight before his liege lady (pp. 9–10).

18. Moore argues: "But it is surely an intolerable supposition that this related series of four aids to Dante should consist of one abstraction and three real persons; and, again, that this one should be just the one to whom the supreme position and the most exalted functions are assigned" (1917, p. 241).

19. Pelikan provides a succinct discussion of Mary as mediatrix (pp. 158–174).

20. Balthasar argues that the importance of Mary actually transcends that of Christ in Dante's poem: "il suo *Paradiso* ha, in fin dei fini, una forma mariana. . . . La croce reale di Cristo non si incontra mai nella *Divina Commedia*" (p. 93). See also Chapters 4 and 6. Although we disagree with this claim, the elevation of Mary in Dante's poem prepares for Beatrice's Christological analogy. Singleton's influential reading of Beatrice "as Christ" (the major argument of *Journey to Beatrice*) does not pay sufficient attention to the importance of Mary as the model for such a formulation.

21. See Masseron: "Ici, le lecteur sursaute: aux yeux de Dante, la martyre de Syracuse . . . est la plus grande sainte de le Loi Nouvelle! Et il n'y a que deux femmes à être au paradis, plus élevées qu'elle en dignité: la Vierge Marie et sa mère!" (p. 372).

22. The Church of Sta. Lucia de' Magnoli (called Sta. Lucia delle Rovinate after the hill in front of the church crumbled in 1547) is one of the oldest churches of the Oltrarno. It was founded in 1098 by Cavalier Uguccione della Pressa and was completed by his son Magnolo. St. Francis was supposed to have stayed in an adjoining "lazzaretto" in 1211 on his first visit to Florence. The church was under the jurisdiction of the Benedictines of San Miniato from 1246 to 1373. Although the church still exists, virtually nothing of its medieval structure remains. We wish to thank Robert Garis and David Alan Brown for their assistance in locating materials about the church.

23. Pézard has a learned, rich, but inconclusive discussion of the passage (pp. 117–205); he explores the relationship between solstice and equinox and between the association of John the Baptist with the summer solstice and Christ with the winter solstice. He notes a variety of associations with Lucy, concluding that she is a doublet of Mary in her role in the *Commedia*.

24. The commentary of Busnelli-Vandelli (Vol. I, 308) does not attempt a rationale for the naming of the cities. The most engaging attempt to deal with this passage that we know is by Jeffrey Schnapp, who generously shared his unpublished thoughts on it with us. Schnapp connects this passage with Dante's discussion in *Convivio* II, xiv, where the visible northern heavens signify the science of Physics and the invisible southern heavens (rotating of course around the southern celestial pole—the axis of Lucia in III, 5) signify Metaphysics. Schnapp suggests that we "retheologize" the allegory here and place it in the context of the Incarnation. "The Incarnation, a passage from 'metaphysics' to 'physics' or 'invisibility' to 'visibility' . . . would represent a movement from Lucy to Mary or South to North: the movement, as a matter of fact, of the sun after the winter solstice. . . . Even without this incarnational symbolism, the allegory of *Convivio* II, 14, complements the Lucy/Mary discussion in III, 5, inasmuch as the two are synonymous (Lucy = lux, Mary = illuminatrix, stella maris), and their hemispheric significance would have the sun shuttling its rays back and forth between their two camps during its yearly cycle."

25. Even though space and time do not have their customary connotations in the Empyrean, it is striking that Dante makes one think about the spatiality of the arrangement; Mary does not take the "shortest" route to Beatrice (who is

seated on the same side of the rose as she herself is), but calls upon Lucy to come across from the opposite side in her role as intermediatrix.

26. The *Passio* itself, along with an abundance of Lucy material, may be found in Beaugrand. Beaugrand reproduces the office for St. Lucy's Day on pp. 154–156. The relation between the Greek and Latin versions of the *Passio* has been studied by Taibbi; the Latin versions appear to be amplifications of the Greek text. See Amore and Celletti for further material on Lucy's legend.

27. For the idea that the story of her plucking out her eyes was grafted on to the older legend from an Indian source, see Delehaye, p. 134.

28. The *Fundamentum Aureum*, a thirteenth-century sermon cycle, contains a series of sermons for St. Lucy's Day which also stress her "fermezza." We thank Robert Kaske for this source. The emphasis on Lucy's fortitude has lasted to the present; in a St. Lucy shrine in Boston's North End we found a prayer to her which begins, "O gloriosa Martire della Cattolica Chiesa, luce di santità ed esempio di fortezza."

29. Petrus Comestor's sermon for St. Lucy's Day refers to her as "magnae . . . virtutis virgo Lucia et virago" (*PL*, 198:1754).

30. "Il concetto di 'fortezza' completa e conchiude in tal modo la nervatura dottrinale dell'episodio; e la sua implicita presenza nel contesto dell'intero canto, riflessa nell'uso di termini che si richiamano al significato di tale virtù come aspre lotte contro il male e la morte, contribuisce a renderne compatta e unitaria la struttura etica" (p. 401).

31. *ST*, 2a–2ae, q. 124, 4, 2. The same passage is quoted again by Thomas in the Supplementum, q. 96, 5, 4.

32. Lucy's status as martyr links her to the powerful theme of martyrdom which is central to the *Paradiso*. On the importance of martyrdom in that *cantica*, see Jacoff (1985) and Schnapp.

33. Bosco (1974) notes the relationship between the crisis of "viltà" in *Inferno* II and the comparable crisis in *Inferno* IX. On the question of magnanimity in Dante, see Forti and Scott, 1977. Hollander argues that there are five "cycles" of pity and fear in *Inferno* (1969, Appendix III, pp. 301–307).

34. When Dante asks Virgil to reconsider "prima ch'a l'alto passo tu mi fidi" (v. 12) most commentators interpret the "alto passo" to mean the journey itself. There is, however, an alternative tradition which regards it as signifying the poem (Mazzoni, p. 180). The possibility of reading it in either way points to the actual doubleness of the enterprise; Dante does use the same language elsewhere about both the journey and the poem, and even here at the beginning, where the roles of the poet and pilgrim seem most separate, he allows for the possibility of seeing them as interrelated.

35. Padoan takes this as a sign that Dante has not yet fully thought through the terms of the poem: "Ed è anche notevole che nelle parole di Lucia a Beatrice non sia accenno alcuno ad una particolare missione da affidare al poeta: come sarà ripetutamente affermato più avanti. . . . Sono non contraddizioni, ma discrepanze estremamente interessanti perchè tracce, se non di stesure precedenti, di incertezze iniziali, quando disegno poetico e anelito escatologico erano già compresenti in Dante ma non ancora compiutamente fusi" (1976, p. 55).

36. The following have been helpful in exploring the history of Lucy's iconography: Kunstle, Vol. II, pp. 408–410; Squarr; Réau, Vol. III, 2, pp. 833–36; Kaftal, 1965, pp. 703–710, and 1952, pp. 643–650; Celletti, pp. 252–258; Capdevila; and Garana. The Princeton Index of Christian Art proved to be a valuable resource. None of the Index's representations of Lucy's martyrdom include anything about her eyes.

37. Moore finds the category of *gratia illuminans* perplexing since it is a general result of any sort of grace rather than a "special kind or type of grace" in the theology of the time. Dante commentators have perpetuated the gloss without reference to extant theological sources (1917, pp. 238–239). But Dante himself uses the term *gratia illuminante* to discuss angelic powers (*Paradiso* XXIX, 61–66).

38. Celletti concludes: "Lucia è divenuta così un segno e una promessa di luce: sia questa la luce materiale che apre gli occhi degli uomini sulle cose create, sia la luce splendente della lampada delle vergini sagge, sia infine, commista alla ancestrale simbologia dei paesi del lungo inverno, il luminoso annuncio della fine delle tenebre invernali" (p. 254). The association of Lucy with the wise virgins no doubt has some relation to the characteristic representation of her holding a lamp.

39. It is not clear whether Lucy's role in *Purgatorio* IX complicates or clarifies her role in *Inferno* II. Most of the early commentators simply reinvoke the gloss "illuminating grace" for *Purgatorio* IX, but her role in the action requires greater specificity, especially because of the complex series of erotic and maternal allusions within and around the dream sequence.

40. Each of the three women is referred to as "donna del ciel": Beatrice (*Purgatorio* I, 53 and 91); Lucy (*Purgatorio* IX, 88); and Mary (*Paradiso* XXIII, 106, XXXII, 29).

41. See *Purgatorio* XXX and XXXI, in particular XXX, 115 ("questi fu tal ne la sua vita nova").

42. For example, Sapegno: "qui siamo riportati nell' ambito della tradizione lirica, raffinata ma altrettanto fragile" (p. 22). See also Chimenz: "Vorrei fare una riserva almeno per questo secondo canto. Senza dubbio, primitivo, ingenuo, e nello stesso tempo, pesante è il mecchanismo di tutta la messa in scena" (p. 40). Chimenz speaks of the canto as "grezzamente medioevale," a reading criticized by Petrini. Della Giovanna regards Canto II as "uno dei più semplici e facili da intendersi"; he thinks it is more poetic than Canto I, but that neither canto is among the "più be[ll]i" of the *Commedia*: "L'autore è alle primissime prove" (p. 6). Padoan, as we have already noted, sees it as full of "discrepanze" (see note 35).

43. Cf. Jacoff, 1980 and Barolini, pp. 3–84.

44. Cf. Freccero, 1968, esp. pp. 85–87. On the homology of "words about words and words about the Word" see Burke.

45. On the relationship between Virgil and John the Baptist, see Hollander, 1969, pp. 261–264, and 1983, p. 77.

46. Boccaccio says, "E in questo lagrimare ancora più d'affezione si dimostra, dimostrandosi ancora uno atto d'amante, e massimamente di donna, le quali,

com'hanno pregato d'alcuna cosa la quale disiderino, incontanente lagrimano, mostrando in quello il disiderio suo essere ardentissimo" (p. 125).

47. One of the most eloquent is by Momigliano: "Questo particolare costituisce l'ultima perfezione del motivo principale del canto: una fugace luce di lacrime in cui si tradisce appena l'umanità dell'anima beata che si allontana. Su questi occhi lucenti si chiude la visione; ma il resto del canto ne rimane tutto ravvivato e commosso" (quoted by Mazzoni, p. 287). The same note is struck by Chimenz, Sapegno, and nearly every single commentator we have read.

48. See Isidore, *PL* 83:105; Jerome, *PL* 25:950; Rhabanus Maurus, *PL* 107:67 and *PL* 107:763; and Rhadbertus *PL* 120:146.

49. See Freccero, 1968, pp. 97–98; reprinted in 1986, pp. 234–235.

50. The three beasts are frequently traced to Jer. 5:6. See Mazzoni, p. 103.

51. We are, of course, aware that the interpretation of Rachel as Contemplation is traditionally invoked here, but we are arguing that it is not the most relevant gloss for this particular passage in the poem. This exegetical commonplace is important for Dante's dream of Rachel and Leah in *Purgatorio* XXVII, but it by no means sufficiently explains the mention of Rachel in *Inferno* II. If one is thinking of Beatrice as an allegory of Theology, as do nearly all the commentators who say that Rachel is Contemplation here, then the association makes sense. But if one is thinking of typological roles, then Beatrice's relation to Rachel weeping for her children is more valid and contextually rich.

52. The motif of the weeping mother is yet another link between Beatrice and Mary. Capone, in a fine and neglected study, relates the tears of Beatrice to those of Mary at the cross, reminding us of the phrase "juxta crucem lacrimosa" in the "Stabat Mater" (p. 519). Capone's major argument about the tears of Beatrice is that they create "la sua analogia recondita e poetica con il Cristo, con il Verbo che prima di redimere sacrificialmente l'uomo, condivide con lui il pianto nella valle dei pianti, che è la terra" (p. 523). He writes eloquently of the relation between the historical and symbolic functions of Beatrice, "le omologie delle funzioni con le funzioni soterico-illuminative del Cristo" (p. 527).

53. On the implications of the maternal in Dante see Shapiro and Stock. The importance of the maternal is also discussed by Palmenta, who follows Papini in connecting the importance of idealized maternal images in the poem with Dante's childhood loss of his real mother (pp. 13–21).

54. Chiavacci Leonardi's argument includes a fine stylistic analysis of the use of the relative pronoun after an apostrophe, noting that it is nearly always used in relation to the person addressed. Among her examples are Dante's farewell apostrophe to Beatrice, which we have already quoted ("O donna in cui la mia speranza vige") and Beatrice's opening address to Virgil ("O anima cortese mantovana / di cui la fama ancor nel mondo dura").

55. Chiavacci Leonardi takes Virgil to be praising Beatrice in her role as "personification" of Revelation, the Wisdom which Virgil himself, along with the entire pre-Christian world, was unable to achieve; in the apostrophe, then, Virgil recognizes Beatrice as a symbol of the Revelation that leads beyond any he might be capable of and thus makes her a fitting guide to the region of the

blessed. Singleton's reading differs by stressing the limits of Virgil's point of view; but even if Virgil were so limited, the reader is not and would immediately see beyond any notion of philosophical Contemplation to the specifically Christian wisdom Beatrice will bear. In the *Commedia*, the capacity for the "umana specie" to transcend its limits must be conceptualized in theological rather than philosophical terms, given the problematic of original sin (see *Paradiso* VII, 28–30).

56. Vellutello's version of a disinterested love for Beatrice as "la virtù" has some affinities with Casella's reading; he says that he who seeks virtue "per edificar se stesso e altri al bene è vero amico di quella, ma chi cerca per acquistar fama, degnità e altre cose sottoparte a la fortuna."

57. As quoted by Russo, 1979, p. 79. In this assessment of recent Dante scholarship, Russo speaks of Mazzoni as "severo custode degli attuali studi di filologia dantesca" (p. 84) and as the "continuatore dichiarato del magistero filologico del Barbi," whom he has earlier referred to as "maestro indiscutibile e indiscusso del metodo filologico" (p. 83). In the same essay, Russo contrasts Singleton's work with Auerbach's, claiming that it has not enjoyed "larga fortuna" among Dantisti. Unfortunately, this does seem to be the case, but the recent translation of Singleton's work into Italian bodes well for the future.

58. At least one commentator reads the lines exactly as Singleton thinks Virgil does. Biagioli glosses them as follows: "figura il Poeta nella bellissima sua Beatrice quella stessa donna, che fu di Boezio consolatrice. Ella è dunque simbolo della Filosofia." Biagioli's interpretation of these lines resembles D'Andria's reading of the *donna gentile* allusion in the description of Mary. See note 15.

59. *Pietà* is one of a number of key words (*cortesia, nobilitade, ingegno*) whose semantic range Dante explores in this canto and throughout the poem. Words such as *pietà* and *cortese* had a limited valence in the lyric register when Dante had used them earlier; in the *Commedia*, he opens them up to more complex meanings, in part by means of their Latinate (and particularly Virgilian) associations.

60. Benvenuto and Lombardi adduce Scripture as the model for the possibility of a character having both a historical and an allegorical identity.

61. On the limits of Auerbach's perceptions, see Freccero: "[Auerbach] suggested that Dante's power of characterization was so great as to overwhelm whatever figural or representative function the souls were meant to have in favor of their irreducible individuality" (1984, p. 780). Auerbach's reading of *Inferno* X ends up with a restatement of a Romantic reading of the canto insofar as it valorizes the secular and humanistic passions of the characters and ignores the context in which they are set.

62. So Benvenuto: "Scilicet Acherontis fluminis, de quo dicitur in capitulo sequenti" [That is, of the River Acheron, which will be mentioned in the following canto] (p. 100).

63. Benvenuto concludes: "sicut per vallem currit flumen, ita per viam viciorum discurrit vita humana, labilis velut aqua" [as a river flows through a valley, so human life, unstable as water, wanders through a way of vices].

L'Anonimo Fiorentino, who does not specify the Acheron, nevertheless attributes to the *fiumana* a similar signification: "Il peccato degli uomini, il vivere vizioso, si può assimigliare alla acqua de' fiumi, ch'è labile e transitoria come il peccare" (p. 51). Two of the poem's early illustrators depict a landscape with an actual river in it: Lombard, ca. 1400, and Lombard called Imperatorum Vitae master, ca. 1480 (reproduced in Brieger, Meiss, and Singleton, vol. II, pp. 52 and 46).

64. Boccaccio calls the river "quello orribile luogo, nel quale l'autore era da quelle bestie combattuto" (p. 125).

65. See also Serravalle, Landino, and nearly all subsequent commentators.

66. For Pagliaro the pilgrim's distress resembles the "situazione di chi, su una fragile imbarcazione trasportata da una fiumana, si trova nel punto in cui . . . questa s'incontra con il mare; le onde fanno contrasto alla corrente, senza riuscire a vincerla" (1961, pp. 237ff. and 1968, pp. 41–42). It is interesting that Pagliaro holds to such a literal reading of the phrase when he is elsewhere a strong advocate of the union of literal and symbolic meaning in Dante's poetry (1961, p. 237).

67. Mazzoni, following Barbi, adds in support a quotation from St. Catherine of Siena, which equates the river and the sea in precisely such a context: "el qual fiume è il mare tempestoso di questa tenebrosa vita" (p. 303). Bruno Basile in his *voce*, "fiumana" in *ED*, cites, in addition to the passage from Catherine, analogous passages from Augustine, Hugh of St. Victor, Nicholas of Lyra, Peter Damian, and the Bernard Silvester commentary on the *Aeneid* to demonstrate how widespread this topos is in medieval tradition.

68. "The River of Rivers in Connecticut," a poem that ends with a line that resembles Dante's description of the "fiumana": "The river that flows nowhere, like a sea."

69. On Exodus typology he cites Singleton (1960); Mazzoni notes that Belloni also identifies the river as Jordan. Battaglia Ricci makes the point as well, noting that Jordan is the only element of the Exodus topography missing from the opening of the poem (pp. 104–105); it is not clear that her position is different from Freccero's although she says that it is. On the "fiumana" as Jordan, see also Hollander, 1969, pp. 262–63; Hollander credits Filippo Villani with being the first to make the identification, as does Basile (*ED*, II, 937b).

70. Freccero implies the lack of a literal sense even as he formulates his thesis: "It is the purpose of this paper to show that when Lucy speaks of the wolf as though it were a *fiumana*, she is glossing the frustrated journey precisely as Beatrice will later gloss its successful counterpart in the *Paradiso*; that is, according to a *figura* which cannot be perceived by the pilgrim on this side of the river" (1966, p. 27). Presumably, if the pilgrim cannot perceive the river as a river, then it is not present to his senses, which one would expect to be heightened beyond the ordinary at this moment of peril.

71. We will not enter into the controversy over whether the line should read "la fiumana *ove* 'l mar non ha vanto" or "la fiumana *onde* 'l mar non ha vanto," both of which are widely diffused in manuscripts of the poem. Petrocchi con-

cludes in favor of the reading "ove" and so it appears in our text, but Mazzoni makes a spirited case for "onde" on philological, paleographical, and interpretive grounds. We would say only that if "onde" were the correct reading, it would make the parallel between the two lines we are here discussing even stronger: both of the "vanto" references would then also occur in lines using the same conjunction: "Per quest' andata *onde* li dai tu vanto" and "su la fiumana *onde* 'l mar non ha vanto."

72. The only other occurrence of "vanto" is in *Inferno* XXXI, 64 ("tre Frison s'averien dato mal vanto"). "Vantare" occurs twice, in *Inferno* XXIV, 85 and *Purgatorio* VII, 129.

73. Although our discussion concentrates on Lethe, there may be another Virgilian river relevant to considerations of the *fiumana*. As Freccero suggested, Canto II recalls the scene in the fourth book of the *Georgics* in which Aristaeus is weeping at the shore of the Penean River. Having just lost his bees, he laments bitterly and petulantly the difference between the promises made to him on account of his divine descent and the reality of his present situation. His lament resembles Venus's complaint to Jupiter at the opening of *Aeneid* I, a text whose importance for *Inferno* II we have already discussed. Aristaeus's lament is heard by the nymph Arethusa who calls upon his mother, Cyrene, in words that resemble Lucy's speech to Beatrice (II, 353–356). Aristaeus's entrance into his mother's watery kingdom is a sign of his divine descent, and, as David Quint has recently shown, an emblem of return to the original source of all being. Since Virgil links this book of the *Georgics* to *Aeneid* VI by means of verbal reminiscence, the connections between Lethe, river of purification, and the rivery home of Aristaeus's mother are already present in Virgil. In both texts, the river crossing is a major feature of an underworld descent. The *Georgics* are not mentioned in connection with *Inferno* II's "fiumana" in the early commentaries, but we were intrigued to find that the scene of Cyrene's parting the waves at Aristaeus's entrance to the underworld is cited by Daniello (1568) exactly at this point in his commentary: "'su la fiumana,' così appresso Virgilio nel 4 della *Georgica*, Aretusa con Cirene madre d'Aristeo parlando," followed by verses 353–356. On this question see Freccero, 1966, pp. 36–37; Quint, 1983, pp. 32–42, 129, and 241 n. 72. On the importance of Daniello's awareness of hitherto unperceived Virgilian allusions, see Hollander, 1983, pp. 132–133.

74. Castelvetro says of the "dilettoso monte": "Non credo adunque che intende [del] monte che chiudeva quella valle, ma del monte di che parla Beatrice nel *Purgatorio* (30.73). . . . Se sposizione sforzata si dee adattare a questi versi, se ne potrebbe adattare una così fatta."

75. Most of the early commentators (Lana, l'Ottimo, Buti, l'Anonimo, Landino) saw these waters as the river described in *Inferno* XIV, the source of all the infernal waters, Acheron, Styx, Phlegethon, and Cocytus, though Benvenuto argues cogently against this position regarding the river at the base of Purgatory: "Nec credas quod iste rivulus manet a Cocyto, sicut aliqui male opiniatur, quia istud est impossibile per naturam, quia tunc aqua ascendet; sed potius et contra, iste rivulus oritur a monte Purgatorii et labitur contra Inferno

usque ad centrum, quia aqua Purgatorii et aqua Inferni sunt contrarie" [Nor should you believe that this stream overflows from Cocytus, as others incorrectly believe, since this is impossible by nature, because then water would ascend; but rather and otherwise, this stream rises from the mountain of Purgatory and descends toward Inferno even to the center, because the waters of Purgatory and the waters of Inferno are opposites]. Benvenuto does not see this body of water as Lethe, however, but as a river whose source is at the foot of the mountain: "illum rivulum . . . nascitur ad radices montis Purgatorii" [that stream is born at the foot of the mountain of Purgatory]. Lia Baldelli's *voce*, "ruscelletto," in *ED* still sees it as one of the infernal rivers.

76. "Failed Exodus" is Freccero's term for Dante's unsuccessful attempt to climb the mountain in *Inferno* I (1966, p. 26). It is interesting that Landino thinks of Exodus in his gloss on the "fiumana," although he does so in a tangential way. The lines remind him of Moses crossing on dry land in the Exodus: "Dobbiamo intendere che Dante era stato ributtato dalla lupa e giù infino al fiume al quale correva appie del colle. Et piglie in questo luogo la fiumana per lappetito concupiscentia delle chose terrene. . . . Onde veggiamo che Moyse pote dividere el mare chon la verga & fare la strada seccha nel mezo dellacque. È la verga la forteza & la continenza con laqual lhuomo virtuoso può seperar de le passioni informa che sanza impedimento pel mezo di quelli puo passare." Thus Landino sees the river as a figure for the tempests and passions of the mind and Moses as a figure of one surmounting such peril. He may be conflating here the "messo del ciel" of *Inferno* IX whose "verghetta" also clears a passage.

77. Freccero suggested to us that Dante's division of the paradisal river into two parts, Lethe and Eunoe, would form yet another connection between Lethe and Jordan since Jordan itself was traditionally thought of as a composite of two rivers, Jor and Dan. The source of this tradition appears to be Jerome, *Liber de situ et nominibus, PL* 23:890. Cf. Rhabanus Maurus, *PL* 112:971.

78. The Princeton Index has separate listings for Jor and Dan. Its collection of photographs shows the wide diffusion of the image, particularly in manuscript illuminations of Psalm 113 and of the baptism of Christ. On Jordan iconography, see Squilbeck.

79. For a discussion of the emblematic significance of this "conversio" of the Jordan, see Stephany, 1983, pp. 155–156.

80. Freccero suggests the importance of the Lethe, though not in exactly the same way as we do here, in a Bonaventuran interpretation of the three stages of the Exodus experience: "Furthermore, this conception of the stages of moral development corresponds to the drama of the *Purgatorio*, from the emergence on the shore, to the ascent of the mountain, to the crossing of the river to Beatrice" (1966, p. 41). In speaking of Dante's failed Exodus of *Inferno* I, Freccero says, "He will be introduced to that *vita nuova* when he is immersed in the river Lethe at the top of Purgatory." But it is also important to note that Dante's Lethe functions in almost the inverse way as Virgil's. In the *Aeneid*, the Lethe is prelude to a rebirth, which means a return to the historical world

of cyclical violence and repetition, while in Dante it presages a rebirth into eternal life.

81. Rossi connects the "fiumana" with Lethe (p. 57). On another possible source for the "fiumana," see Witke's discussion of the river of light in the *Anticlaudianus* and the *Divine Comedy*.

82. Perhaps what Dante here presents is an example of fourfold allegory. Historically, the *fiumana* is a river in the Holy Land; allegorically, it is the river of baptism in Christ; morally, the river in Dante's heart to which he is reacting inappropriately; and anagogically, the "river" of paradise. The suggestion was made to us by Robert Hollander.

83. On the connection of rivers and rhetoric, see *Inferno* I, 80, where Virgil is "quella fonte / che spandi di parlar sì largo fiume."

CHAPTER THREE: Pilgrim and Poet

1. This is the central argument of Freccero's seminal essay, "Dante's Firm Foot and the Journey without a Guide" (1959). See also "The Prologue Scene" (1966).

2. On the relation of autocitation and autobiography, see Barolini, pp. 3−84, and Contini, 1958, pp. 14−16.

3. To Graziolo, the Guelph chancellor of Bologna, this passage reveals Dante's early Guelph allegiances. Graziolo's reading has had many adherents but is now generally rejected on two grounds. First, the congruence between Dante's position on the providentiality of the empire in *Inferno* II with his earlier references in the *Convivio* (e.g., IV, iv, 8−9), suggests that this is an aspect of Dante's mature political thought. And second, as Torraca has shown, the identity of imperial with papal Rome was a staple of Ghibelline political theory (Mazzoni, p. 214). Perhaps Dante is here telling this "truth," not only to Virgil, who would perforce have been innocent of this reading of Roman teleology, but also to himself, since Dante's mature thought on the empire contains a revisionary relation to his own earlier position that Rome had achieved its hegemony by force rather than providentially. Dante speaks of the change in his understanding of Rome in *Convivio* IV, iv, 8−11. In rejecting the theory of Rome's domination by force, Dante is also rejecting Augustine's position in the *City of God*. On the Virgilian dimension of Dante's polemic with Augustine, see Mazzotta, 1979, pp. 147−191. See also Davis, and Ferrante, 1984, esp. her chapter "City and Empire in the *Comedy*," pp. 44−75.

4. Charity concurs with the analysis of Nardi (1942, pp. 282−286) in arguing that "from the very first (*Inferno* II, 10−36) it is in this connection with 'missions,' much more than in connection with 'modes of vision,' that Dante treats Paul and Aeneas as 'types' for the journey which he is making" (p. 233n).

5. In a similar analysis, Kleinhenz comments: "It is commonly agreed that, by citing the first verse of a hymn, psalm, or poem in the *Divina Commedia*, Dante expects his reader to recall and to think in terms of the entire composition. . . . By employing this 'extended context,' or 'extra-textual' reference,

Dante is able to heighten our understanding of the immediate episode and, in some cases, of its place and role in the *Commedia*" (p. 71).

6. Pietro di Dante in all three redactions, along with Benvenuto who follows him, cites St. Jerome's reference to Paul as "vas legis et sacrarum . . . scripturarum armarium" [vessel of the law and container of holy scripture]. The reference may be found in a letter of Jerome included in the Clementine edition of the Vulgate (Tournai, 1894), p. xi.

7. This would be to respond in strict literalness to the antecedent of "Andovvi" as the same place that Aeneas went. Mazzoni provides one of his most useful *excursus* on this topic (pp. 223–231). Among the early commentaries which claim that Paul went to hell (although some make the claim in qualified fashion) are those of Jacopo di Dante, Graziolo, Lana, the Chiose Selmiane, Guido da Pisa, Buti, l'Anonimo Fiorentino, and Serravalle. Among the early commentators who believe that Dante refers here to Paul's journey to the third heaven—for Mazzoni (and for us) those "chi aveva visto giusto" (p. 226)—are l'Ottimo, Pietro, Boccaccio, and Benvenuto.

8. The *Visio Pauli* was originally written in Greek, probably in the fourth century, and survived in Latin translation in more than fifty manuscripts of various transcriptions and redactions. The legends that evolved in the various redactions of the *Visio Pauli* provide a wealth of fantastic detail concerning what Paul is alleged to have seen and heard during his rapture.

9. D'Ovidio (1897) was arguing against the position of such scholars as Villari (1865, p. xxxiv), D'Ancona (1874, pp. 43–48), and Graf (1893, pp. 241–270). They in turn were following Ozanam's suggestion of Dante's familiarity with the *Visio Pauli* (1839, pp. 331–333). Silverstein (1932, 1937) makes a spirited case for Dante's indebtedness to the *Visio Pauli*. For the text of the *Visio* in nine of its different redactions, see the appendix to Silverstein (1935).

10. Jerome stands alone in the patristic tradition for remaining open to an alternate reading: "Sive humilitatis causa de se in alterius persona loquitur: sive de alio: verum potest utrumque constare" (*PL* 30:802) [Either he speaks of himself in the persona of another for the sake of humility, or he speaks of someone else: in truth, either can be the case].

11. Many of the earliest commentators glossed the reference to "quella fede / ch' è principio a la via di salvazione" with the commonplace that salvation can be found only within the church. Buti, who is representative of this position, also takes this opportunity to strike a blow in the faith-works dispute: "Ben dice che la fede è principio: imperò che sanza la fede nessuno può piacere a Dio, e benchè sia principio non salva però l'uomo: però che la fede sanza l'opera è morta." See also Lana, l'Ottimo, Guido, Benvenuto, and l'Anonimo Fiorentino. Nearly all of them cite words that were attributed to Paul in the Middle Ages, "sine fide autem impossibile est placere Deo" (Heb. 11:6) [but without faith it is impossible to please God].

12. "Et hoc insinuatur nobis per Apostolum ad Corinthios loquentem, ubi dicit: 'Scio huiusmodi hominem (sive in corpore, sive extra corpus, nescio; Deus scit), quoniam raptus est in Paradisum, et audivit arcana verba, quae non licet homini loqui' " (Epistle XIII, paragraph 28) [And this idea is implied to us

⅃ and the *Doctor gentium* but the *pater Romanorum* and the *Doctor*
⅃ 101–102).

ᴀzzoni, Dante mentions the two together "col preciso scopo di
ᵉsperienza tutta naturale di Enea quella soprannaturale del *Vas*
ᵐᵉndo così, fin dall'inizio dell'opera, due termini di conforto ben
ᵃlessero a indicare non solo il senso della duplice esperienza che
ᵉlla *Commedia*, ma anche precedenti, le fonti ideali (e le sole ri-
plicitamente) cui il poeta si richiamava" (p. 230). Mazzoni en-
ᵍgestion—which he attributes to Pascoli—that nel *Inferno* and
ᴐ Dante is like Aeneas, while in the *Paradiso* he is like Paul, as a
ᵉr capire il senso dell'esperienza dantesca entro la machina del
ᵼ2).

Inferno II, where Beatrice commissions Virgil to serve as guide,
ᴐo the beginning of Anchises' speech; in *Purgatorio* XXX, when
ᵛay to Beatrice, the angels quote the end of this same speech,
date lilia plenis," Anchises' tribute to Marcellus.

ʰe early commentators understand Dante to be here alluding to
ᵢn *Aeneid* VI. For Livy's version, see *Ab urbe condita*, I.iii.6–7.
ᴵter summarizing the difference between the versions of Livy and
ᴐusly finesses the whole question of disagreement by pointing out
ᐟ in the phrase "di Silvïo il parente" could as easily mean grand-
ᵣ (pp. 80–81). Dante presumably does intend father here: he calls
ᶠ Anchises in *Inferno* I and father of Silvius in *Inferno* II, thus
ᵐeas, as the *Aeneid* itself does, in his relationship to a male line

ᴵon about the ways in which this high idealism is qualified and
ᵉ *Aeneid* is the subject of a number of recent studies of the poem.
ᴵar, Putnam (1965) and Johnson.
ᵐo Fiorentino and Boccaccio both provide the etymology of Sil-
from *selva*, since Lavinia had to go into the woods to bear and
ᵢm lest the newborn child be assassinated.
discusses this question in some detail (pp. 185–186), concluding
ᴄe to "il differenziare e gerarchizzare, mediante una opportuna
ᴄa ('tu dici . . .'; ma 'Andovvi . . .'), la menzione dei precedenti
ᴵere idealmente la dimensione del suo inventare e narrare: quello
ᵐo, quello biblico, divino." See also D'Ovidio, 1926, pp. 115–116,
, "*Inferno* II: The Canto of the Word."
explains the discrepancy as follows: "The temporal institution of
ᴐends not on Paul but on Aeneas's heirs, which is why Dante
ᵊes to describe the reasons for Aeneas's journey and only three
ᵼ, p. 139).
ᴐrophecy at the outset of the *Aeneid* suggests that for Virgil, too,
ᴐosen in heaven," but for Dante the true nature of the mission is
ʰt of redemption history.
ᴐo differentiates between these as the remote and proximate
ᵻs's journey to the underworld.

by the Apostle, addressing the C
(whether in the body or out of th
up to the third heaven, and heard
to utter']. As translated in Haller,

13. In II Cor.: 3:7ff., Paul recal
haps Moses is also recalled in Dar
mission. When Yahweh, speaking
to lead his people to freedom, M
four separate ways (Exod. 3:11–4
that God could be seen directly
words to him in Exod. 33:20: "n
shall not see me and live].

14. The *locus classicus*, Thomas's
a summary of this tradition. Thor
(art. 3, reply 1–2), in an ecstasy
of the state of blessedness perm
(reply 3–4). Paul's claim of raptu
sion of how God is known (*ST* I

15. Mazzeo wisely notes that tl
sarily imply a similar claim on b
man had a vision of God's esse
question. But that Dante as a
claims and describes such a vis
heaven, so that he is committe
rendering of such a vision, and
commenting on the final part o
gether with those of the *Comed*
sees" (p. 106).

16. Sarolli also argues that D
own, as of Paul's journey; for
Aeneas "corruttibile ancora, ac
has as its real significance the
(p. 114). Earlier in our century,
as model. Padoan (1977) argu
Dante intends the *Paradiso* to
(pp. 30–63). Newman argues
forms the whole of Dante's *vis*
Paul") the concurrence of wate
as well as the coincidence of ti
into the Empyrean both occu
Aeneas and Paul parallel, that
noon. (See Hollander, 1983, p.

17. Mazzeo calls attention t
Aeneas, pointing out that "t
mystical thought was not Ae
pology and parallelism of his

tor Judaeoru
gentium" (p

18. For N
affiancare a
d'elezione; p
precisi, che
Dante vive
conosciute
dorses the s
the *Purgato*
"chiave ...
poema" (p.

19. Here i
Dante refers
Virgil gives
"*Manibus*, o

20. All of
this moment
Benvenuto, a
Virgil, ingen
that "parente
father as fath
Aeneas son
bracketing A
of *pietas*.

21. Specula
undercut in t
See, in partic

22. L'Anon
vio as derivec
then conceal

23. Mazzon
with a refere
scelta linguist
ai quali apper
letterario, um
and Hollande

24. Ferrant
the church d
takes fifteen
for Paul's" (19

25. Jupiter's
Aeneas was "c
clear only in l

26. Benven
causes of Aen

Epist. II ad Cor., PL 112:229–234; and Haymo of Halberstadt, *Opera. Pars I: Comment. Bibl., Expositio in Epp. S. Pauli: In Epist. II Ad Cor., PL* 117:660–668.

39. The word *stimulus* also occurs in association with Paul's moment of conversion, but not in Acts 9. Rather, in one of Paul's own subsequent accounts of that experience, in what Acts presents as his testimony before Herod Agrippa II, he quotes the voice that spoke to him from the great light as having said to him, "Saule, Saule, quid me persequeris? durum est tibi contra stimulum calcitrare" (Acts 26:14) [Saul, Saul, why persecutest thou me? It is hard for thee to kick against the goads]. Paul thus acknowledges that he was in reality already called—or rather, driven, since the goad metaphor is related to the motivation of oxen—even before his moment of conversion.

40. Paul's humility became the model for others in the mystical tradition. St. Bernard, for example, in *De gradibus humilitatis*, discusses why Paul says he was "raptus" and not "ductus," caught up, that is, rather than brought up: "Ut videlicet si tantus Apostolus raptum se dicit fuisse, quo nec ductus scivit, nec ductus potuit ire; me, qui procul dubio minor sum Paulo, ad tertium coelum nulla mea virtute confidam, vel pro labore diffidam" [In order that, if so great an apostle says that he was *caught up* there whither he could not go by being taught or brought, I who am surely less than Paul shall not presume to be able to attain the third heaven by any strength of my own, and so shall be neither confident of my strength nor diffident because of the toil]. We cite the text and translation of Burch, pp. 166–167.

41. Aeneas and Paul are also related by the fact that Paul's final suffering came at the hands of Aeneas's descendants: not only "lo vas d'elezione," but "il maggior Piero" as well, were martyred during Nero's persecution.

42. The other three effects, in order, are "the efficacious performance of the good willed," "perseverance in the good," and "the attainment of glory." The five effects are sequential so that the grace to will the good can be said to be prevenient with respect to the grace to perform that good and subsequent with respect to the grace that healed the soul. If Dante has come to accept the grace of spiritual healing in *Inferno* I, Canto II begins the process of identifying the unique good he is called to perform, a process that culminates in *Paradiso* XV–XVII. To continue the analysis, the composition of the *Commedia* may be seen as evidence of the third and fourth effects of grace, performance of and perseverance in the good, and Dante's ultimate hope is the fifth effect, the attainment of glory. For Thomas's discussion of prevenient and subsequent grace, see *ST* I.ii. quest. III, art. 3.

43. The centrality of this episode has been perceived by several recent studies. See, for example, Hollander, 1969, pp. 67–69; Mazzotta, 1979, pp. 219–226; Ball, p. 77; and Barolini, pp. 256–269. For a recent reading of *Inferno* II related to ours, see Robin Kirkpatrick: "The theme of this canto is the inadequacy of heroic and rational modes of conduct in the light of Christian humility and Christian faith" (p. 50).

44. See Stephany's conclusion: "Dante's *Commedia* is his attempt to do with his own writing what Statius had failed to do and what Virgil had accom-

plished, albeit unintentionally, with his. It is Dante's public response to his own conversion" (1983, p. 162). See also Padoan: "Il poeta è riuscito a far vivere intensamente la commozione di Stazio di fronte a Virgilio, perchè si potrebbe quasi affermare che dietro Stazio è Dante stesso che parla. Anche Dante, come Stazio, può dire di Virgilio: 'per te poeta fui, per te cristiano,' perchè la *Commedia* dà una illuminante rilettura dell'*Eneide* in chiave escatologica" (1970, p. 354).

45. Goldstein, who makes the case for Paul as "perfect writer and perfect voyager" (p. 326 n. 25), cites Augustine's *De Doctrina Christiana* 4, 14, 7 on the contrast between the pagan rhetorical desire to display eloquence and Christian writers such as Paul, who "possess, but do not make a display of eloquence" (p. 319).

46. For the story of Victorinus's public and heroic conversion, see Augustine's *Confessions*, VIII, 2.

47. L'Anonimo presumably refers here to the apocryphal exchange of correspondence between Paul and Nero's tutor, the moral philosopher Seneca, which is supposed to have taken place at the time when Paul was imprisoned in Rome and shortly before Seneca's fall from imperial favor and subsequent execution. For the text of this third-century document, see Hennecke, Vol. II, pp. 133–141. In his subsequent analysis, l'Anonimo suggests another common way of relating the two Pauline passages Dante evokes, namely, by seeing the moment of Paul's blinding and conversion as concurrent with the spiritual rapture discussed in II Corinthians: "ma comprendesi che quando Cristo gli apparve si dice ch' elli fu rapito infino al terzo cielo, et in quello stante egli ficcasse l'occhio nella individua Trinità, nella vera Sapienza del figliuolo di Dio, et quivi vedesse et lo inferno et il purgatorio, et il paradiso tanto pienamente quanto vedere si puote" (p. 39).

48. As Singleton puts it: "Dante abandoned the *Convivio* because he came to see that in choosing to build this work according to the allegory of the poets, he had ventured down a false way; that he came to realize that a poet could not be a poet of rectitude and work with an allegory whose first meaning was a disembodied fiction" (1957, p. 93).

49. This position, that the *Commedia* dramatizes a recantation of the *Convivio*'s fundamental artistic stance, has received widespread but by no means complete acceptance in the scholarly community. For a strong statement of an opposing view see Picchio Simonelli.

50. As Freccero has said, "the landscape in which the pilgrim finds himself [in *Inferno* I] bears a striking, indeed at times a textual, resemblance to the 'region of unlikeness' in which the young Augustine finds himself in the seventh book of the *Confessions*" (1966a, p. 1). To the person Dante had become by the time he wrote the *Commedia*, the *Convivio*'s intellectual premises may well have seemed to provide evidence that he was at that time "smarrito" in a spiritual wilderness. Freccero's speculations later in the essay are germane to our consideration: "If Dante chose to echo Augustine's attempt to reach the truth through Philosophy alone, then the implication is that Dante undertook a similar at-

tempt and also met with failure. For all of his efforts in the *Convivio* to define philosophical truth in theological terms, Dante's philosophical experience may have been as ultimately disillusioning for him as was Augustine's with the neoplatonists" (p. 19).

51. Pine-Coffin's analysis (in the introduction of his translation) of Augustine's harsh judgment of his past may, *mutatis mutandis*, have some relevance for Dante. "Perhaps [Augustine's] training as a teacher of rhetoric accounts for this. He was, after all, trying to make out a case against himself before an audience which was predisposed to believe him a saintly man. When he wrote the *Confessions* he already had a considerable reputation for sanctity, and one of the reasons why he wrote was to persuade his admirers that any good qualities he had were his by the grace of God, who had saved him so often from himself" (p. 12).

52. On the polyvalence of recantation, see Jacoff: "The notion of recantation implies not only retraction, but also resinging, singing again. In a broader sense, we might say that palinodic language is part of the poet's motivation for continuing to write" (1980, p. 117).

53. Trecento commentaries are generally content to paraphrase the terms of the comparison. L'Anonimo makes explicit the attitude that the others take for granted: "chiaro appare la comparazione" (p. 52). Of modern critics, Apollonio senses the significance conferred on the simile by its emphatic position and startling beauty but offers no explanation of its function, calling it "un *topos* della poesia cortese che, in sè e nel suo compito tradizionale, non avrebbe che un assunto decorativo; ma la maniera della composizione dantesca è assai più robusta di quel che comporterebbe la semplice imitazione di una maniera (p. 18). For a recent alternate reading, see Cornish.

54. In *Purgatorio* XXX, Beatrice defines Dante's transfer of allegiance from her memory to the other lady as an anticonversion, a "turning" (*volse*) from the true path: "e volse i passi suoi per via non vera, / imagini di ben seguendo false, / che nulla promissïon rendono intera" (*Purgatorio* XXX, 130–132). Dante's subsequent inability to recall this estrangement (XXXIII, 91–93) is greeted as proof positive that his love for the *donna gentile* was sinful, for it is memory only of former sin that is obliterated by the waters of Lethe (XXXIII, 94–99). Later in the same speech (XXX, 136–141), Beatrice attributes to Dante's infidelity the necessity of her own intervention, the central event described in *Inferno* II. It is appropriate that in *Inferno* I, at the moment when Virgil describes this encounter with Beatrice, Dante's response recalls and as it were "corrects" the *Convivio*'s figure of speech.

55. This recantation works in a way precisely parallel to *Paradiso* II's recantation of *Convivio* I, i, the passage analyzed in Ransom's "Panis Angelorum." The line "Voialtri pochi che drizzaste il collo / per tempo al pan de li angeli" (*Paradiso* II, 10–11), evokes the *Convivio*'s constitutive metaphor of intellectual feasting, and in particular its first chapter, in which Dante had considered himself among the "beati pochi" fortunate enough to eat the symbolic bread of angels. For a discussion of the way this thirst spoken of at the beginning of the *Convivio*

is presented in a "corrected" way in *Purgatorio* XXI's reference to the Samaritan woman, see Stephany 1983.

56. The verb "drizzare" is repeated in both passages. In the *Convivio*, Dante had expressed the hope that through his efforts, "la gente . . . per diritto calle si dirizzasse"; in the *Commedia*, he is himself like the flower which "si drizzan tutti aperti" at the spiritual sunlight conveyed to him through the canto's chain of intermediaries.

57. The traditional description of Boethius as the last Roman philosopher and the first medieval theologian (Rand, pp. 155–156) is not without merit. Boethius was the last western European of cultural significance to be educated at the Platonic Academy, was universally accepted in the Middle Ages as the author of a series of theological tractates, and was believed to have been martyred as an orthodox Christian by the Arian Theodoric. Reiss provides an excellent recent summary and analysis of Boethius's life and cultural significance, which judiciously balances the Boethius of tradition against modern historical evidence. See also Francesco Tateo's *voce*, "Boezio," in *ED*, as well as the studies by Courcelle, Murari, Kranz, Scuderi, D'Alverny, and Gualtieri.

58. The *Commedia*'s trecento commentators identify Boethius as a great scholar who wrote the *Consolation* while exiled for his opposition to Theodoric's Arianism (Pietro di Dante) or to Theodoric's injustice and misrule (Buti) or to both (l'Ottimo). L'Ottimo's summary of Boethius's accomplishments is representative: "nelle scienze di tutte le liberali arti ammaestratissimo; così in greco come in latino compose libri, e comentò li altrui, o traslatò di greco in latino, delle dette scienze; in sapienza di teologia fu nobilissimo, libri di scienza naturale e morale recò di greco in latino."

59. Barolini provides an excellent discussion of this part of the *Convivio* (pp. 14ff.).

60. To borrow Freccero's well-known distinction, *paideia* fails to achieve what *askesis* allows. See also Jacoff, 1980, pp. 115–116.

61. See Hollander: "It was not Boethius who was at fault so much as Dante's reading of Boethius. For it led him away from Beatrice to an attempt at a neoplatonizing *folle volo*" (1980, p. 102). For a discussion of the importance of the word "cacciare," used in the sense of "scacciare," in Dante's lexicon of exile, see Stephany (1985), pp. 27–30.

62. For Augustine's argument about "Egyptian gold," see *On Christian Doctrine*, pp. 75–78 (2.40.60–63).

63. Dante even claims to perceive in this process the working out of Providence, "divino imperio," concealed in the hidden cause, the "occulta cagione." If Providence does eventually work things out in Dante's best interests— as Cacciaguida assures him that it will—it does not do so in the ways he thought he perceived in the *Convivio* to be the secret significance of "Voi ch' intendendo."

64. Hollander has argued on several occasions that the "serena" of the dream of *Purgatorio* XIX and the "serene" of *Purgatorio* XXXI are recollections of the harlot Muses which Lady Philosophy drives from Boethius in the opening

episode of the *Consolation of Philosophy*. See, for example, Hollander, 1969, pp. 136–144, 162–163; 1975, pp. 348–363; and 1983a, pp. 79–80. The dream of *Purgatorio* XIX, in which Dante's gaze makes the ugly "femmina balba" appear to be beautiful, is perhaps a recollection of the earlier episode from the *Convivio*, where it is also Dante's gaze that made the *donna gentile*, there interpreted as Philosophy, seem beautiful. Dante converts her, by means of an emotional short circuit, into an image of what, seeking to console himself, he had been seeking: "per che sì volontieri lo senso di vero la mirava, che appena lo potea volgere da quella" (II, ii[xiii], 6). In the *Vita Nuova*, too, Dante seems almost to "create" the *donna gentile* when he looks up for her and finds her. "Levai li occhi per veder se altri mi videsse," he says, and immediately sees the *donna gentile* looking at him. She mirrors his emotional needs, and her pity releases his self-pity (See Robert P. Harrison, pp. 114–116). Hollander connects the dream of *Purgatorio* XIX with *Inferno* II: the "donna . . . santa e presta" who asks Virgil to expose to Dante the hidden reality of the transformed hag "should be seen as recreating the offstage encounter of Virgil and Beatrice as this was narrated by his *autore* in *Inferno* II" (1983a, p. 79). If Hollander is right, all three of the purgatorial dreams look back to *Inferno* II: the eagle as Lucy in Canto IX and the Leah/Rachel dream of Canto XXVIII both have their obvious echoes in the ladies of *Inferno* II.

65. One is permitted to talk about oneself "quando, per ragionare di sé, grandissima utilitade ne segue altrui per via di dottrina; e questa ragione mosse Agustino ne le sue Confessioni a parlare di sé, ché per lo processo de la sua vita, lo quale fu di [non] buono in buono, e di buono in migliore, e di migliore in ottimo, ne diede essemplo e dottrina, la quale per sì vero testimonio ricevere non si potea" (I, ii, 14).

66. Dante proposes this patent misreading of Boethius while defending himself against what he claims (unpersuasively) to be a misinterpretation of his own poems.

67. "Veramente io sono stato legno sanza vela e sanza governo, portato a diversi porti e foce e liti dal vento secco che vapora la dolorosa povertade" (I, iii, 5). For an interesting discussion of "The Rudderless Ship and the Sea," see the chapter "The Man of Law's Tale" in Kolve, pp. 297–358. For a consideration of *Inferno* I's "pelago" in relation to the language of the *Convivio's* opening sequence, see also Jacoff, 1980, p. 116.

68. The similarity of this portion of the *Convivio* to *Consolation* I, pr, iv is widely recognized. See, for example, Moore, 1896, pp. 282–288. (See also Boethius's lament over what he perceives as his undeserved suffering at the hands of Providence, in the famous ode, "O stelliferi conditor orbis," I, m. 5.)

69. An additional reason why Dante might have thought of these two great scholar-saints together is the coincidence that they were buried in the same church, a point noted by both Benvenuto and Serravalle in their commentaries on *Paradiso* X, 127–128. Although it is a surprise that Dante reserves no place for Augustine among *Paradiso* X's philosopher-saints, he does place Boethius there immediately after the character who is identified indirectly as "quello av-

vocato de' tempi cristiani, / del cui latino Augustin si provide" (X, 119–120). For a recent discussion of Augustine's influence on Boethius, see Fleming, pp. 38–63.

70. In the *Confessions*, Augustine makes the same point by using the Prodigal Son as a structural parallel to his own spirtual "erring." The connection is made explicit in its first occurrence, where we are told that the Son, to reach the distant land in which he dissipated his birthright, "non . . . equos aut currus vel naves quaesavit aut avolavit pinna visibili; aut moto iter egit . . . ; in affectu ergo libidinoso, id enim est tenebroso atque id est longe a vultu tuo" (I, 18). Pine-Coffin offers a helpful elaboration rather than a strict translation: [the Prodigal Son] "did not hire horses, carriages, or ships: he did not take to the air on real wings or set one foot before the other. . . . But he set his heart on pleasure and his soul was blinded, and this blindness was the measure of the distance he travelled away from you, so that he could not see your face" (p. 38). See Ferrari for an excellent study of this motif.

71. Those such as ourselves who see the *Commedia* as recanting attitudes formerly espoused in the *Convivio* need to acknowledge that this creates an awkward problem with the poem's fictional time. The *Convivio* is a product of, and in many ways a response to, Dante's exile from Florence, but the *Commedia*'s fictional setting is 1300, a time before the exile, when Dante was at his political zenith within his commune. In its palinodic moments, therefore, the *Commedia* recants positions formerly held with respect to the literary career of the poet but expressed in a work not yet written with respect to the *Commedia*'s setting. The attitudes expressed in the *Convivio* might well have antedated that work, but the palinodic references to specific passages in the *Convivio* require some degree of mental gymnastics: the poet recants a work that, in the life of the pilgrim, has not yet been written.

72. On the interrelationship of exile and language (with particular emphasis on Augustine but with implications for Dante), see Ferguson and also Ladner.

73. Benvenuto's précis of the *Consolation* in his note on *Paradiso* X sums up the work's main themes with brilliant conciseness: "In quo quidem libro probat quae sit falsa felicitas, et quae vera; et quomodo temporalia fortuita non possunt conferre beatitudinem homini, immo potius faciunt ipsum infelicem" (V, 45) [In this book he examines what is false felicity and what true; and how temporal things derived from fortune cannot confer happiness upon a person, but rather make one unhappy].

74. The feminine endings of the emphatic pronouns "ella" and "essa" emphasize the separation between Boethius's "corpo," which lies buried "giuso," "down there," and his soul (the antecedent for those pronouns), which "came from suffering and exile to this peace."

75. The question of whether Dante wrote the whole of this Epistle is still not closed. Mazzoni has written several studies over the past three decades arguing for Dante's authorship of the entire Epistle, an argument we find persuasive and congenial. For an extended discussion of the controversy, see Manlio Pastore Stocchi's *voce* on "Epistole" in *ED* and Padoan's extended discussion in his

chapter "La 'mirabile visione' di Dante e l'Epistola a Cangrande," in *Il pio Enea*, pp. 30–63. Peter Dronke has recently engaged the question anew, arguing on the basis of his analysis of *cursus* that only the initial dedicatory sequence of the letter is authentic and that the expository sequence is not by Dante.

76. Here and subsequently we cite Haller's translation of the Epistle.

77. In this paragraph, in response to those who would remain skeptical about mystical experiences of knowledge such as he proposes, Dante cites three other works, Richard of St. Victor's *De Contemplatione* (also known as the *Benjamin Major*), Augustine's *De Quantitate Animae*, and Bernard's *De Consideratione*. All three texts discuss the soul's ascent through successive stages of knowledge to a final resting in an act of contemplative identification with God. These references suggest how widely Dante had read in the mystical tradition of Christianized Neoplatonism into which he places his *Paradiso*. In all three of these works, Paul's ascent is the canonically sanctioned model of mystical rapture. Cf. Padoan, "La 'mirabile visione' di Dante e l'Epistola a Cangrande" (1977, pp. 30–63).

78. Courcelle speaks of the importance of these lines: "À l'époque du Haut Moyen Âge le passage qui rencontra le plus d'écho dans les textes littéraires est l'invocation finale, qui pouvait aisément passer pour chrétienne" (p. 177), and he devotes an entire chapter to III, m. ix (pp. 159–199). Courcelle's collection of glosses on this passage (which includes Peter Abelard, John of Salisbury, Alain de Lille, Geoffrey of Vinsauf, Vincent of Beauvais, Albertus Magnus, and Thomas Aquinas) concludes with an allusion to the passage from the Epistle to Cangrande: "On ne s'étonnera pas, avec de tels antécédents, de voir Dante placer son *Paradis* sous le signe du *Te cernere finis* boécien; il semble s'être assimilé très intimement cette Prière et n'hésite pas à mettre le vers de Boéce sur le même plan que le verset de saint Jean relatif à la vie éternelle" (p. 184).

79. Beatrice *does* respond with justice in *Purgatorio* XXX, when her doing so will be of benefit to Dante. Lucy here elides the whole composition of the *Convivio*, recalling Beatrice to the *Vita Nuova* experience.

80. In commenting on Paul's journey in II Corinthians, the exegetical tradition devised several ingenious interpretations of the meaning of the third heaven, but in none of them is it associated with secular knowledge. The Pseudo-Hugh of St. Victor's *Questiones in Epistolas Pauli*, which comes late enough in the tradition to attempt an organizational summary of earlier readings, differentiates among four interpretations of the passage, but in all of them the third heaven is a place of spiritual knowledge: "per tertium vero coelum, et paradisum, in quem raptus est, idem intelligit, videlicet plenam divinitatis intelligentiam, vel cognitionem" [the third heaven indeed and paradise, into which he was transported, he (Paul) understands in short to be the full understanding or apprehension of divinity] (*PL* 175:552). In the third heaven, as the *Glossa Ordinaria* sums up the traditional reading, "angeli et sanctae animae Dei fruuntur contemplatione" [the angels and sainted souls take pleasure in the contemplation of God] (*PL* 114:568).

81. Dante may have heard an etymological pun in the word *Commedia*

whereby it may actually "recant" the title of the *Convivio,* Dante's intellectual "banquet": perhaps *Commedia* puns on the Latin word *comedere,* to eat together. Instead of a banquet in which Dante's own literary accomplishments are distributed, the *Commedia* offers the true "pane de li angeli." If Dante intends this pun, he recalls a word that is a scriptural and liturgical commonplace, as, for example, in Jesus' words instituting the Eucharist, "accipite et comedite" [take it and eat]. This idea was suggested to us by Daniel P. Daley.

82. In a sense, Cacciaguida stands in figural relation to the spiritual guides in the background of *Inferno* II: he is like Anchises, Ananias, and Lady Philosophy. If "nomina sunt consequentia rerum," Cacciaguida is indeed, as his name etymologically suggests, the exile's guide. Ferrante, whose reading has a more political orientation than ours, suggests that his name implies one who hunts for a leader (1984, p. 282).

83. See Hollander, 1983a, p. 136n; and Schnapp.

84. Again, as in *Inferno* II, the tentativeness of the *Aeneid*'s authority is emphasized. The comparison to Anchises in the first and third lines of the *terzina* are qualified by the middle line, "se fede merta nostra maggior musa."

85. Virgil had promised that Beatrice would be the one to clarify this prophecy, but it turns out, surprisingly, to be Cacciaguida who does so. Chiarenza observes that Dante is even here following a Virgilian model: "In Book III of the *Aeneid* (441–660), Helenus instructs Aeneas to go to the Sibyl, from whom he will hear of the wars to be waged and the future glories of his people. In fact, his words are inaccurate, for in Book VI it is not the Sibyl but Anchises, to whom Aeneas is led by the Sibyl, who speaks of these things. The well-known inconsistency in the *Divine Comedy* between *Inferno* X, 130–32, where the pilgrim is told that Beatrice will give him the final account of the voyage of his life, and *Paradiso* XVII, where it is his ancestor, to whom she has quite purposefully led him, who offers the long awaited forecast, is too similar to the one in the *Aeneid* to be a coincidence; especially if we consider how Dante introduces Cacciaguida's prophecy" (1983a, p. 28).

86. The connection of Cacciaguida's words with Paul's two journeys to heaven is also noted by Ferrante (1984, p. 282, n. 33), and by Padoan (1977, pp. 33–34).

87. *Homil. in Evangelia* II, 35 (*PL* 76:1259). For the first of these references in *Paradiso* XVII, Chiarenza (1983b, p. 139) cites John of Salisbury, *Policraticus* III.xi: "iaculae quae previdentur feriunt minus" [spears which are foreseen inflict lighter wounds].

88. Cacciaguida speaks of his own martyrdom during the Second Crusade, and he warns Dante of the necessity of his impending suffering. As we saw in our second chapter, it is during the course of this discussion that Thomas cites the defiant words of St. Lucy to her tormentors (*ST* II–ii, q. 124, a. 4). We are reminded once again that her *fermezza* provides a contrast to Dante's timidity in *Inferno* II.

89. See Appendix III, "Fear, Pity, and Firmness," in Hollander (1969).

90. Cacciaguida begins his discourse on the loneliness and alienation of exile

(*Paradiso* XVII, 37–60) with a discussion of contingency, which he says does not extend beyond the "quaderno" of the material world (where each page, the metaphor suggests, conceals the sheaf of still unturned leaves to follow). Cacciaguida's consideration of freedom and foreknowledge (and even the nature of his example of the ship floating downstream) is an adaptation of the *locus classicus* on this question, the *Consolation*, Book V, meter 2.

91. After a draft of our book had been submitted for publication, Schnapp's excellent book on the Cacciaguida cantos was published. His final chapter, esp. pp. 215–238, provides a persuasive study of the centrality of martyrdom to the poem. Martyrdom is, Schnapp argues, an inherently discursive act (p. 218); Dante is summoned not only to a life of suffering but to one of witness, of prophecy. See Jacoff, 1985.

92. The heaviest burden of exile will be the ungrateful company of fellow exiles, those whom Dante might have expected to be friends, from whom he will be isolated as a party of one. His first comfort will come from the Scaligeri, the first to offer shelter to the powerless exile (vv. 70–75). It hardly seems accidental that Dante places this moment at the precise midpoint of his final *cantica*: sixteen cantos precede and sixteen follow *Paradiso* XVII; the canto consists of forty-seven *terzine*, with this the twenty-fourth *terzina*, therefore, the exact midpoint of this central canto. The twenty-third *terzina* foretells Dante's isolation from the *bestialità* of the other exiles; the twenty-fourth foretells "la cortesia del gran Lombardo"; the twenty-fifth balances the loneliness of the "parte per te stesso" with the intimacy "tra voi due" between Dante and his Scaliger host. The importance of the Epistle to Cangrande for clarifying Dante's typological evaluation of his exile may here be implied within the narrative architecture of his poem.

BIBLIOGRAPHY

COMMENTARIES CITED

For a somewhat longer list of commentaries arranged in chronological, rather than alphabetical, order, see R. Hollander, "A Checklist of Commentators on the *Commedia*," *Dante Studies*, 101 (1983[= 1988]), and A. Cassell, *Lectura Dantis Americana*: Inferno *I* (Philadelphia: University of Pennsylvania Press, 1989).

ANDREOLI (1856)	*La Divina Commedia di Dante Alighieri col Commento di Raffaello Andreoli.* Firenze, G. Barbèra, 1887.
ANONIMO FIORENTINO (1400 ca.)	*Commento alla Divina Commedia d'Anonimo Fiorentino del secolo XIV, ora per la prima volta stampato a cura di Pietro Fanfani.* Bologna, G. Romagnoli, 1866–74.
BENNASSUTI (1864–68)	*La Divina Commedia di Dante Alighieri col commento cattolico di Luigi Bennassuti, arciprete di Cerea.* Verona, G. Civelli, 1864–68.
BENVENUTO (1371–80)	*Benevenuti de Rambaldis de Imola Comentum super Dantis Aldigherij Comoediam, nunc primum integre in lucem editum sumptibus Guilielmi Warren Vernon, curante Jacopo Philippo Lacaita.* Florentiae, G. Barbèra, 1887.
BIAGIOLI (1818–19)	*La Divina Commedia di Dante Alighieri col comento di* G[iosafatte] *Biagioli.* Milano, G. Silvestri, 1820–21.
BOCCACCIO (1373)	*Esposizioni sopra la Comedia di Dante,* a cura di Giorgio Padoan, vol. VI of *Tutte le opere di Giovanni Boccaccio,* a cura di Vittore Branca. Milano, Mondadori, 1965.
BUTI (1385–95)	*Commento di Francesco da Buti sopra la Divina Commedia di Dante Allighieri . . . per cura di Crescentino Giannini.* Pisa, Fratelli Nistri, 1858–62.
CASTELVETRO (1570 ca.)	*Sposizione di Lodovico Castelvetro a XXIX Canti dell'Inferno dantesco, ora per la prima volta data in luce da Giovanni Franciosi.* Modena, Società tipografica, 1886.

DANIELLO
(1568)

Dante con l'espositione di M. Bernard[in]o Daniello da Lucca sopra la sua Comedia dell'Inferno, del Purgatorio, & del Paradiso. . . . Venetia, Pietro da Fino, 1568.

DEL LUNGO
(1926)

La Divina Commedia commentata da Isidoro del Lungo. Firenze, F. Le Monnier, 1926.

GMELIN
(1954−57)

Die Göttliche Komödie, ubersetzt von Hermann Gmelin. Kommentar. Stuttgart, Klett, 1954−57.

GRANDGENT
(1909−13)

La Divina Commedia de Dante Alighieri, edited and annotated by C. H. Grandgent. Boston, D.C. Heath, 1909−13. [See also the revised ed. of 1933, *ivi.*]

GRAZIOLO
(1324)

Il Commento dantesco di Graziolo de' Bambaglioli, dal 'Colombino' di Siviglia con altri codici raffrontato. Contributi di Antonio Fiammazzo all'edizione critica. Savona, D. Bertolotto e C., 1915.

GUIDO DA PISA
(1327−28)

Guido da Pisa's Expoistiones et Glose super Comediam Dantis, or Commentary on Dante's Inferno. Edited with Notes and Introduction by Vincenzo Cioffari. Albany, N.Y., State University of New York Press, 1974.

JACOPO
ALIGHIERI
(1322)

Chiose Alla Cantica dell'Inferno di Dante Alighieri scritte da Jacopo Alighieri, pubblicate per la prima volta in corretta lezione con riscontri e facsimili di codici, e precedute da una indagine critica per cura di Jarro [Giulio Piccini]. Firenze, R. Bemporad e figlio, 1915.

LANA
(1324−28 ca.)

Comedia di Dante degli Allaghieri col Commento di Jacopo della Lana bolognese, a cura di Luciano Scarabelli. Bologna, Tipografia Regia, 1866−67.

LANDINO (1481)

Comento di Christophoro Landino fiorentino sopra la Comedia di Danthe Alighieri Poeta fiorentino. Firenze, Nicholò di Lorenzo della Magna, 1481.

LOMBARDI
(1791)

La Divina Commedia, novamente corretta, spiegata e difesa da F. B. L. M. C. [i.e., Fra Baldassare Lombardi, minore conventuale]. Roma, A. Fulgoni, 1791[−92].

MATTALIA
(1960)

La Divina Commedia a cura di Daniele Mattalia. Milano, A. Rizzoli, 1975.

MOMIGLIANO
(1946−51)

La Divina Commedia commentata da Attilio Momigliano. Firenze, G.C. Sansoni, 1946−51.

OTTIMO (1333)

L'Ottimo Commento della Divina Commedia [Andrea Lancia]. *Testo inedito d'un contemporaneo di Dante* . . . [ed. Alessandro Torri]. Pisa, N. Capurro, 1827−29.

PIETRO DI
DANTE (1340)

Petri Allegherii super Dantis ipsius genitoris Comoediam Commentarium, nunc primum in lucem editum . . . [ed. Vincenzo Nannucci]. Florentiae, G. Piatti, 1845 [see also *Il "Commentarium" di Pietro Alighieri nelle redazioni ashburnhamiana e ottoboniana*, ed. R. della Vedova & M.T. Silvotti. Firenze, L. S. Olschki, 1978, *Inf.* only].

PLUMPTRE
(1886–87)

The Commedia and Canzoniere of Dante Alighieri; a New Translation with Notes, Essays and a Biographical Introduction by E. H. Plumptre, D.D., Dean of Wells. London, Wm. Isbister, 1886–87.

SALINARI (1980)

La Divina Commedia, a cura di Carlo Salinari, Sergio Romagnoli, and Antonio Lanza. Vol. I. Roma, Riuniti, 1980.

SAPEGNO (1955)

La Divina Commedia a cura di Natalino Sapegno. Milano-Napoli, R. Ricciardi, 1957 [see also 2nd ed., Firenze, La Nuova Italia, 1968, and 3rd ed. of 1985].

SCARTAZZINI
(1874–82)

La Divina Commedia di Dante Alighieri, riveduta nel testo e commentata da G.A. Scartazzini. Leipzig, Brockhaus, 1874–90 [and see the greatly revised 2nd ed., *ivi*, 1900, repr. Bologna, Forni, 1965].

ANON.
SELMIANO
(1337 ca.)

Chiose anonime alla prima Cantica della Divina Commedia di un contemporaneo del Poeta, pubblicate . . . *da Francesco Selmi.* . . . Torino, Stamperia Reale, 1865.

SERRAVALLE
(1416–17)

Fratris Johannis de Serravalle Ord. Min. Episcopi et Principis Firmani Translatio et Comentum totius libri Dantis Aldigherii, cum textu italico Fratris Bartholomaei a Colle eiusdem Ordinis, nunc primum edita [a cura di Fr. Marcellino da Civezza & Fr. Teofilo Domenichelli]. Prati, Giachetti, 1891.

SINGLETON
(1970–75)

The Divine Comedy, Translated, with a Commentary, by Charles S. Singleton. Princeton, Princeton University Press, 1970–75.

TOMMASEO
(1837)

La Divina Commedia con le note di Niccolò Tommaseo e introduzione di Umberto Cosmo. Torino, UTET, 1927–34 [repr. of 2nd (definitive) ed., Milano, F. Pagnoni, 1865].

TORRACA (1905)

La Divina Commedia di Dante Alighieri nuovamente commentata da Francesco Torraca, 4th ed. Milano-Roma-Napoli, Albrighi, Segati, 1920.

VELLUTELLO
(1544)

La Comedia di Dante Alighieri con la nova espositione di Alessandro Vellutello. Vinegia, Francesco Marcolini, 1544.

VILLANI (1391)   Filippo Villani, *Il comento al primo canto dell' "Inferno,"* *pubblicato ed annotata da Giuseppe Cugnoni*. Città di Castello, Lapi, 1896.

WORKS CONSULTED

Abbadessa, Silvio. "Trame dantesche: onore e fama," *Italianistica: Rivista di letteratura italiana*, 8 (1979), 465–489.

Amore, Agostino, and Eugenio Battisti. "Lucia," in *Enciclopedia cattolica*, VII. Firenze: Sansoni, 1951.

Amore, Agostino, and Maria Chiara Celletti. "Lucia," in *Biblioteca sanctorum*, VIII. Roma: Città Nuova, 1966.

Angiolillo, Giuliana. "Noterella dantesca: 'e durerà quanto il mondo (moto) lontana,'" *Misure critiche*, 5 (1975), 16–17, 19–27.

Apollonio, Mario. "Il canto II dell' *Inferno*," *Lectura Dantis Romana*. Torino: SEI, 1965, 5–23.

Auerbach, Erich. "Figura" (1944), in *Scenes from the Drama of European Literature*. Trans. Ralph Manheim. New York: Meridian, 1959, 11–76.

———. "Sermo Humilis," in *Literary Language and Its Public in Late Latin Antiquity and the Middle Ages*. Trans. Ralph Manheim. Princeton: Princeton University Press, 1965.

Augustine. *On Christian Doctrine*. Trans. D. W. Robertson, Jr. Indianapolis: Bobbs-Merrill, 1958.

———. *Confessions*. Loeb Classical Library. London: Heinemann, and Cambridge: Harvard University Press, 1968.

———. *The Confessions of Augustine*. Trans. R. S. Pine-Coffin. Harmondsworth: Penguin, 1961.

Ball, Robert. "Theological Semantics: Virgil's *Pietas* and Dante's *pietà*," *SIR*, 2 (1981), 59–71.

Ballerini, Carlo. "Il canto del ricordo (II dell'*Inferno*)," *L'Albero*, 12 (1962), No. 36–40, 26–42.

Balthasar, Hans Urs von. *Dante*. Trans. Giuseppe Magagna. Brescia: Morcellina, 1973.

Barbi, Michele. "Per il testo della 'Divina Commedia,'" *SD*, 18 (1934), 5–57.

———. *Problemi fondamentali per un nuovo commento della Divina Commedia*. Firenze: Sansoni, 1956.

Barolini, Teodolinda. *Dante's Poets: Textuality and Truth in the "Comedy."* Princeton: Princeton University Press, 1984.

Battaglia Ricci, Lucia. *Dante e la tradizione letteraria medievale: Una proposta per la "Commedia."* Pisa: Giardini, 1983.

Beaugrand, Augustine. *Sainte Lucie, vièrge et martyre de Syracuse*. Paris: Tardieu, 1882.

Bernard of Clairvaux. *De consideratione*, in *Tractatus et Opuscula*, S. Bernardi Opera, Vol. III. Ed. Jean Leclercq and H. M. Rochais. Roma: Editiones Cistercienses, 1963.

————. *The Steps of Humility*. Trans. and ed. George Bosworth Burch. Cambridge: Harvard University Press, 1950.

Bernardo, Aldo S., and Anthony L. Pellegrini, eds. *Dante, Petrarch, Boccaccio: Studies in the Italian Trecento in Honor of Charles S. Singleton*. Binghamton: MRTS, 1983.

Boethius. *The Consolation of Philosophy*. Trans. Richard Greene. Indianapolis: Bobbs-Merrill, 1962.

————. *The Tractates and The Consolation of Philosophy*. Ed. E. K. Rand and H. F. Stewart. London: Heinemann, and New York: Putnam, 1918.

Bosco, Umberto. "La 'follia' di Dante," *Lettere italiane*, 10, iv (1958), 417–430.

————. "Il tema della magnanimità nella Commedia," *L'Alighieri* 15, ii (1974), 3–13.

Boyde, Patrick. "Style and Structure in Dante's Canzone, 'Doglia mi reca,'" *IS*, 20 (1965), 26–41.

Brieger, Peter, Millard Meiss, and Charles S. Singleton. *Illuminated Manuscripts of the Divine Comedy*. 2 vols. Princeton: Princeton University Press, 1969.

Brown, Peter. *Augustine of Hippo*. Berkeley: University of California Press, 1970.

Burke, Kenneth. *The Rhetoric of Religion: Studies in Logology*. Berkeley: University of California Press, 1970.

Busnelli, Giovanni, and Giuseppe Vandelli, eds. *Il Convivio*. 2nd ed. Firenze: LeMonnier, 1964.

Caligari, Pietro. *Commento ai primi tre canti dell' "Inferno." Avvio ad una nuova lettura di Dante*. Novara: Tip. S. Gaudenzio, 1965.

Capdevila, Miguel. *Iconografia de Santa Lucia*. Barcelona: Laboratorios del Norte de España, 1950.

Capone, Vittore Ugo. *Civiltà teologica e civiltà cortese*. Roma: Instituto Editoriale del Mediterraneo, 1974.

Casella, Mario. "L'amico mio e non della ventura," *SD*, 27 (1943), 117–134.

————, "Le guide di Dante nella DC," *Atti e Memorie dell' Accademia Fiorentina di Scienze Morali La Columbaria*, n.s., 1 (1943–46), 3–51.

————. "Interpretazione III. Tre donne intorno al cor mi son venute," *SD*, 30 (1951), 5–22.

Cassell, Anthony K. *Dante's Fearful Art of Justice*. Toronto: University of Toronto Press, 1984.

Charity, A. C. *Events and Their Afterlife: The Dialectics of Christian Typology in the Bible and Dante*. Cambridge: Cambridge University Press, 1966.

Chiarenza, Marguerite. "Boethian Themes in Dante's Reading of Virgil," *SIR*, 3, i (1983a), 25–35.

————. "Time and Eternity in the Myths of *Paradiso* XVII," in Bernardo and Pellegrini (1983), 133–150.

Chiari, Alberto. "Il preludio dell'*Inferno*," *Lectura Dantis Romana*. Torino: SEI, 1966.

Chiavacci Leonardi, Anna Maria, ed. *La Commedia. Inferno* I–V. Pavia: Tip. del Libro, 1979.

————. *La guerra de la pietate: saggio per una interpretazione dell'Inferno di Dante*. Napoli: Liguori, 1979.

————. "Questioni di punteggiatura in due celebri attacchi danteschi (*Inf.* II, 76–78 e X, 67–69)," *Lettere italiane*, 36, n. 1 (Genn.–Marzo 1984), 3–24.

Chimenz, Siro A. "Il canto II dell'*Inferno*," in *Letture dantesche*, ed. Giovanni Getto. Firenze: Sansoni, 1964, Vol. I, 27–41.

Cicchitto, Leone. *Il canto II del Purgatorio.* Torino: SEI, 1965.

Cioffari, Vincent. "Guido da Pisa's Basic Interpretation: Translation of the First Two Cantos," *DS*, 93 (1975), 1–26.

Consoli, Andrea. "Postilla dantesca. *Inferno* II, 88–90," *Aspetti letterari*, 5 (1965), 58–60.

Contini, Gianfranco. "Introduzione," *Rime.* Torino: Einaudi, 1946, rept. 1970. Trans. Yvonne Freccero in *Dante: A Collection of Critical Essays*, ed. John Freccero. Englewood Cliffs, N.J.: Prentice-Hall, 1965, 28–38.

————. "Dante come personaggio-poeta della *Commedia*," in *Un'idea di Dante.* Torino: Einaudi, 1976, 33–62. Originally in *L'approdo letterario*, 4 (1958), 19–46.

Cornish, Alison. "'Quali i fioretti': Euryalus, Hyacinth, and the Pilgrim," *SIR* 7 (1987), 205–215.

Courcelle, Pierre. *La Consolation de philosophie dans la tradition littéraire.* Paris: Centre des Etudes Augustiniennes, 1967.

Croce, Benedetto. *La Poesia di Dante.* Bari: Laterza, 1921.

Curtius, Ernst Robert. *European Literature in the Latin Middle Ages.* Trans. Willard R. Trask. New York: Harper, 1963.

D'Alverny, Marie Thérèse. "Notes sur Dante et la Sagesse," *Revue des études italiennes*, 11 (1965), 5–24.

D'Ancona, Alessandro. *I precursori di Dante.* Firenze: G. C. Sansoni, 1874.

D'Andria, Michele. *Beatrice simbolo della poesia: con Dante dalla terra a Dio.* Roma: Edizioni dell'Ateneo e Bizzarri, 1979.

D'Aramengo Balbiano, Maria Teresa. *Tre donne intorno al cor. Saggio di psicologia dantesca.* Mantova-Verona: Valdonega, 1958.

Davis, Charles Till. *Dante and the Idea of Rome.* Oxford: Clarendon Press, 1957.

Delehaye, Hippolyte. *Cinq leçons sur la méthode hagiographique.* Bruxelles: Societé des Bollandistes, 1934.

De Robertis, Domenico. *Il Libro della "Vita Nuova."* 2nd ed. Firenze: Sansoni, 1970.

Di Scipio, Giuseppe C. "Dante and St. Paul: The Blinding Light and Water," *DS*, 98 (1980), 151–157.

————. *The Symbolic Rose in Dante's "Paradiso."* Ravenna: Longo, 1984.

D'Ovidio, Francesco. "Dante e San Paolo," *Nuova Antologia*, 4th ser., 67 (1897), 214–238.

————. *Nuovo volume di studi danteschi.* Caserta-Roma: A.P.E., 1926.

Dronke, Peter. *Dante and Medieval Latin Traditions.* Cambridge: Cambridge University Press, 1986.

Durling, Robert M. "The Ascent of Mt. Ventoux and the Crisis of Allegory," *Italian Quarterly*, 18 (1974), 7–28.

Durling, Robert M., and Ronald L. Martinez. *Time and the Crystal: Studies in Dante's "Rime petrose"* (Forthcoming).

Enciclopedia dantesca. Direttore, Umberto Bosco; Giorgio Petrocchi, redattore capo. 6 Vols. Roma: Istituto della Enciclopedia italiana, 1970–78.

Fallani, Giovanni. *Il canto II dell'Inferno*. Firenze: Le Monnier, 1960.

Ferguson, Margaret W. "St. Augustine's Region of Unlikeness: The Crossing of Exile and Language," *Georgia Review*, 29, iv (1975), 842–864.

Fergusson, Francis. *Dante*. New York: Macmillan, 1966.

Ferrante, Joan. *Woman as Image in the Middle Ages from the Twelfth Century to Dante*. New York: Columbia University Press, 1975.

———. *The Political Vision of the Divine Comedy*. Princeton: Princeton University Press, 1984.

Ferrari, Leo Charles. "The Theme of the Prodigal Son in Augustine's *Confessions*," *Récherches augustiniennes*, 12 (1977), 105–118.

Fisher, John H., ed. *The Complete Poetry and Prose of Geoffrey Chaucer*. New York: Holt, Rinehart, and Winston, 1977.

Fleming, John V. *Reason and the Lover*. Princeton: Princeton University Press, 1984.

Fletcher, Jefferson B. *The Symbolism of the Divine Comedy*. New York: Columbia University Press, 1921; rept., New York: AMS Press, 1966.

———. "Dante, Aeneas, and Paul," in *Todd Memorial Volumes*, ed. John D. Fitzgerald and Pauline Taylor. New York: Columbia University Press, 1930, Vol. I, 153–170.

Forti, Fiorenzo. *Magnanimitade: Studi su un tema dantesco*. Bologna: Pàtron, 1977.

Foster, Kenelm, and Patrick Boyde, eds. and trans. *Dante's Lyric Poetry*. 2 vols. Oxford: Clarendon Press, 1967.

Franchetti, Domenico. *Maria nel pensiero di Dante*. Torino: Ed. di Torino Grafica, 1958.

Freccero, John. "Dante's Firm Foot and the Journey without a Guide," *Harvard Theological Review*, 52, no. 3 (1959), 245–281; reprinted in *Conversion*, 29–54.

———. "Dante's Prologue Scene," *DS*, 84 (1966a), 1–25; reprinted in *Conversion*, 1–28.

———. "The River of Death: *Inferno* II, 108," in *The World of Dante*, ed. S. Bernard Chandler and J. A. Molinaro. Toronto: University of Toronto Press, 1966b, 25–42; reprinted in *Conversion*, 55–69.

———. "*Paradiso* X: The Dance of the Stars," *DS*, 86 (1968), 85–111; reprinted in *Conversion*, 221–244.

———. "Casella's Song (*Purg*. II, 112)," *DS*, 91 (1973), 73–80; reprinted in *Conversion*, 186–194.

———. "Infernal Irony: The Gates of Hell," *MLN*, 99, iv (1984), 769–786; reprinted in *Conversion*, 93–109.

———. *Dante: The Poetics of Conversion*. Ed. Rachel Jacoff. Cambridge: Harvard University Press, 1986.

Garana, Ottavio Capodieci. *Santa Lucia nella tradizione, nella storia, nell'arte*. Siracusa: Mascali, 1958.

Gardner, Edmund G. *Dante and the Mystics*. London: Dent, 1903; rept. New York: Octagon, 1968.

Getto, Giovanni. "Dante e Virgilio," *Il Veltro*, 3 (Oct. 1970), 11–20.

Giglio, Raffaele. "Il prologo alla *Divina Commedia*," *Critica letteraria*, 1 (1973), 131–159.

Giordano da Rivalto. *Prediche de Beato Fra Giordano da Rivalto*. Firenze: Stamperia Pietro Gaetano Viviana, 1738.

Giovanna, Ildebrando della. *Lectura Dantis*. Firenze: Lectura Dantis Fiorentina, 1925.

Goldstein, Harvey. "*Enea e Paolo*: A Reading of the 26th Canto of Dante's *Inferno*," *Symposium*, 19 (1965), 316–327.

Graf, Arturo. *Miti, leggende, e superstizioni del Medio Evo*. 2 vols. Torino: E. Loescher, 1892–93; rept., Bologna: Forni, 1965.

Greene, Thomas. *The Descent from Heaven: A Study in Epic Continuity*. New Haven: Yale University Press, 1963.

Gualtieri, A. "Lady Philosophy in Boethius and Dante," *Comparative Literature*, 23 (1971), 141–150.

Haller, Robert, trans. *Literary Criticism of Dante Alighieri*. Lincoln: University of Nebraska Press, 1973.

Hanning, Robert W. *The Individual in Twelfth-Century Romance*. New Haven: Yale University Press, 1977.

Harrison, Robert Pogue. *The Body of Beatrice*. Baltimore: Johns Hopkins University Press, 1988.

Hawkins, Peter S. "Virtuosity and Virtue: Poetic Self Reflection in the *Commedia*," *DS*, 98 (1980), 1–18.

Hennecke, Edgar. *New Testament Apocrypha*. Ed. Wilhelm Schneemelcher. 2 vols. Trans. R. McL. Wilson. Philadelphia: Westminster, 1964.

Hollander, Robert. *Allegory in Dante's Commedia*. Princeton: Princeton University Press, 1969.

———. "*Purgatorio* II: Cato's Rebuke and Dante's *scoglio*," *Italica*, 52 (1975), 348–363.

———. *Studies in Dante*. Ravenna: Longo, 1980.

———. *Il Virgilio dantesco*. Firenze: Olschki, 1983a.

———. "*Purgatorio* XIX: Dante's Siren/Harpy," in Bernardo and Pellegrini (1983), 77–88.

———. "Dante's Pagan Past: Notes on *Inferno* XIV and XVIII," *SIR*, 5 (1985), 23–36.

———. "*Inferno* II: The Canto of the Word," in *Lectura Dantis Californiana* (forthcoming).

———. "*Purgatorio* II: The New Song and the Old," in *Lectura Dantis Californiana* (forthcoming).

Iannucci, Amilcare A. "Beatrice in Limbo: A Metaphoric Harrowing of Hell," *DS*, 97 (1979), 23–45.

Inguagiato, Vincenzina. "Come Dante col Poema rinovelli l'azione d'Enea e di S. Paolo," *Giornale dantesco*, 18 (1909), 193–199. Jacobus de Voragine. *The Golden Legend of Jacobus de Voragine*, trans. Granger Ryan and Helmut Ripperger. New York: Arno Press, 1969.

Jacoff, Rachel. "The Post-Palinodic Smile: *Par.* 8 and 9," *DS*, 98 (1980), 111–122.

———. "The Tears of Beatrice," *DS*, 100 (1982), 1–12.

———. "Sacrifice and Empire: Thematic Analogies in San Vitale and the *Paradiso*," in *Renaissance Studies in Honor of Craig Hugh Smyth*. Firenze: Giunti, 1985, Vol. 1, 317–331.

Johnson, W. Ralph. *Darkness Visible: A Study of Virgil's Aeneid*. Berkeley: University of California Press, 1976.

Kaftal, George. *Saints in Italian Art: Iconography of the Saints in Tuscan Painting*. Firenze: Sansoni, 1952.

———. *Iconography of the Saints in Central and South Italian Schools of Painting*. Firenze: Sansoni, 1965.

Kennedy, Vincent L. *The Saints of the Canon of the Mass*. Studi di antichità cristiana, 14. Città del Vaticano: Pontificale Istituto di Archeologia Cristiana, 1963.

Kirkpatrick, Robin. *The Divine Comedy*. Cambridge: Cambridge University Press, 1987.

Kleinhenz, Christopher. "Food for Thought: *Purgatorio XXII*, 146–147," *DS*, 95 (1977), 69–80.

Kolve, V. A. *Chaucer and the Imagery of Narrative*. Stanford: Stanford University Press, 1984.

Kranz, W. "Dante und Boethius," *Romanische Forschungen*, 63 (1951), 72–78.

Kunstle, Karl. *Ikonographie der Christlichen Kunst*. Vol II. Freiburg im Breisgau: Herder, 1928.

Ladner, Gerhart. "Homo Viator: Mediaeval Ideas on Alienation and Order," *Speculum*, 42 (1967), 233–259.

Lansing, Richard. *From Image to Idea: A Study of the Simile in Dante's "Commedia."* Ravenna: Longo, 1977.

Laurano, Renzo. "I 'fioretti chiusi . . . '" *Persona*, 7 (1966), 3, 8–9.

Leo, Ulrich. "The Unfinished *Convivio* and Dante's Rereading of the *Aeneid*," *Mediaeval Studies*, 13 (1951), 41–64.

Locke, F. W. "Dante's Perilous Crossing," *Symposium*, 19 (1965), 293–305.

Lucrezi, Bruno. "Un'interpretazione dantesca: Lucia (*Inferno* II)," *Atti dell'Academia Pontaniana*, 12 (1962–63), 173–180.

Masciandaro, Franco. "*Inferno* I–II: il dramma della conversione e il tempo," *SD*, 49 (1972), 1–26.

Masseron, Alexandre. "Quelques énigmes hagiographiques de la 'Divine Comédy,'" *Analecta Bollandiana*, 65 (1950), 369–382.

May, Herbert G., and Bruce M. Metzger, eds. *The New Oxford Annotated Bible*. New York: Oxford University Press, 1973.

Mazzeo, Joseph Anthony. "Dante and the Pauline Modes of Vision," in *Structure and Thought in the Paradiso*. Ithaca: Cornell University Press, 1958, 84–110.

Mazzoni, Francesco. "Il canto II dell' *Inferno*," in *Saggio per un nuovo commento alla "Divina Commedia." Inferno, Canti I–III*. Firenze: Sansoni, 1967.

Mazzotta, Giuseppe. *Dante, Poet of the Desert*. Princeton: Princeton University Press, 1979.

———. "Dante and the Virtues of Exile," *Poetics Today*, 5, iii (1984), 645–667.

Moore, Edward. *Studies in Dante, First Series*. Oxford: Clarendon Press, 1896; rept. New York: Haskell, 1968.

————. *Studies in Dante, Fourth Series*. Oxford: Clarendon Press, 1917; rept. New York: Haskell, 1968.

Morghen, Raffaelo. "Dante tra 'l'umano' e la storia della salvezza," *L'Alighieri*, 21, i (1980), 18–30.

Murari, Rocco. *Dante e Boezio*. Bologna: Zanichelli, 1905.

Myerowitz, Molly. *Ovid's Games of Love*. Detroit: Wayne State University Press, 1985.

Nardi, Bruno. *Dante e la cultura medievale*. Bari: Laterza, 1942.

————. "Dal *Convivio* alla *Commedia*," in *Dal Convivio alla Commedia*. Roma: Istituto storico italiano per il medio evo, 1960, 37–150.

————. "Due brevi note alla *Commedia*. I. 'La fiumana ove 'l mar non ha vanto' (*Inf.* II, 108). II. 'Il nome che più dura e più onora' (*Purg.* XXXI, 85)," *L'Alighieri*, I, i (1961), 21–26.

————. "Tre momenti del incontro di Dante con Virgilio," *L'Alighieri*, 6, ii (1965), 42–53.

————. *Saggi e note di critica dantesca*. Milano-Napoli, 1966, 309–313.

Negri, G. *Le tre donne benedette*. Parma: Bedonia, 1929.

Newman, Francis X. "St. Augustine's Three Visions and the Structure of the Comedy," *MLN*, 82 (1967), 56–78.

Nohrnberg, James. *The Analogy of "The Fairie Queene."* Princeton: Princeton University Press, 1976.

————. "The Inferno," in *Homer to Brecht: The European Epic and Dramatic Traditions*, ed. Michael Seidel and Edward Mendelson. New Haven: Yale University Press, 1977.

Nuvoli, Giuliana. "Le tre guide: Per una precisazione sul ruolo di Virgilio, Beatrice, e Bernardo all'interno della *Commedia*," *Italianistica: Rivista di letteratura italiana*, 7 (1978), 499–513.

Ozanam, A. F. *Dante et la philosophie catholique au XIIIe siècle*. Paris: Débécourt, 1839.

Paasinen, Aino Anna-Maria. "Dante at the Turning Point: The Canzone 'Tre donne intorno al cor mi son venute' as a New Key to the *Commedia*." *DAI*, 37, v (Nov. 1976), 292.

Padoan, Giorgio. "*Purgatorio XXI*," in *Nuove letture danteschi*, Vol. III. Firenze: Le Monnier, 1970.

————. "Il canto II dell' *Inferno*," *Letture Classensi*, 5 (1976), 41–56.

————. *Il pio Enea, l'empio Ulisse: Tradizione classica e intendimento medievale in Dante*. Ravenna: Longo, 1977.

Pagliaro, Antonino. "Io non Enea, io non Paolo sono," *Il Veltro*, 1, i (1957), 7–14.

————. "' . . . ove 'l mar non ha vanto,' (Dante, *Inf.* II, 108)," in *Studi in onore di Angelo Monteverdi*. Modena: Soc. Tipografica Editrice Modenese, 1959, Vol. II, 543–548.

————. *Altri saggi di critica semantica*. Messina and Firenze: D'Anna, 1961.

————. "Il testo della *Divina Commedia* e l'esegesi," in *Saggi e problemi di critica testuale*, ed. Raffaele Spongono. Bologna: Commisione per i testi di lingua, 1961, 326–331.

————. "'. . . chi per lungo silenzio parea fioco,'" *Saggi e ricerche in memoria di Ettore LiGotti*. Palermo: Centro di Studi Filologici e Linguistici Siciliani [Bolletino 6], 1962, Vol. II, 417–428.

————. "Proemio e Prologo della *Divina Commedia*," in *Atti del Convegno di studi su Dante e la magna curia*. Palermo: Centro di Studi Filologici e Linguistici Siciliani, 1965, 4–29.

————. *Ulisse: Ricerche semantiche sulla Divina Commedia*. Firenze-Messina: D'Anna, 1966.

————. "Il Canto II dell'*Inferno*," *Nuove letture dantesche*. Firenze: Le Monnier, 1967, Vol. I, 17–46.

Palmenta, Giuseppe. *La vergine madre nella Divina Commedia*. Catania: Pia Società San Paolo, 1971.

Pasquazi, Silvio. "Il Prologo in Cielo," *Critica letteraria*, 2 (1974), 163–188; rept. in "Il canto II dell'*Inferno*," *Inferno: Letture degli anni 1973–76*, a cura di S. Zennaro Roma: Bonacci, 1977, 35–65.

Pearce, Richard. "The Eyes of Beatrice," *New Blackfriars*, 54 (1973), 407–416.

Pelikan, Jaroslav. *The Growth of Medieval Theology (600–1300)*, Vol. III of *The Christian Tradition, A History of the Development of Doctrine*. Chicago: University of Chicago Press, 1978.

Pellegrini, Flaminio. "Canto Secondo," *Lectura Dantis Genovese*. Firenze: Le Monnier, 1904, vol. I, 83–109.

Pellegrini, Silvio. "*Inferno*, II. 59–60," in *Studi di varia umanità in onore di Francesco Flora*. Milano: Mondadori, 1963.

Petrarca, Francesco. *Canzoniere*. Ed. Gianfranco Contini. Torino: Einaudi, 1968.

Petrini, Mario. "Situazione e poesia nel secondo canto dell' *Inferno*," *Belfagor*, 15, ii (1960), 205–212.

Petrocchi, Giorgio, ed. *La Commedia secondo l'antica vulgato*. 4 vols. Milano: Mondadori, 1966–67.

Pézard, André. "Marie et Lucie," in *La rotta gonna: gloses et corrections aux textes mineurs de Dante*. Vol. I, 117–205. Publications de l'Institut Francais de Florence, 17. Florence: Sansoni, 1967.

Picchio Simonelli, Maria. "La prosa nutrice del verso: Dal 'Convivio' all 'Divina Commedia,'" in *Aquila: Chestnut Hill Studies in Modern Languages and Literatures*, 2 (1973), 117–176.

Poletto, Msgr. Giacomo. "Gli occhi di Beatrice nella *Divina Commedia*," *Scritti vari*. Siena: Tip Pont. S. Bernadino, 1910, 25–48.

Puppo, Mario. "Beatrice," *Cultura e Scuola*, 4 (1965), 356–361.

Putnam, Michael C. J. *The Poetry of the Aeneid*. Cambridge, Harvard University Press, 1965.

————. *Virgil's Poem of the Earth: Studies in the "Georgics."* Princeton: Princeton University Press, 1979.

Quinones, Ricardo. *Dante Alighieri*. TWAS 563. Boston: G. K. Hall, 1979.

Quint, David. "Epic Tradition and *Inferno* IX," *DS*, 93 (1975), 201–207.

———. *Origin and Originality in Renaissance Literature*. New Haven: Yale University Press, 1983.

Rand, E. K. *Founders of the Middle Ages*. Cambridge: Harvard University Press, 1928.

Ransom, Daniel. "Panis Angelorum: A Palinode in the *Paradiso*," *DS*, 95 (1977), 81–94.

Réau, Louis. *Iconographie de l'art Chrétien*. 3 vols. Paris: Presses Universitaires de France, 1958.

Reiss, Edmund. *Boethius*. *TWAS* 672. Boston: G. K. Hall, 1982.

Roedel, Reto. "'Quali i fioretti . . . '," *Svizzera italiana*, 20, cxlix, (1960), 27–39.

Rossi, Albert. "'A l'ultimo suo': *Paradiso* XXX and Its Virgilian Context," *Studies in Medieval and Renaissance History*, n.s. 4 (1981), 39–88.

Russo, Vittorio. "Timor, audacia, e fortitudo nel canto II dell' *Inferno*," *Filologia e letteratura*, 11, iv (1965), 391–408. Rept. in *Sussidi di esegesi dantesca*. Napoli: Liguori, 1966, 9–32.

———. "Prospettive di lettere della *Commedia*," *Atti del convegno internazionale di studi danteschi*, a cura del commune di Ravenna e della Società Dantesca Italiana. Ravenna: Longo, 1979, 73–94.

Sanguineti, Edoardo. "Dante, *Inferno* I–III." *Tre studi danteschi*. Firenze: Le Monnier, 1961, 1–24.

Sarolli, Gian Roberto. *Prologomena alla Divina Commedia*. Firenze: Olschki, 1971.

Schnapp, Jeffrey. *The Transformation of History at the Center of Dante's Paradiso*. Princeton: Princeton University Press, 1986.

Scott, John F. "La contemporaneità Enea-Davide," *SD*, 49 (1972), 129–134.

———. *Dante magnanimo*. Firenze: Olschki, 1977.

Scuderi, Ermanno. "Dante e Boezio," *Orpheus*, 9 (1962), 105–107.

Seznec, Jean. *The Survival of the Pagan Gods*. Princeton: Princeton University Press, 1972.

Shapiro, Marianne. *Women Earthly and Divine in the "Comedy" of Dante*. Lexington: University Press of Kentucky, 1975.

Silverstein, Theodore M. "Dante and the *Visio Pauli*," *MLN*, 47 (1932), 389–399.

———. *Visio Sancti Pauli: The History of the Apocalypse in Latin Together with Nine Texts*. London: Christophers, 1935.

———. "Did Dante Know the Vision of St. Paul?" *Harvard Studies and Notes in Philology and Literature*, 19 (1937), 231–247.

Simonelli, Maria, ed. *Il Convivio*. Bologna: Pàtron, 1966.

Singleton, Charles S. "'Su la fiumana ove 'l mar non ha vanto' (*Inf.* II, 108)," *Romanic Review*, 39, iv (December, 1948), 269–277.

———. "Virgil Recognizes Beatrice," *ARDS*, 74 (1956), 29–38.

———. *Dante Studies 1: Elements of Structure*. Cambridge: Harvard University Press, 1957.

———. *Dante Studies 2: Journey to Beatrice*. Cambridge: Harvard University Press, 1958.

———. *An Essay on the "Vita Nuova."* Cambridge: Harvard University Press, 1958.

———. "In Exitu Israel de Aegypto," *ARDS*, 78 (1960), 1–24; rept. in *Dante: A Collection of Essays*, ed. John Freccero. Englewood Cliffs, N.J.: Prentice-Hall, 1965, 102–121.

Squarr, Christel. "Lucia," in *Lexikon der Christlichen Ikonographie*. Vol. VII. Freiburg: Herder, 1974.

Squilbeck, Jean. "Le Jourdain dans l'iconographie mediévale du Baptême du Christ," *Bulletin des Musées Royaux d'art et d'histoire*, 4th ser., 38–39 (1966–67), 69–116.

Steinberg, Leo. *The Sexuality of Christ in Renaissance Art and in Modern Oblivion*. New York: Pantheon, 1983.

Stephany, William A. "Biblical Allusions to Conversion in *Purgatorio* XXI," *SIR*, 3, ii (Fall 1983), 141–162.

———. "'Tristo annunzio di futuro danno': Dante's Harpies," *Italica*, 62 (1985), 24–33.

Stock, Lorraine Kochanske. "Reversion for Conversion: Maternal Images in Dante's *Commedia*," *Italian Quarterly*, 23 (Fall 1982), 5–15.

Taibbi, Giuseppe Rossi. *Martirio di Santa Lucia: Vita di Santa Siciliana*, II. Palermo: Istituto Siciliano di Studi Bizantini e Neogreci, 1959.

Thompson, David. *Dante's Epic Journeys*. Baltimore: Johns Hopkins University Press, 1974.

Toynbee, Paget. *Dictionary of Proper Names and Notable Matters in the Works of Dante*. Oxford: Oxford University Press, 1898.

Vallone, Aldo. "Interpretazione del Virgilio dantesco," *L'Alighieri*, 10, i (1969), 14–40.

Vettori, V. "Il prologo dell' *Inferno*," in *Letture dell' Inferno*, ed. V. Vettori. Lectura Dantis Internazionale. Milano: Marzorati, 1963, 7–27.

Villari, P. *Antiche leggende e tradizioni che illustrano la Divina Commedia*. Pisa: Tip. Nistri, 1865.

Wind, Edgar. *Pagan Mysteries in the Renaissance*. New Haven: Yale University Press, 1958; rept. New York: Norton, 1968.

Witke, Edward C. "The River of Light in the *Anticlaudianus* and the *Divine Comedy*," *Classical Review*, 11 (1959), 144–156.

INDEX

Abelard, 45
Acts of the Apostles, 61, 62, 70, 71, 115, 117
Aelred of Rievaulx, 45
Aeneas, 3, 11, 17, 21, 51, 57–61, 64–68, 69, 87–89, 96, 97, 98, 99, 113, 117, 124
Aeneid, 11, 20–22, 24, 29, 41, 51, 64–66, 70, 75, 96, 97, 98, 99, 108, 109, 110, 114, 115, 116, 124
allegory, 24–26, 43–50, 55–56, 100, 101, 106, 107, 111, 116, 118
allusion, 10–11, 60–61, 64, 98
Ambrose, St., 116
Amore, A., 104
Ananias, 11, 65–67, 88, 114
Anchises, 38, 63, 69, 71, 88
Andreoli, R., 52
Anonimo Fiorentino, 108, 109
Apollonio, M., 119
Aristotle, 97
Auerbach, E., 15, 43, 47, 95, 99, 107
Augustine, St., 18, 45, 64, 79, 81, 100, 108, 111, 118, 119, 120, 122, 123

Ball, R., 12, 29, 98, 117
Ballerini, C., 97
Balthasar, H. Urs von, 103
Barbi, M., 43, 44, 46–48, 107, 108
Barolini, T., 76, 99, 102, 105, 111, 117, 120
Battaglia Ricci, L., 108
Beatrice, 1, 3, 5–7, 10, 12, 15–19, 25, 38, 43–48, 50, 54, 55, 56, 63, 68, 76–79, 84–86, 97, 99, 106, 107
Beaugrand, A., 104
Bede, 115
Bennassuti, L., 14

Benvenuto da Imola, 15–17, 37, 45, 48, 59, 95, 96, 107, 109, 112, 114, 121, 122
Bernard, St., 28, 45, 117, 123
Bernard Silvester, 108
Biagioli, G., 107
Boccaccio, G., 37, 41, 44, 48, 97, 99, 101, 105, 108, 112, 114
Boethius, 23, 44, 46, 58, 77–89, 107, 120, 121
Bosco, U., 104
Boyde, P. *See* Foster
Brieger, P., M. Meiss, and C. S. Singleton, 25, 101, 108
Burke, K., 105
Busnelli, G., and G. Vandelli, 103
Buti, F. de, 37, 44, 48, 101, 109, 112

Cacciaguida, 12, 58, 71, 87–89, 120, 124, 125
Capdevila, M., 105
Capone, V., 106
Casella, M., 45, 107
Cassell, A., 116
Castelvetro, L., 15, 19, 27, 109
Catherine of Siena, St., 108
Celletti, M. C., 104, 105
Charity, A. C., 111, 116
Chaucer, G., 98
Chiarenza, M., 115, 124
Chiavacci Leonardi, A., 44, 46, 106
Chimenz, S., 105, 106
Chiose Selmiane, 112
Cioffari, V., 102
Confessions, 18, 79, 81, 100, 118, 119, 122
Consolation of Philosophy, 23, 46, 77–82, 84–86, 121, 123, 125
Contini, G., 16, 39, 99, 111

conversion, 18, 57, 58, 71, 73, 74, 77, 78
Convivio, 15, 23, 24, 26–27, 30–32, 39, 46, 48, 58, 60, 68, 75–86, 91, 102, 103, 111, 115, 118, 119, 120, 121, 122
Corinthians (Second Epistle to), 62, 63, 70, 113, 116
Cornish, A., 119
Courcelle, P., 120, 123
Croce, B., 45
Curtius, E. R., 59, 98, 102

D'Alverny, M., 120
D'Ancona, A., 112
D'Andria, M., 102, 107
Daniello, 109
Davis, C. T., 111
De Doctrina Christiana, 118
De Monarchia, 24, 60
De Robertis, D., 45, 46
De vulgari eloquentia, 16
Del Lungo, I., 101
Di Scipio, G., 113
donna gentile, 24, 26–27, 30, 46–48, 84–85, 102, 107, 119, 121
Donne, J., 32
D'Ovidio, F., 62, 112, 114
Dronke, P., 123
Durling, R., 99, 100

Epistle to Cangrande, 19, 43, 63, 83, 113, 122, 123, 125
exile, 50, 77, 80–84, 88–89, 97, 120, 122, 124
Exodus, 50, 53, 108, 110, 113

fear, 9–10, 35, 99
Ferguson, M., 122
Ferrante, J., 111, 114, 124
Ferrari, L., 122
fiumana, 48–50, 54–56, 108, 109, 111
Fleming, J., 122
Fletcher, J., 25
Forti, F., 104
fortitude, 33–36, 88, 104, 115, 124
fortune, 44–46, 85, 86, 107
Foster, K., and P. Boyde, 100, 102
Freccero, J., 2, 23, 45, 49, 50, 51, 53, 54, 56, 95, 105, 106, 107, 108, 109, 110, 111, 118, 120
Fundamentum Aureum, 104

Gafurius, 101
Garana, O., 105
Gardner, E., 113
Georgics, 109
Giglio, R., 101
Giordano da Rivalto, Fra, 34, 35
Giovanna, I. della, 105
Gmelin, H., 12, 98
Goldstein, H., 118
grace, 9, 17–18, 24, 27–29, 37, 68–72, 92, 101, 105, 116, 117
Graf, A., 112
Grandgent, C. H., 52
Graziolo, 30, 111, 112, 116
Greene, T., 100
Gregory, St., 64, 88, 115
Gualtieri, A., 120
Guido da Pisa, 27, 44, 112

Haller, R., 123
Hanning, R., 99
Harrison, R., 121
Hawkins, P., 13, 98
Haymo of Halberstadt, 117
Hennecke, E., 118
Hollander, R., 13, 14, 15, 20, 23, 41, 98, 99, 100, 104, 105, 108, 109, 111, 113, 114, 117, 120, 121, 124
Hous of Fame, The, 108
Hrabanus Maurus, 116
Hugh of St. Victor, 108

Iannucci, A., 40, 100
iconography, 33, 36, 105
Index of Christian Art, Princeton, 105, 110
Inferno
  I, 1–2, 3–4, 10, 20, 25, 35, 38, 40, 48–51, 53, 54, 56, 58, 68, 72–73, 75, 78, 84, 95, 96, 99, 100, 102, 105, 110, 111, 113, 114, 117, 119, 121
  III, 2, 35, 48
  IV, 35, 42, 100
  V, 18, 27
  IX, 100, 104, 110
  X, 13, 98, 107, 124
  XIV, 109
  XVIII, 16
  XXIV, 109
  XXV, 13, 98

XXVI, 98
XXVIII, 99
XXXI, 109
XXXIV, 55
ingegno, 13–15, 99
interpretation, 8–9, 68
invocation, 10–15, 28, 55
Isidore, St., 53, 106

Jacobus de Voragine, 33, 36
Jacoff, R., 104, 105, 119, 120, 121, 125
Jacopo di Dante, 30, 37, 48, 112
Jeremiah, 41, 42, 106
Jerome, St., 53, 102, 106, 110, 112, 116
John the Baptist, St., 33, 40, 103, 105
John of Salisbury, 124
Johnson, W. R., 114
Jordan River, 49–50, 53, 108, 110

Kaftal, G., 105
Kirkpatrick, R., 117
Kleinhenz, C., 111
Kolve, V. A., 121
Kranz, W., 120
Kunstle, K., 105

Ladner, G., 122
Lana, J. della, 44, 112
Landino, C., 44, 101, 108, 109, 110
language, 5–7, 15–19, 91–92, 122
Lansing, R., 96
Leo, U., 115
Lethe, 51–55, 64, 87, 109, 119
Limbo, 40, 56
Livy, 65, 99, 114
Lombardi, B., 107
Lorenzetti, Pietro, 36
Lucy, St., 3, 6, 18–19, 25, 29, 45, 48, 50, 54, 84–85, 105, 124
Lucy (degli Ubaldini), St., 31

Martinez, R., 99. *See also* Durling
Martini, Simone, 36
martyrdom, 33–36, 87–88, 102, 124, 125
Mary, St., 3, 6, 18–19, 25, 26–29, 45, 46, 84–85, 96, 102, 103, 106
Masseron, A., 103
Mattalia, D., 44
Mazzeo, J., 64, 113

Mazzoni, F., 9, 11, 14, 16, 27, 43–46, 48, 49, 59, 64, 95, 96, 97, 98, 106, 107, 108, 109, 112, 114, 122
Mazzotta, G., 15, 99, 111, 116, 117
mediation, 18, 22, 28–29, 38, 42, 54, 58, 68, 73–74, 77, 84, 91, 102
Momigliano, A., 106
Moore, E., 22, 27, 28, 30, 31, 46, 102, 121
motion, 4–6, 18, 97
Murari, R., 120
Myerowitz, M., 99

Nardi, B., 49, 50, 75, 111
Newman, F. X., 113
Nicholas of Lyra, 108
Nohrnberg, J., 95, 100, 101

Ottimo, 44, 109
Ozanam, A. F., 112

Paasinen, A., 100
Padoan, G., 24, 41, 45, 100, 101, 104, 105, 113, 118, 122, 123, 124
Pagliaro, A., 49, 108
Palmenta, G., 102, 106
Paradiso
I, 63
II, 23, 119
III, 30, 31
IV, 34
VII, 107
X, 82, 83, 88, 121, 122
XV, 87, 117
XVII, 16, 89, 117, 124
XXI, 63
XXII, 15
XXIII, 28
XXVI, 38, 63
XXX, 54–56, 63, 101
XXXI, 28–29, 39, 55, 96
XXXII, 28–29, 30, 33, 96, 105
XXXIII, 6, 28–29, 96, 102
Pasquazi, S., 31, 34, 35, 95, 96
Paul, St., 3, 17, 38, 57–64, 66, 69–71, 73, 86, 87–89, 112, 113, 116, 117, 118
Pelikan, J., 102
Peter Damian, St., 108
Petrarch, 27, 97, 99, 101
Petrini, M., 105

Petrocchi, G., 43, 108
Petrus Comestor, 104
Pézard, A., 103
Piccarda Donati, 31
pietà, 6, 12, 25–27, 91, 107
pietas, 12
Pietro di Dante, 11, 23, 46, 101, 112
Pine-Coffin, 119
poet, role of, 5, 12–13, 57–58, 72–74, 91
Purgatorio
  I, 53, 55
  II, 23
  VII, 109
  IX, 29, 37, 38, 98, 105
  XIV, 49
  XIX, 120, 121
  XXI, 120
  XXIV, 39
  XXVII, 106
  XXIX, 24
  XXX, 26, 31, 38, 105, 114, 119, 123
  XXXI, 26, 101, 105, 120
  XXXII, 100
  XXXIII, 25, 55, 100
Putnam, M., 114

Quinones, R., 116
Quint, D., 100, 109

Rachel, 41, 42, 50, 106
Ransom, D., 23, 119
reader, role of, 18–19, 82, 92, 97
Réau, L., 105
Reiss, E., 120
Rhabanus Maurus, 106, 110
Rhadbertus, 106
Richard of St. Victor, 123
Rossi, A., 111
Russo, V., 35, 107

San Apollinare Nuovo, 36
San Sebastiano al Palatino, 36
Sanguineti, E., 96
Santa Lucia de' Magnoli, 31, 35, 36, 103
Santa Maria Maggiore, 36
Sapegno, N., 101, 102, 105, 106
Sarolli, G. R., 101, 113
Scartazzini, G. A., 101
Schnapp, J., 103, 104, 124, 125

Scott, J., 104
Scripture, 17, 40, 41, 50, 53, 62, 113, 115
Scuderi, E., 120
Seneca, 118
Serravalle, G., 108, 112, 121
Seznec, J., 101
Shapiro, M., 106
Silverstein, T., 112
Simonelli, M., 118
Singleton, C. S., 44–47, 49–51, 95, 103, 107, 108, 118
Squarr, C., 105
Squilbeck, J., 110
Steinberg, L., 47
Stephany, W., 110, 116, 117, 120
Stevens, W., 49
stilnovo, 48
Stock, L., 106
structure, narrative, 2–3, 5, 18, 96, 125

Taibbi, G., 104
Thomas, St., 35, 37, 71, 88, 102, 104, 113, 116, 117
Thompson, D., 96
three graces, 100, 101
Tommaseo, N., 27, 28, 102
Torraca, F., 101, 111
Toynbee, P., 52
"Tre donne intorno al cor," 24
typology, 40–43, 48–56, 64, 68, 100, 106, 113

Vallone, A., 101
Vellutello, A., 107
Villani, F., 108
Villari, P., 112
Vincent of Beauvais, 33
Virgil, 1–7, 9–12, 14–17, 20–23, 25, 35, 38–44, 46, 51–52, 56, 58–61, 65–69, 72–74, 76, 81, 84, 87, 88, 91, 97, 105
Visio Pauli, 62, 112
Vita Nuova, 16, 26–27, 30–31, 38–39, 45–48, 56, 84–85, 91, 121
vocation, 12, 15, 39, 60–61, 64–74, 87–89, 91–92

Wind, E., 101
Witke, E., 111